Asghar and Zahra

# Asghar and Zahra

*Sameer Rahim*

JM ORIGINALS

First published in Great Britain in 2019 by JM Originals
An Imprint of John Murray (Publishers)
An Hachette UK company

1

A CIP catalogue record for this title is available from the British Library

Trade Paperback ISBN 978-1-473-69722-5
eBook ISBN 978-1-473-69723-2

Typeset in Minion Pro by
Palimpsest Book Production Ltd, Falkirk, Stirlingshire

Printed and bound in Great Britain by Clays Ltd, Elcograf S.p.A.

John Murray policy is to use papers that are natural, renewable and recyclable
products and made from wood grown in sustainable forests. The logging
and manufacturing processes are expected to conform to the environmental
regulations of the country of origin.

John Murray (Publishers)
Carmelite House
50 Victoria Embankment
London EC4Y ODZ

www.johnmurray.co.uk

*In loving memory*
*of my father*
MOHAMMED SADIQ RAHIM
6 February 1945, Zanzibar
19 February 2000, London

*With Islam the ideal and the real are not two opposing forces which cannot be reconciled. The life of the ideal consists, not in a total breach with the real which would tend to shatter the organic wholeness of life into painful oppositions, but in the perpetual endeavour of the ideal to appropriate the real with a view eventually to absorb it, to convert it into itself and to illuminate its whole being.*
– Muhammad Iqbal


*Art thou real, my ideal?*
– James Joyce

# Chapter One

A sghar swayed happily on his garden swing in a cream-and-gold frock coat, gently sweating in the warm sun. His wedding clothes fitted perfectly, apart from the tight red shoes curling at the toes. He twirled his wrist to check the time on his chunky, loose-fitting silver watch – a present from Zahra's father. The rest of the family were taking ages. His sister Fatima claimed to have religious objections to layered make-up and fancy hairstyles; but she had still spent forever in the shower, leaving him only lukewarm water. After his mother took twenty minutes compacting his father's hair with hairspray – making the hazy corridor impassable – she needed an hour to make herself beautiful. On her son's wedding day, helped by a hairdresser from the community, that hour naturally became two.

Asghar didn't really mind waiting. Even as a boy, he had many times sat patiently for his family on the same garden swing – a three-seater with faded yellow cushions and rusted springs – playing his Game Boy or, more recently, messing around with his mobile phone. Slowing down, he pushed the swing back again and, as the clouds passed, he watched the garden's well-tended sunflowers burst into bright halo and back into shadow. Checking his phone, he saw that Zahra hadn't sent any more messages. He hoped he had said the right thing about that sari-top; the last thing he wanted was to put her under any pressure.

On his lap was a tatty red booklet entitled *The Making of an Islamic Marriage*. Two days earlier his best man – an older cousin he hardly knew – had awkwardly thrust it into his hands, before telling him to send any queries via email. Asghar had accepted this infamous work with proper awe. At Sunday madressa, he had heard rumours that it described in unblushing detail the true path to satisfying marital sex. Once someone had claimed to have seen it tucked in the jurisprudence section of the madressa's mobile library; another said that a liberal-minded teacher had read his class extracts. But neither report had ever been confirmed. Over the years, the booklet had gained an aura of erotic secrecy – like a sharia-compliant *Kama Sutra*, which would be solemnly revealed only on the eve of marriage.

When Asghar finally got his hands on the booklet, though, he found it disappointingly tame. Written by a Pakistani mullah and printed in Birmingham in the early 1990s, it was mostly a rundown of the prayers to be performed on the wedding night, with only a few bald pages on the mechanics of human intercourse. The diagrams seemed to have been cribbed from the same biology textbook he knew from school. And its language was euphemistic to the point of obscurity (there was much talk of 'tillage' and 'cultivation'). Still, Asghar

2

tried to remain cheerful. He was aware, roughly speaking, of what needed to be done that night and assumed – or at least hoped – that once everything got going, instinct would take over. As family legend had it, back in old Zanzibar days, his uncle had been so horrified by what his wife had suggested on their wedding night that he had run to the balcony and threatened to commit suicide. But the couple had been married for thirty-three years and had two children – one of whom was now Asghar's best man – so clearly they had worked things out in the end.

It was a typically variable English spring morning. The sun disappeared and the sky turned a cool metallic grey. Asghar watched as the scrappy clouds absorbed the sun's rays. Before getting engaged he had felt a bit like one of those clouds – floating unremarked until caught by Zahra's brightness. Now, though, he walked round the new mosque with a masculine strut, while the boys who had once bullied or ignored him rushed to offer their congratulations. At the miraculous age of nineteen, Asghar had ensnared the most beautiful and charismatic girl in the community. The girl he had first seen as a little boy at the rickety old mosque, upstairs, escaping the tense vote on whether to move to Manor Grove. He recalled peering round the door and spotting Zahra sitting on the crèche floor as she removed her hijab. She had fiddled with her pins and clips and then used her fingers to comb her long, curly, reddish-brown hair – before she tossed it back in slow waves.

That Zahra was three years older than him only added to the delicious scandal. How *had* he managed it, everyone wondered? Some suggested it was a political match between his father and Zahra's – the respective leaders of the new

3

mosque and the old. Perhaps their engagement presaged a reunion of the divided community? Asghar informed them that neither family had anything to do with arranging the marriage. It was, he told them shyly, a love match.

Asking for Zahra's hand had been the boldest move of his life. When the risk came off, it changed the way the world looked at him, and the way he looked at the world. His teenage melancholy disappeared so fast he could barely remember what it meant to be unhappy. The short time between getting back in contact that autumn and the engagement – just two dates – made it all the more stunning. It was as though he had aced an exam without studying, or won a marathon with only a day's training.

'You never thought I'd be the first to get married, did you?'

A few suburban streets away, Zahra was chatting on the phone to Andrea. She checked her sharply manicured nails while she listened to her friend's reply.

'Marrying out? That's all a bit pre-9/11,' she continued, doing her best to sound insouciant.

Andrea, she knew, wasn't happy that Zahra was marrying someone to whom she had never been introduced – and therefore was unable to pass judgment. Zahra checked herself in the mirror. She had to admit that the hairdresser had done a good job – but only after being forced to listen to her precise instructions.

'Yes, we must. We will. You'll like him, I'm sure. Just a second, I can hear Mum coming. Probably wants to perfume my knickers or something. Must go, darling.' She put down the phone.

Her mother knocked gently before entering. Zahra overheard

two cousins in the corridor arguing over a hair straightener. Some brides crave quiet but she enjoyed the chaos her wedding was stirring. Through the week, she had welcomed a host of East African and Canadian cousins, who all seemed hyperactively excited by her 'love match'. They had demanded every last detail. Who was he? Where did they meet? How did he propose? She had the story honed to a few dramatic lines that provoked the right amount of 'oohs' and 'aahs' but also left it tantalisingly incomplete.

'I've given it more oud,' said Mrs Amir, hanging up the cream sari on the wardrobe. Zahra coughed. 'It needed to be smoked a bit longer,' said her mother defensively, 'or the smell doesn't come through.' She surveyed Zahra with satisfaction. 'And now it's your turn,' she said.

The previous evening Zahra had sat before the oud burner without complaint, letting it smoke her hair, but she knew something more thorough was planned for this morning. Asghar's mother had dropped round a basket of strong-smelling oils and unguents for Mrs Amir to rub on her daughter before the wedding night. This was traditional, apparently, though Zahra had never heard about it from any of her married cousins. 'I was rubbed down by my mother,' Mrs Amir claimed, 'and she was rubbed down by hers. All from oils sent by your grandmother.'

Zahra said she would have nothing to do with this perfuming business. 'It's textbook orientalism, Mummy.'

'It's not oriental, it's Indian,' said Mrs Amir.

'It's the kind of thing *they* think we would do. Like white men painting brown women.'

'No white men will be painting you: *I* will be rubbing you with the oils.'

'It's not religious,' said Zahra, trying a different tack. 'It's cultural. They're two different things.'

'Not for us they're not,' she said, sorting through the basket of oils.

'And anyway,' Zahra added, giving it another push, 'you're always saying we should be more modern.'

'It is a bit old-fashioned,' admitted her mother before turning her irritation towards the groom's family. 'But what do you expect from such people?' She shook her head. 'The Dhalanis were the most traditional of the traditional, even in East Africa.'

'That's what I mean, Mummy, we can't let them push us around.'

'I suppose they'll never know,' Mrs Amir replied, as though contemplating retreat. 'But,' she continued, swerving to mother-knows-best mode, 'it'll make things easier on the wedding night if you smell nice – you know what I mean?'

'I do know, but I really wish I didn't.'

Zahra stood up to give her mother a hug and a kiss. 'Why don't you go and have your make-up done, and I'll rub these on myself. I promise.' Her mother headed off, grateful for the compromise, leaving Zahra with the brown and white tubs. She opened up and sniffed each one. Then she stepped back and surveyed her childhood bedroom for the last time. On the dressing table was a cherished photo of her as a little girl, sweetly beaming for her father's camera, her thick hair curled in glossy bunches. Pinned to the wall was a poster of Millais's lazily drowning Ophelia she had bought in Cambridge. Next to the tatty economics textbook was a popular biography of the Prophet and an English translation of the Quran – books she rarely opened. Her mother had told her she would happily keep her room intact and her

6

belongings secure even after she had moved out, but Zahra wanted everything – the red armchair, the large mirror, the Millais poster, the Moroccan side table – taken to her new house in Kilburn. There would be enough space, she had insisted, and Asghar wouldn't mind. She smiled to herself. Just one more day and she would be mistress of her own home.

Her mother came back in complaining that her brother's wife – a middle-aged Englishwoman from Exeter – was hogging the make-up girl. 'Let's get you dressed,' she said. After smoothing down the cream sari, Mrs Amir stood behind her daughter and tickled her neck. Zahra giggled when she saw her mother's mischievous face in the mirror. Her own features were slightly misshapen: narrow and jagged with an aquiline nose. But she had a fairish complexion, almost Kashmiri her grandmother told her, that became even fairer when she dusted it with foundation – covering up the red blotches left over from her teenage years. Her mother told her she was beautiful and, though Zahra insisted she didn't agree, she knew that boys found her attractive. She could have picked any of the community's prime bachelors: the heir to a clarified-butter fortune who had entertained her at a wedding reception with import-export tales of woe; the budding cricketer with powerful shoulders who invited her and her younger brother Mohsen to watch him play for Middlesex's second eleven; the Iraqi maulana's son dressed stylishly in black jeans and black shirt, whom she liked to distract with a flirty smile whenever he walked past her outside the old mosque. Before going to Cambridge, she had chatted to her mother about all three. They had agreed she should go to university first and settle into a job before getting engaged.

This was almost exactly as things had turned out. Except that rather than her mother nudging Maryam Auntie, the community matchmaker, into arranging meetings with an eligible family, a few short months after graduating Zahra had defiantly announced to her father that she had got engaged to Asghar Dhalani, a boy who seemed to have nothing special or appealing about him at all. When he heard the news, Mohsen was aghast: Asghar was that sad sack who was always bullied at madressa. Her mother worried that the Dhalanis came from a rough Zanzibarian family, in contrast to her husband's refined upbringing on the banks of Lake Victoria in Uganda. For his part, Dr Amir was terribly disappointed that his favourite child, as he always whispered to her that she was, had betrayed him so badly. The Dhalanis were the Amirs' arch rivals. During the great community schism ten years earlier, Asghar's father had founded the new mosque at Manor Grove, while Dr Amir had stayed on with the old mosque – and the bitterness still lingered.

It wasn't just Zahra's family who were worried. Andrea told her straight-up that she was on the rebound, and that Asghar didn't sound right for her at all. But Zahra had ignored everyone; in fact, she had relished the astonishment she had caused. Only now, on her wedding day, with the reality of married life stretching before her, had the anxious tremors truly begun.

'How are you feeling?' asked Mrs Amir.

'Never better. I don't really have to do anything today; it'll all be done for me.'

'I've laid out both sari-tops for you: the covered-up one and the less covered-up one,' she replied cautiously. 'It's your choice which one to wear.'

Traditionally, the groom's family chose the bride's clothes, though nowadays there was more leeway. Zahra had gone to the dressmaker, picked the material, suggested the cut and sent the bill to Asghar's mother. All had seemed fine until a week earlier when Mrs Dhalani called Mrs Amir. Asghar's mother had visited the dressmaker to check on her own wedding clothes, and while she was there she couldn't help enquiring about Zahra's sari. The dressmaker showed her the page Zahra had marked in *Indian Bride*. Mrs Dhalani thought it was far too exposing of the back and shoulders: she had conservative relatives from Dar-es-salaam to consider. On the phone, with Zahra hovering in the background trying to listen in, Mrs Amir protested that Zahra's choice was fashionable, adding in frank Gujarati that her son would definitely appreciate how beautiful his wife looked, especially on the wedding night.

Zahra mimed puking with two fingers.

Yet Mrs Dhalani was unmoved. Zahra saw her mother's face crease in frustration as the phone's corkscrew curls bobbed against the fridge. In the end, they deferred the decision and ordered two sari-tops: one naked round the shoulders and one demurely covered up.

'I think I'll go for the longer one,' said Zahra, going over to the bed, where they lay spread out like lifeless puppets. 'The bay windows at the new mosque are so draughty. And if you're going to go traditional, then why not go the whole way?'

'I thought you wanted to wear the short one!' her mother said in surprise. 'Your father wouldn't mind you wearing anything you wanted, you know that.'

'Oh I know he would prefer it. It would show off how terribly modern his family is.'

'He would,' said Mrs Amir putting a hand on her daughter's cheek. 'He would have loved to see the nikah ceremony. But you know how stubborn he can be.'

Her voice had the breathless, pleading tone Zahra knew well.

'Don't worry, Mummyji,' she said, striving for a gracious tone. 'I understand. Dad said he'd never set foot in the new mosque – even for his daughter's wedding. That's his right.'

'Come,' said Mrs Amir, bustling her daughter back towards the mirror, 'let's get you ready.' She noticed the unscooped oil tubs but decided not to say anything; instead she opened a box filled with gleaming silver pins.

Zahra stood up and faced her mother. 'Dad always says how bad Asghar's family is – how Mr Dhalani took his rightful place as mosque leader. Like he was Abu Bakr, and Dad was Imam Ali. That's really hurtful to Asghar.'

'You haven't told him he says that?'

'He picks up the vibe. Dad's always squeezing Asghar's shoulders, tapping him on the chin, throwing pretend punches.'

'He's known him since he was a baby. He can't see him as a grown-up.'

'How do you think that makes me feel?'

'Your father agreed in the end, didn't he?' She started sorting through the lipsticks lined up like little rockets on the dressing-table. 'Let him have his head; let him enjoy teasing Asghar. Men need to feel like they've won, even when they've lost.'

'Not exactly my style,' murmured Zahra.

'Husbands are simple creatures,' she said, a pin in her mouth. 'A nice cooked meal in the evening, and always tell them they're taller than they are.'

A cousin burst in dramatically. Auntie was needed now –

the make-up girl had dropped nail polish on the carpet. Mrs Amir bustled out of the room quickly, telling Zahra she needed to decide which sari-top to wear. Just then her phone buzzed. It was Asghar texting a good luck message with a smiley face. He sent a picture of the sunflowers from his garden. She replied telling him to wait a second. Pulling off her green T-shirt, she tried on the more revealing sari-top. The material was stiff and the hooks at the back tough to cleanly connect. She photographed herself in front of the mirror, before doing the same with the long sari-top, sending Asghar both images and asking which he preferred. She felt a thrill sending him vaguely revealing pictures. Waiting for his response, she texted again: *Why don't I tell you which one is easier to undo? xxx*

Sitting on his swing, Asghar responded: *They both look v pretty.*

New message: *Your choice.*

Zahra slumped in her armchair. Asghar's declarations of undying love were courtly and chaste, which was lovely and romantic – up to a point. That point, she thought, had surely been reached on their wedding day. She was disturbed by an unruly memory of Krish's warm hands on her leg. Putting the phone away, she walked round the room to clear her head. That boy had had no respect for her boundaries; he had treated her like his property. The man about to become her husband, though, would wait until they had bound themselves in the eyes of Allah before giving her everything he had – body and soul.

# Chapter Two

Zahra arrived at the new mosque in a cream sari brocaded with a hundred tiny mirrors. The long top she had chosen covered her arms and shoulders thoroughly. Her hands were painted with dark branches of henna and her entire body smelled sweetly of oud. She felt as though she were performing in a television show she had seen many times, but one which she had never imagined she would be starring in – making the same moves as a thousand brides before her. She had always told her mother that when she got married everything would be different. And indeed she had charmed her way into getting the bridal train to wear matching blue and gold outfits – not the garish designs suggested by Asghar's mother. (His pious little sister Fatima, who had insisted on wearing a full black abaya and black scarf over her bridesmaid's dress, was looking awkward and hot.) But she hadn't had it all her own way. Mrs Dhalani was upset at Zahra's suggestion that she wear her grandmother's red wedding sari. Western white was the appropriate colour these days – red was far too Hindu. Her wish to be driven to the mosque in a horse-drawn carriage was stymied by both the mosque sub-committee for marriages and deaths – which was worried about the hygiene implications – and by Asghar's father, who had insisted on picking her up in his dented Mercedes.

Her most daring challenge to convention had what she believed was the best religious grounding. Rather than have a male representative speak her marriage vows for her, she wanted to recite them for herself. However, this would entail her voice being broadcast from the women's section into the men's – something the new mosque had never entertained. In an email sent to the sub-committee, she cited the example of the Prophet's wife Lady Khadija, a wealthy businesswoman who had married her younger employee on her own terms. 'Was she ever silenced?' she asked pointedly. She received no reply. After three days she emailed again. Eventually, Maulana Haider responded that although it was religiously acceptable for her to recite her own marriage contract (as long as her Arabic was perfect), it was wrong for a woman's voice to be so brazenly broadcast to the men. It would be improperly distracting. She shot back asking for textual evidence. Where was it written that it was fine for a man's voice, like his own, to be heard by women but not for a woman's to be heard by a man? Weren't both sexes liable to the same distractions? In a spirit of compromise, she added that she would be happy to recite without having her voice broadcast into the men's section – the women on her side could be witnesses. But the mosque still refused. She complained to Asghar about the unfairness of it all, threatening to move the wedding to the old mosque, where they were more relaxed about such matters.

'But sweetheart, you know the problem with the old mosque. We agreed it wasn't big enough.'

'Why don't you ask your dad? He's meant to be the president.'

'Dad said it wasn't his decision,' he said. 'It's for the maulana to decide. It's okay. When Faisal Uncle is reciting your vows, I'll imagine in my head that I'm hearing your voice.'

The thought of Faisal Uncle – an elderly man with a high-pitched voice and betel nuts permanently lodged between his teeth – channelling her voice was not especially appealing.

'Darling,' he continued quickly, nervous of her silence, 'why don't we say the vows ourselves later, in the hotel? We can practise them together?' He took Zahra's hand and kissed it. 'You're better at reading Arabic than I am,' he said, his eyes brimming at the thought of her unhappiness.

She kissed his hand back, pleased that, even if she hadn't got her own way, he had acknowledged the injustice.

Stepping out of the Mercedes, Zahra's sari train was rescued from the dusty white gravel by a parade of flapping aunties. They were quickly shooed away by the older married cousin who had been assigned to take care of her. Zahra had wanted someone she knew better as her maid-of-honour – had they not fallen out, it would have been Andrea – instead of this woman from Minnesota she barely knew. Once again, though, she had been overruled by her mother who insisted that she needed someone who could tell her where to sit and when to stand on her big day. Zahra smiled broadly for the video camera that was catching her every step and gesture – grateful, at this point, for the Minnesotan's advice to kick out her feet to avoid tripping over her heavily embroidered sari.

Walking slowly across the courtyard, Zahra looked round

the new mosque curiously. When Asghar's family had founded the place, they had taken more than half the community with them; but her own family had stayed resolutely loyal to the old hall. On the few occasions she had been here for weddings or funerals, she had been struck by its strange hybrid nature. The new mosque's website said that Manor Grove had been built by a minor Georgian earl, and been put on the market by his last female descendant, who couldn't afford the inheritance bill after the last earl – Octavian Michael – had passed away. The large estate overlooked a pleasant spread of fields and farm cottages; in the distance sheep grazed bucolically next to a private tennis court. Inside the grounds she saw a square of faded brown grass where the earl had once played croquet – or was it bowls? She couldn't remember. Now it was a cricket pitch where the new mosque competed against other mosques from around the country. As she passed through the courtyard, Zahra noticed a dry fountain encircled with empty plinths that had once supported semi-naked Greek statues. On the website she had seen photographs of Mr Dhalani and a teenage Asghar pulling white sheets over the women whose improbably round stone breasts, Zahra couldn't help think, echoed the shape of the mosque's recently installed dome. (The picture caption said they were following in the footsteps of the Prophet who, when he reclaimed Makkah, had ordered the city's idols destroyed.) Other pictures showed the courtyard on Eid ul-fitr covered with green tarpaulin for open-air morning prayers, with stalls selling snacks and religious trinkets.

Inside, there were a few signs that the mosque had once been a grand house. Behind the side door was a row of defunct servants' bells. The two large reception rooms had been converted into the gents' and ladies' sections; and the two sets of French windows, which once opened on to the garden, now led to the car park. She walked along the plastic strip laid out on the carpet, scanning the crowd for people she knew: aside from her cousins, and the girls from madressa looking in admiration – and perhaps envy – at one of the first of their cohort to get married, there was also Andrea in a pink sari, filming the whole thing on her phone. Zahra gave her a little wave, and then did the same for her mother – plus a wink. Her mum shook her head, as if to indicate that she should remain demure on her wedding day, but Maryam Auntie, ever the community matriarch, gave her an encouraging smile, seemingly delighted she was animating the wedding by pushing at its strictures. Where was the fun in a bride who did everything by the book?

Zahra approached the raised dais where she would be sitting on a large white sofa. (The other bride getting married that day was at the other end of the room on her own sofa: they exchanged brief smiles.) She imagined the posh parties once held at the house: perhaps this dais was where string quartets and jazz bands had played? Her cousin nudged her; it was time to reapply her lip-gloss. She pulled out a small tube and hastily dabbed Zahra's lips, something she would repeat every half-hour for the rest of the day. 'They're already practically dripping,' she whispered to the Minnesotan, who replied that the more she talked the more her make-up would look bad in the photos. The photographer, an Englishwoman dressed in jeans and a black T-shirt, squeezed round the seated ladies, looking for the best angle from which to shoot the bride.

The boy reciting Quran in the men's section finished his

portion. Zahra watched the action from the men's side on the large television screens mounted inside the ladies' section. Maulana Haider clambered up the pulpit's dark green steps. When Zahra had last seen him at the old mosque, his beard had only been edged with orange henna; now it was fully orange with grey patches at the tips. She was surprised when he began speaking in English, rather than Urdu, although rather laboriously.

'The holy verses we have just heard mean the following,' said the maulana. '"Among His signs is that He matched you with spouses from among yourselves to live in tranquillity and contentment with one another; and He placed between you love and care towards your spouses. These are clear signs for people who reflect."'

These words, which needed no hedging or contextual quali-fication, spoke to Zahra with a moving directness.

After the lecture – the rest of which Zahra barely listened to, instead pretending to read the white-embroidered Quran she had been given – the camera panned down to where the two grooms were leaning back on purple cushions. Their best men were older married cousins who, so it was assumed, would initiate them into the secrets of successful married life. She saw Asghar's cousin whisper in his ear and watched as her soon-to-be husband clumsily adjusted the red and gold scarf hanging raggedly around his neck.

The other marriage ceremony began. Zahra listened to the austere, un-poetical vows: no 'for better, for worse' or 'for richer, for poorer'; no 'love, honour and obey'. Private emotion was downplayed in favour of brisk ritual. Maybe formality was for the best. When she and Asghar had tried to come up with their own vows for the civil marriage ceremony two weeks earlier, they had had no clue where to begin. In the end they had gone with one of the standard formulas.

Now it was their turn. In place of her missing father, her representative was Faisal Uncle with the betel-nut teeth. Zahra caught Andrea's eye as she mouthed, 'Who's that?' She could only shrug and smile in response. In the crowd she spotted Asghar's mother crying, her eyeshadow smudging. The uncle asked Maulana Haider three times whether Asghar was willing to marry Zahra at the agreed bridal price. Three times Asghar, via the maulana, confirmed that he accepted Zahra. It all went by in a blur. When it was over, the congregation cried blessings on the couple, while the women began ululating joyfully in the way their servants had done back in East Africa.

Through the thick walls, Asghar heard the women's muffled cries. His fellow groom, a handsome man with wolfish sideburns, leaned over to congratulate Asghar.

'Well done, mate,' he said, putting a hand on his shoulder.

'Thanks, you too,' replied Asghar.

'It's even better than you think,' he whispered. Asghar shook his head, puzzled. 'You'll see what I mean,' he added with a grin, before standing up to respectfully embrace his new father-in-law.

Asghar's best man nudged him to also rise. Asghar embraced Maulana Haider followed by his own father. He was relieved nothing had gone wrong. In the minutes before the ceremony, he had been convinced that a message would arrive to say that Zahra had pulled out of the wedding. When the vows were complete, his heart lifted and a powerful surge of confidence ran through him. He joined the line where the guests shuffled past to congratulate him. Beside him, his father was openly campaigning for re-election, clasping the elders closely and speaking quietly in their ears. Asghar felt flattered that his father, who always urged him to get more involved in mosque affairs, was able to use his wedding to help with his campaign. It made him feel useful. Asghar knew he had disappointed his father on many occasions, especially during that dark time when he was forced to leave Enfield House. Yet by marrying the daughter of his chief rival, Asghar felt like he had won through love what his father had not managed through cunning.

An hour later, Asghar was sitting in the back of the hired Bentley and waiting for Zahra. He checked his phone for the address of the hotel where they would be spending their wedding night. He had searched dozens of places in the area; in the end he chose Foxfield Lodge, the first place he had looked, in fact, which was a popular destination for the mosque's other newlyweds. Foxfield was so used to Muslim guests that they put little watering cans in the bathrooms and served halal English breakfasts without you even having to ask – 'even beef sausages!' he had boasted to Zahra. Asghar raised his eyes from his phone as Zahra emerged from the mosque. She looked like a film star. Night had fallen and the cameraman flooded her in a pool of light. Family and friends snapped with their cameras and phones. As planned, Asghar got out and joined his wife. He pecked her on the cheek and demurely held her hand. They spent an hour posing for photographs with the family, and then returned to the car. The English driver – wearing a peaked cap whose brass insignia had been rubbed clean – held the backseat door open for Zahra, while Asghar lifted her sari to safety. Everyone cheered as they were driven past the wrought iron gates and down the dark country roads to begin a new life.

'You okay?' asked Asghar.

'I can't see you,' she said.

'Turn the lights on,' said Asghar authoritatively. The driver flicked a switch and the back seat lit up.

'That's better,' she said, putting her hand on Asghar's arm and giving it a proper squeeze.

The couple walked into Foxfield's pillared hall and waited at the empty reception. Asghar rang the bell gently. From the back wall a variety of stuffed fox heads stared glassily down.

'God, English people are weird,' said Zahra, looking up. The receptionist appeared and checked them in. Walking to the lifts, they passed the smoking lounge where people were no longer allowed to smoke. Zahra pointed with her primped eyelashes to the beetroot-faced man asleep in front of the fire and giggled. The man looked up and stared, and they both hurried on.

Earlier that day, Zahra had texted to say that she didn't want anything tacky in the hotel; so Asghar frantically phoned to cancel the balloons and banners his mother had ordered. Softly lit by the bed's sidelights, the bridal suite looked rather plain to him. The only signs that this was no ordinary occasion were the red roses on the table and the heart-shaped chocolates on their pillows.

'Are you hungry? Shall I order something?' he asked.

'No, I'm fine. Luckily, I managed to get some biryani. Usually brides don't eat anything because it doesn't look dignified, apparently. So they sit on the sofa starving, staring into space looking sad while everyone else stuffs themselves. But last year, a bride fainted so Maryam Auntie changed the policy.'

'So you got to eat with the others?'

'Not exactly,' she said, taking off her earrings and bracelets. '"You have to keep your respect," Maryam Auntie said. So they set up a table and chair in the corridor. I spent the whole time staring at buckets and mops in the cupboard, trying not to get rice on my sari, while the women pushed past me getting to the toilet.' She picked up her towel from the bed. 'How about you?'

'I sat with the maulana. They served me even before him.'

'What a *privilege*,' she said in a mock-Indian accent and shut the bathroom door behind her.

Asghar, after hauling their suitcases on to the rack, lay on the immaculate sheets and unwrapped his melting chocolate. He pulled out *The Making of an Islamic Marriage* hoping to find some last-minute advice. He flicked to the final page and found some faded quotations he hadn't noticed before. His heart beat faster. Maybe this was the secret knowledge for which the booklet had been famed? He read the first saying: 'When a man sits amid his wife's four parts and presses her to the limit, a ritual bath becomes obligatory on him. From *Sahih Muslim*.'

What on earth were these 'four parts'? Unless he had been drastically misled there was only one part to worry about. The line below was bracingly clear. According to the Holy Prophet: 'Allah is not shy of the truth: do not enter women from behind.' The note below said that he was replying to a question from his companion Umar, who later became the second caliph.

Why was Asghar not surprised that it was rough-tongued

Umar who had asked such a question? One jurist apparently said that sex with your spouse was superior to one thousand years of worship. (That sounded promising.) Another that before sex each partner should prepare the other with 'kissing and words'. Kissing he got, but which words? Did he mean a special prayer? It was not specified. There was, however, right at the end, the prayer to be recited as the couple reached orgasm together: 'Oh Allah, protect our offspring from the touch of Satan. From *Sahih al-Bukhari*.' He tried memorising the Arabic but it didn't stick. Never mind; they wouldn't be trying for children that evening in any case. That prayer could wait for the future.

Now Asghar examined the condom packet. It had been just his luck that the chemist serving him had been a hijabi girl – possibly even from the community, he wasn't sure. She had sold him the condoms – and toothpaste, dental floss, cold-sore cream and hay-fever tablets – without much interest. No coy smile or bitten lip. She was wearing a wedding ring and for one mad moment, Asghar had thought of asking her what sex was really like. Was it as functional as cleaning your teeth or curing a sore? Would it feel different from masturbation? Searching online, he had found a Christian blog that said married sex elevated base desires into something sacred; no longer was the orgasm provoked for its own sake – as was the case with self-pollution or casual sex – but to achieve 'ecstatic intimacy'. Asghar started to sweat.

Zahra emerged from the bathroom wrapped in a white dressing gown with a head towel. She sat next to him on the bed and dried her long, thickly matted hair. Her movements loosened her gown and her breasts slowly shook free. Asghar stretched out his hands, and playfully covered them up. She

22

caught his hands and pulled herself on top of him; as she kissed him her wet hair lashed his neck.

'Wait,' he said, pulling away. 'We must do the prayers first.'

'We'll do them later,' she replied urgently, tearing off her gown and straddling his thighs. Feeling the expectant heat between her legs, he wriggled free from his clothes and slipped under the sheets. When she joined him, he felt the sensational newness of her naked body. She grabbed his penis – slightly too roughly – with her hands. The thought of Zahra touching him turned him on more than her actual touch. He tore open the condom packet and rolled the sheath on swiftly – he had practised this part many times. Rolling on top of her he began thrusting wildly. He felt a pleasant friction.

'I'm in!' he cried.

'Those are my thighs,' she said gently. She tried to direct him with her hands but he carried on thrusting.

'Sweetheart,' she said. 'We might need to slow down . . . I'll need some attention first.'

'Of course,' he said, feeling immediately guilty. His erection humbly retreated.

Guided by her hand he rubbed her for a few minutes.

'Try again now,' she said. By now his withdrawn penis barely supported the condom. She brushed her hand over the empty plastic.

'Do I need to touch you again?' she asked.

'No, I can get it back,' he said, hoping that tensing his whole body might help.

'Don't you like touching me?'

'I'm sorry,' he said. 'When I'm on my own this never happens.'

'Don't worry,' she said, slipping out of bed to pull on a pair of oversized pyjamas. 'I suppose we've got our whole lives to make this work.'


Zahra woke up early the next morning to find Asghar's hand draped over her waist and his neck nestled in her shoulder. She pulled away and busied herself getting ready. She fixed her hair and ironed the long blue dress she had brought for the wedding breakfast at the Dhalanis. Asghar was still asleep. She boiled the hotel's travel kettle and made him a small cup of tea.

'Asghar,' she said quietly, 'we need to get going.'

He opened his eyes and instinctively covered his sprawling naked body with the sheet.

'Yes, yes, I'm coming,' he said. 'Five minutes.'

'But we'll be late for your parents.'

'Okay,' he said, wrapping the sheet around him and sitting up. His tired eyes and messy hair made him look like a lost little boy. She ruffled his hair and he looked back, playfully grumpy. For the first time she noticed that his placid hairless chest was dotted with beauty spots. She kissed her finger and touched each one. 'That tickles!' he said, almost rolling off the bed.

As Zahra had predicted, they were late to the breakfast. Mrs Dhalani had already cooked an oily banquet of fried eggs and fried bread. Asghar apologised for keeping them waiting.

'No, no, it's fine,' said his mother, wiping her hands on a faded royal wedding tea towel. 'It's better sizzling, but you must be so tired from yesterday.'

'You must be exhausted, no?' asked Mr Dhalani. Was it Zahra's imagination or had he exchanged a naughty glance with his wife?

'Zahra,' said Fatima, turning to her new sister-in-law, 'which prayers did you recite before your wedding night?'

'I'm not sure. The usual ones,' she answered. Asghar had warned her about his father's creepy jokes; he had not mentioned anything about his irritatingly devout sister. She seemed like the kind of girl who spent her nights leaving comments on religious websites.

'I've got a special version for my wedding night,' said Fatima. 'On such a night nothing is more important than Allah's blessings.'

'We're trying to find a boy Islamic enough for Fatima,' Mr Dhalani told Zahra. 'It's very hard. She keeps on saying their beard isn't long enough.'

'Aren't you still at school?' Zahra asked.

'I can get engaged now and get married later,' she said. 'That's how everyone does it these days.'

'We'll see about that,' said her mother.

'The last boy who visited was very good: tall, handsome, full beard,' Mr Dhalani said. 'Guess what she said? He wears too tight trousers!'

'They were awful!' exclaimed Fatima.

'They are the latest fashion,' protested Mrs Dhalani.

'I don't want some fashion boy,' she said. 'I want a serious guy to study with in Iran.'

'Why not wait until you get out there?' Zahra suggested. 'You'll find lots of seriously religious guys.'

'There might be joint seminars,' said Fatima dreamily.

'Don't encourage her,' said Mrs Dhalani. 'First Asghar is disappearing, living God-knows-where in London, when there is a lovely upstairs bedroom for you here—' She stopped herself just in time, refocusing her annoyance at the safe target of her daughter. '—And now you want to go gallivanting to Iran. Let's stay a family a bit longer.'

As Zahra ate her cold eggs she noticed that Asghar had hardly spoken during the family exchange. He seemed comfortable sitting quietly and occasionally checking his phone under the table. Clearly the Dhalani family had large personalities jostling for attention; perhaps Asghar had decided there was no point competing. In her own home everyone was expected to speak up. Her father made sure she was allowed the time to say what she thought as much as her brother – whether the discussion was about current affairs or what they should watch on television that evening. The Dhalanis seemed to speak all at once and past each other. She thought back to the failure of the previous night. Maybe she had been too insistent. They were both tired and under pressure. Asghar, she was starting to realise, needed careful handling.

'When's the flight to Spain?' asked Mrs Dhalani.

'Asghar's arranged all that,' said Zahra, putting a hand on her husband's knee.

'Wednesday,' said Asghar, looking up. 'Straight to Granada.'

'The caliph's last sigh as he left Islamic Spain,' said Fatima. 'How tragic!'

'We're staying in the Arab quarter,' said Asghar. 'Really close to the Alhambra.'

Zahra had been excited when Asghar had suggested southern Spain: it was somewhere she might easily have chosen herself – rather than the Maldives or Bali, where other community couples went. 'I've heard it's an amazing mix of cultures,' she said. 'There's even a mosque that's also a cathedral.'

'What's that?' said Mr Dhalani, puzzled.

26

'The Christians destroyed the city and captured the mosque, putting idols in the prayer hall,' said Fatima. 'It's incredibly sad.'

'Really?' asked Asghar. 'We have to see that.'

'Christians have always been at war with us – even today,' Fatima said. 'Look at Iraq.'

'The weather will be wonderful this time of year,' Zahra interrupted. 'I've seen beautiful pictures of the Alhambra gardens.'

'Send us a postcard,' said Mr Dhalani with a wink.

# Chapter Three

The bus from Granada airport dropped them on a busy central boulevard. Asghar pulled down his baseball cap to shield his eyes from the sun, and squinted at his directions to the guesthouse. According to the map, they needed to take the road opposite the bus stop. Carrying Zahra's heavy canvas bag on his shoulder, as well as dragging his own suitcase, he led her up a cobbled slope to the Albayzin – the old town over which the Alhambra fortress loomed. He had booked a guesthouse that claimed to be a historical Arab house. He had the address but the streets were poorly marked and the place was tough to find. For twenty minutes they scraped their suitcases over the uneven stones, until Zahra spotted a small sign for Casa Benengeli written in a sinuous Latin font designed to evoke the Arabic script. He gripped the doorknocker – an iron hoop running through a pig's nose – and banged loudly. There was no answer.

'God, I hope the guy's in,' said Zahra, flapping her loose shirt in the heat.

'He promised he would be,' Asghar said confidently. 'He's called Ian.' He looked round the hot deserted streets. It was late afternoon and he guessed most people were taking siestas. Suddenly, a panel in the wooden door shot back and a smiling bronze face appeared.

'Ahoy there,' said Ian.

Leading them up a narrow staircase, Ian explained how he had come to be running a guesthouse in Granada. He had been born in Portsmouth fifty-three years earlier. His English family, not to mention the English weather, did not agree with him, and the day after graduating from Chelsea School of Art, he moved to Spain with no money and a vague plan. He taught English in Barcelona and then Seville, painting in his spare time. Fifteen years ago, he was going through a painful divorce from his Spanish wife and spent what was left of his savings on the Casa Benengeli in Granada – a city whose oriental splendour he had always admired. It doubled as his studio. In his top-floor workshop, he spent his mornings designing geometric patterns for glazed tiles and painting fantastical scenes of Islamic Spain.

'We'd love to see them,' said Asghar, always keen to please.

'I keep examples of my work in each room for guests to peruse. They are also available for purchase.' He spoke with a slight Spanish accent.

Asghar asked how often he returned home.

'Home? Here is home,' he said, sounding slightly annoyed to be asked. He showed them into a large, furniture-heavy bedroom with Arabesque fretting on the wooden blinds. On the wall was a large canvas depicting an Eastern harem.

'Is that yours?' asked Zahra, dropping her rucksack to take a closer look.

'For my sins,' said Ian, looking pleased with himself.

'It's very . . . atmospheric,' said Asghar, immediately absorbed by the scene: a fair-skinned woman was stretched out beside a steaming bathing pool, while a black maid poured water over her. The bather's wet dress hugged her fulsome outline.

'That's a special one for me,' said Ian. 'The girls who modelled for it were guests of mine.'

'Really?' said Zahra, an eyebrow raised.

'Two girls from France: close friends. They were so happy they bought the original but I made a copy. Anyway,' he continued, 'let me not keep you. You must be tired. There is bread in the cupboard and cheese in the fridge. On the table is all the information you need about the Alhambra.' Ian bustled back upstairs.

'Oh. My. God,' said Zahra, falling on the bed laughing. 'Who the hell is this guy?'

'I have no idea,' said Asghar.

'Look at it,' she said pointing, almost gleeful at how easily condemnable the painting was.

'Sweetheart, do you want to go somewhere else?'

'No, let's stay. It's a beautiful house. We can ignore it.'

Asghar turned on the plastic ceiling fan and, as it stuttered into life, joined her on the bed. He leaned forward and kissed her gently, then pressed his clammy body close to hers.

'Not now,' she whispered, 'I'm so tired.'

'No need to say another word,' he said. He mimed zipping his mouth shut and then, without quite knowing why, mimed zipping his fly.

Next morning, they climbed up to the Alhambra through the misty dawn. Already there were a hundred or so tourists queuing at the entrance, like medieval petitioners waiting for an audience. Standing with Zahra, Asghar read aloud from the Islamic history book he had borrowed from the new mosque's library, authored by one Dr R. S. Hassan, PhD.

After the conquest of Spain eighty years after the Prophet's death, Asghar informed Zahra, the Muslims created the first multi-faith society, in which Jews and Christians were free to practise their religions.

'It says here,' said Asghar, 'that even the Jews call it their Golden Age.'

'Some amazing Muslims were Spanish – Averroes and all that lot,' said Zahra. 'They were close enough to the Europeans, you see, to pick up their learning.'

'Wasn't it the other way round?' asked Asghar. He quoted Dr R. S. Hassan's words: 'The Muslims translated ancient Greek works – Plato, Aristotle – when Europe was still in the Dark Ages. They were the best for poetry, medicine and philosophy, while the Christians were busy fighting each other.'

'Well, I'm sure it was a two-way process.'

'Dr Hassan says Granada fell in 1492 *because* people like Ibn Rushd were too Westoxified. They became too settled in their ways and soft – not like the old tribal warriors of the desert.'

'Have you read any Averroes?' she asked.

'I haven't,' he admitted. 'Why, what does he say?'

'Well, it's very complex,' she said vaguely. 'Look – we're nearly at the entrance.'


By the time they reached the head of the queue, the sun was beating down hard. Entering the cool palace was a welcome balm. The buildings were smaller than Asghar had expected and not as impressive as the monumental shrines in Iran he had visited. Zahra informed him that the subtle beauty of the courtyards lay in their perfect proportions – the bright ponds and intricately carved calligraphy. Perhaps that was why, she said, after quickly glancing at Wikipedia on her phone, that the conquering Castilian monarchs Ferdinand and Isabella did not destroy the Alhambra as they had the other Muslim splendours of Granada. Instead they took up residence and frolicked about in Moorish dress.

Asghar and Zahra left the palace and climbed the crowded tower where Boabdil, the last caliph of Spain, had been forced to surrender the city's keys to the Christians. Looking out at the stunning mountain landscape that had once belonged to the Muslims, Asghar felt incredibly sad. He had hoped that visiting Granada would make him feel proud of these early European Muslims, whom he regarded as his spiritual ancestors. Yet he found the city suffused with melancholy: every church was built on a destroyed mosque; the palace of Charles V, next to the Alhambra, was a grey stone monstrosity that had replaced the grand mosque. All that was left of a great civilisation were a few quaint tourist spots: all Spain's Muslims had either been converted or expelled. It might have been a long time ago but Asghar took the *reconquista* personally. For him it recalled the ethnic cleansing of the Bosnians only a few years earlier; perhaps, he thought gloomily, given the way things were going, something similar could happen in Britain. He looked at the Western tourists sitting on the floor scoffing crushed ham sandwiches. They seemed oblivious to the tower's significance or else saw it as a relic of a lost world that could be admired only because it had been defeated. Asghar, though, looked at the Alhambra as a warning from history. He wanted to explain all this to Zahra, but she was too busy re-tying her hair into a bun. She pushed her large sunglasses over her head.

'Time for a selfie?' she asked.

After wandering in the gardens for a while, they returned to the Albayzin for lunch. Moroccan immigrants had recreated a souk-like atmosphere among the steep alleys, and opened halal places to eat. They spent a pleasant hour at Ricote's Cafe where they ate chicken wraps and chips, and spoke to the waiter in madressa Arabic. Returning to Casa Benengeli, they lay in bed and dozed.

Asghar woke up feeling aroused. He put an arm on Zahra's shoulder and pulled her round to face him. Still half-asleep, she resisted at first but then gave way into his arms. He kissed her neck and she gave a little moan. He stroked her shoulders with his hands. She seemed aware of what he was doing, but didn't open her eyes. He carried on for a bit and then stopped, feeling both disappointed and relieved. Their failed wedding night had raised the stakes for every subsequent physical intimacy. One misplaced word or misperceived gesture could make a fragile situation worse. Zahra snoozed with her mouth slightly open – a picture of innocent pliability. He touched her cheek with the back of his hand and slowly disentangled his body from hers. She must be just as nervous, he thought – all this was new to her as well. He tried to be cheerful: if they both kept taking small steps, they would eventually meet in the middle. He turned away distractedly from Ian's harem painting, and fell into a troubled sleep.

That evening they walked hand-in-hand from Casa Benengeli to a plateau from where, Ian had told them, they could get an excellent view of the Alhambra. Under a cold moon the Moorish palace was bathed in golden light. Zahra was wearing a floral-pattern summer dress just above the knee; it looked pretty daring to Asghar, but no one knew them in Spain so he figured it didn't matter. And it did make her look achingly sexy.

Just then a familiar sound drifted on the wind: a muezzin reciting the call to prayer. They followed the voice down an alleyway and round the corner, where they found a brightly lit mosque. Asghar saw a man standing by the entrance; noticing his curiosity, the man beckoned them to come forward.

'As-salaam aleikum,' said the man, who had fair skin and a wispy ginger beard.

'Wa aleikum salaam,' replied Asghar in his best accent. The man told them his name was Tariq, and that he was the mosque's guardian. Asghar said they were visitors from England.

'Welcome,' he said, inviting them inside and staring disapprovingly at Zahra's legs. 'Please come for Isha prayers.'

'I'm not dressed properly,' said Zahra, crossing her bare arms self-consciously.

'Don't worry,' said Tariq. 'My wife will bring proper clothes for you.' He phoned his wife and spoke a few words in Spanish. Asghar glanced at Zahra but she betrayed little emotion. Other worshippers rushed past them – including, Asghar noticed, the Moroccan waiter who had served them that afternoon. After a minute or two, Tariq's wife emerged with a bag of clothes. Her face was veiled except for her startling blue eyes. Zahra wore the scarf she was offered and wrapped another round her exposed legs. Following Tariq's wife, she walked awkwardly towards the ladies' entrance. Tariq directed Asghar to where he could perform wudhu. Inside, the mosque was

34

beautifully decorated with a low chandelier and bejewelled prayer niche. He joined the prayers, which were led by an imam wearing a brown cloak and green fez.

Outside, Asghar found Tariq speaking to Zahra alone. She looked uncomfortable wearing a large green woollen cloak.

'Wow, you look like a Jedi!' he said. Zahra tilted her head at him sarcastically.

'I was telling your wife the history of our Granada mosque,' said Tariq, whose English was fluent but accented. The mosque, he told them, had been the first built in Spain since 1492. Planned since Franco's death, it had only been completed a few years earlier, in the teeth of opposition from the Church and conservative Spaniards. That was why he, Tariq, stood guard at the entrance during the call to prayer.

'I do not look for trouble,' he said, 'but we must be careful.' The imam and most of the congregation were Moroccan; but Tariq was a Spanish convert to Islam – the word he used was 'revert' – who claimed he could trace his ancestry to before the Christian reconquest.

'My family were forced to practise Islam in secret, praying and fasting behind closed doors. Eventually, the pressure was too much and they forgot where they came from. But they were Muslim for hundreds of years—'

'Longer than ours!' said Asghar, enchanted by the story.

'—so it could not all be erased.'

'We're staying in an old Arab guesthouse,' said Zahra.

'Casa Benengeli!' said Asghar.

'Just like the one my ancestors lived in,' said Tariq. 'Did you notice the door?'

'The big black one?' asked Asghar.

35

'You will find a hatch,' he said, framing his face with his palms, 'built by the Catholics to spy on Muslims. They checked to make sure that you were drinking wine and eating pigs – that you weren't fasting in Ramadan or celebrating Eid.'

'Astaghfirullah,' said Asghar, tutting in the way his father did whenever he heard about some shameful calamity that had befallen Muslims.

'Even today you can't eat in a Spanish restaurant without pig meat in your food.' Tariq's grey eyes glistened. 'They slip it in the soup even if you say you're Muslim – *especially* if you say you're Muslim. That's our situation in al-Andalus. Nothing has changed in five hundred years. The Castilians will never accept this is our land, not theirs.'

Asghar felt a rush of vindication. Tariq was articulating exactly what he had felt on Boabdil's tower.

'Tell me,' continued Tariq, turning to Asghar, 'will you visit Qurtuba?'

'Where?'

Tariq looked briefly vexed but then regained his composure. 'Cordoba. It's a famous city, not far from here. There is a wonderful *mesquita*.'

'Is that the Cordoba Mosque?' asked Asghar. 'Apparently it's amazing.'

'Some of us are going there tomorrow for Friday prayers. You must join us.'

'That sounds great,' said Asghar. 'We planned to go anyway.'

'We'll try to make it,' said Zahra.

Tariq insisted on walking them back to Casa Benengeli. On the way he told them the story of his reversion to Islam. Visiting his grandfather in the countryside as a boy, Tariq had seen him wake before dawn and wash his face and arms at the farm faucet in the yard, and then do some stretches – 'a bit like yoga'. Only years after his death did Tariq see Moroccans performing wudhu and praying salaat; and only then did he recognise these half-remembered rituals as unconsciously preserved from his Muslim ancestors.

'I pray for my grandfather every day. I say the prayers he wanted to speak but he never knew the words.'

Opening the black door, Ian looked surprised to see Tariq and greeted him warily. They spoke in Spanish while Asghar and Zahra stood quietly. When Tariq was ready to leave, Zahra remembered she was still wearing the green woollen cloak from the mosque. She told him she would go and change and bring it back.

'Keep it,' he replied. 'You can wear it tomorrow. Women are welcome.' She protested but he insisted.

'Let's swap numbers,' said Asghar, already looking forward to the Friday adventure.

Once the door was closed, Asghar told Ian he thought Tariq was an interesting guy.

'What did he tell you?' asked Ian. Asghar repeated the story about his Spanish Muslim ancestors. Ian chuckled.

'His name isn't Tariq,' he said, 'it's Alonso. I've known him since he was a teenager. His parents are lawyers from downtown – Catholic as the hills, especially the mother. They helped me buy this place.'

'What's his deal?' asked Zahra.

'Alonso always changes his story. First he was a surrealist, then a punk, and now he's a Muslim. His parents sent him to an American school in Madrid, away from a bad crowd. He met a Turkish boy whose father was some big cleric. When he returned to Granada he claimed he was now a Muslim –

and that his family was descended from *Mudéjars*. *Al*-onso, do you get it? We thought it was another phase, but this time it appears to have stuck.' Ian ran his fingers through his slicked-back hair. 'For me all religions are the same: money-making schemes run by powerful men with beards. The stories I could tell you about the Church.' He stopped on the stairs and half turned around. 'But still, you hear funny things about his mosque.'

'What things?' said Asghar, alert to Ian's suspicious tone.

'Someone told me they invited a preacher who wanted Muslims to reconquer Spain, bring back the caliphate – that sort of thing.'

'We didn't hear anything strange,' said Zahra.

'I'm not saying Alonso is into anything dodgy – he's always been a polite kid. But a couple that stay with me every summer, their cousin was killed on the trains in Madrid. So we have to be vigilant.'

Now the atrocity had been invoked, the conversation had nowhere to go.

Back in their room, undressing in front of Ian's harem painting, Asghar said he thought it was inspiring that Islam was finding a home where once it had been so ruthlessly suppressed. Zahra said Tariq was creepy. She hadn't liked how close he had stood to her while they were alone in the mosque's courtyard. And why had he insisted on walking them home?

'He's standing up for Muslims – in a place they were ethnic-ally cleansed, just like in Bosnia.'

'Those things were five hundred years apart.'

'Tariq said people hate the mosque. They had a pig's head thrown in the courtyard.'

'Why are you suddenly in love with Tariq?' She started to take off her Jedi cloak.

'Just because he reverts to Islam, that makes him bad?'

'He's not a revert; he's a convert.'

She was struggling with the cloak and so he came over to help. 'When one member of our family is being oppressed,' he said, 'we have a responsibility to support them. That's all Tariq's doing.'

They finally got the cloak off. Zahra scrunched it up and threw it under the bed.

'I'm hungry,' she said. 'Is there anything to eat?' Asghar took the hint and said nothing.

After finding some bread and cheese in the kitchenette, she sliced the dark loaf and unwrapped the vacuum-packed hard cheese.

'I'm making a sandwich – do you want one?' she asked.

'What kind of cheese is it? Is it halal?'

'It's cheese,' she said. 'It's made from milk. How can it be halal or haraam?'

'Sometimes they wrap it in pig bladder – especially Spanish cheeses, I'm sure. You remember what Tariq said?'

'I doubt this cheese comes from an Islamophobic farm.'

'Let me look at the ingredients.' Unable to read Spanish, Asghar couldn't work out if the cheese was vegetarian. He was always careful with halal food; he had given up his favourite brand of fruit pastilles after his mum forwarded him an email saying they contained gelatine.

'Can't we give it the benefit of the doubt?' said Zahra. 'I'm really hungry.'

'I'll just have the bread,' Asghar replied.

'Suit yourself,' she said sharply. She took a bite of bread

and cheese. 'Our parents never cared about eating English meat, you know', she ventured, her mouth still full. 'They only started making a fuss when halal butchers opened.'

'What do you mean?' he asked.

'Our families would never go without meat.'

'Have you ever eaten non-halal?'

'I once ate a chicken curry in the college canteen.' She cut some more bread and handed him a dry slice.

'Really?' he said, his curiosity overcoming his disapproval. 'What did it taste like?'

'Exactly the same!' she said. 'Except it was cooked by English people, so it was bland as hell.'

The thought of his wife eating haraam meat made him feel strangely homesick. He watched her chew her bread and cheese and consoled himself with a bite of his own plain leathery crust.

Tariq texted him saying they should meet at the *mesquita* at midday. There was a coach very early the next morning. Asghar said he was going to bed right away; he wanted to be fresh. She asked to borrow his book on Islamic Spain by Dr R. S. Hassan; she always needed something to read before bed. She had brought her own reading material – a detective novel and *The Economist* – and so Asghar took her request as a gesture of reconciliation. Giving her the book, he pecked her lightly on the lips.

# Chapter Four

Zahra had risen at dawn but Asghar had taken so long to get ready they almost missed the coach to Cordoba. Taking her seat, she was sweaty and palpitating – definitely in no mood to chat about what the day might bring. After attempting to share his excitement a few times, Asghar got the message and, after closing his eyes, slumped awkwardly on his side, fast asleep. Once she was awake, Zahra couldn't nap and reading on coaches always made her feel sick. She stared out of the window. In the distance the snowy tips of the Alpujarras looked majestic above the lemon trees. She wondered about Tariq. Was he rebelling against his Catholic parents, as Ian had said, or was he seriously exploring his Islamic heritage? Either way there was something disconcerting about his harping on 1492. Surely, she thought, history was the story of one group of people conquering another, from east to west and west to east? How did Asghar think Spain had become Islamic in the first place?

They arrived in Cordoba late morning, and followed the pretty streets towards the *mesquita*. They walked along the river bank, watching smaller vessels trying to navigate around the larger tourist boats. 'Tariq said he would be leading Friday prayers at the mosque,' Asghar said. 'We should hurry up.'

'We have time,' said Zahra, who would not have minded missing Tariq.

At the *mesquita*, Zahra was surprised to see signs announcing it as a cathedral. She had assumed both religions shared the space, but Tariq had given the impression that the mosque predominated. Stepping inside the imposing walls, there didn't seem to be anywhere to put their shoes. She picked up a leaflet printed by the Church authorities. Upon their conquest of the region, it read, the Moors destroyed the Visigothic church that had stood on the site and built a mosque in its place. When the Church reclaimed the building in 1236, it reconsecrated the site and built a cathedral within the old mosque walls. Where they were standing, the pamphlet made clear, was a purely Christian place of worship. Zahra felt like an interloper. Tariq's green cloak stayed tucked in her bag: the stern guards patrolling the place did not look like they would appreciate her wearing it.

Further inside, they saw the red-and-white banded pillars sprouting from the floor like palm trees.

'That's the mosque part,' whispered Asghar. A statue of a man riding a horse caught Zahra's eye. A sign described him as 'Santiago Matamoros'; below the horse's hooves were the crushed bodies of Muslim soldiers. She shivered. Back home, her family would sometimes visit old churches, and she would happily rest on the pews while her mother lit a candle. Mrs Amir had been to a Catholic school in Nairobi and liked to say a prayer for the nuns who taught her. But here the ghost of the Moorish mosque was discomfiting: taking a pew would mean taking sides in an ancient battle; lighting a candle meant approving what the Church had done to the place.

She left Asghar staring upwards at the wave of pillars, and took refuge in a museum-like display in a nearby alcove. A glass case housed medieval gravestones, which had Latin inscriptions on one side and Arabic words on the reverse. Rather than make new tombstones, the sign said, the Christians had reused the Islamic monuments for their own purposes. She felt relieved to find a place that offered some anthropological neutrality. The only reason the Muslim tombstones had been saved was because – like the building itself – they had been too valuable to discard. The gravestones, she concluded, were moving emblems of the true multicultural inheritance of Muslim Spain. She circled the stones respectfully.

Asghar, however, did not see the gravestones in the same way.

'It makes me want to cry,' he said when he saw them. 'Our Muslim brothers dug up and disrespected so Christians can steal their treasures.'

'The gravestones must have been lying around.'

'Now they display their triumph over us, for all and sundry to witness. Just like the statue of Santiago Matamoros – Moor Killer.'

'That statue must have been put up ages ago,' she said, although she too had felt a chill when faced with the gold-flecked stone saint, his sword raised in triumph.

'They should pull it down. It's offensive to Muslims.' After knuckling the glass where the gravestones were kept, he went round to the Arabic side and recited prayers for the dead. Zahra spied a portly security guard looking at them. She pulled Asghar's sleeve. 'Let's see what's over there,' she said.

They found the large glass screen that protected the old prayer hall. There was a magnificently inlaid mihrab – the niche from where the imam led the congregation – whose design the new Granada mosque had imitated. She pressed her nose to the glass trying to make out the Arabic words framing the arch, which was engraved with flowers. The ebb and flow of its pattern was hypnotic – inspired by a love that had never waned or faded.

'Tariq's going to lead prayers here,' said Asghar. He looked at his heavy silver watch, still loose round his wrist. 'I wonder when they open the place up?'

'It's very open-minded that the Church lets Muslims pray here,' said Zahra, still hoping Tariq wouldn't come.

'This isn't a church: it's a mosque,' said Asghar emphatically. 'You can't stop a Muslim praying in a mosque.'

'Well, it looks a lot like a church to me.' She waved her hand towards the grey walls and plaster saints.

'You know they changed all the mosques in Granada to churches? Every one.'

'How do you think Christians felt when the Turks took Istanbul?' asked Zahra, who was determined to be the reasonable, rational one in the conversation. 'Weren't their churches turned into mosques – wasn't this originally a church?'

'That was different.'

'Well how?'

'Islam spread peacefully. You could keep your religion if you wanted.'

'You sound like bloody Tariq,' she muttered.

44

Their voices attracted the attention of the security guard, who pointed to the ceiling as a reminder of the cathedral's sanctity, before putting a finger to his lips. Zahra raised a pacifying palm and drew Asghar away from the prayer hall. Just then she heard a loud cry from the entrance. Three men dressed in knee-length white robes and Palestinian head-scarves were arguing with a black-cassocked priest. She recognised Tariq's voice.

'They've come!' cried Asghar. Zahra stood paralysed as Tariq and his sidekicks wrestled their way past the protesting priest, and strode towards them. The security guard kept his distance but spoke a few panicked words into his walkie-talkie. In front of the prayer hall, Tariq unfurled a red and gold mat, touched his earlobes with his stretched thumbs, and called out 'Allah-u-akbar, Allah-u-akbar!' in poorly accented Arabic. The two followers behind him crossed their arms. Before he started the prayers, Tariq turned round to invite Asghar and Zahra to join them. Zahra, still holding her husband's sleeve, felt a strong tug. Fearing he was about to join the prayer invasion, she pulled him back. Asghar stumbled and looked over angrily. Taking out his phone, he began filming Tariq bowing and kneeling as he led the others in prayer. Other tourists appeared and started taking pictures. For a few moments all was calm.

Suddenly, a dozen Spanish policemen rushed towards them, their boots clacking menacingly on the stone floor. The secur-ity guard shouted with relief. Tariq continued praying, serenely oblivious to what was happening. Asghar and the other tour-ists raised their phones again. Without allowing them to finish praying, the policemen grabbed Tariq and his followers. There was chaos and shouting as blurry batons struck the men's robed bodies. As he was being put in handcuffs, Tariq shouted something in Spanish. Zahra shrank back, fearing he might have something more spectacular planned.

Once Tariq had gone she felt ashamed of her fears; she had reacted just like those prejudiced people who avoided Asian men on the Tube. Asghar was watching the footage he had just shot on his phone. She was about to say something, when the security guard ordered them and the other tourists out of the cathedral and into the harsh afternoon sun.

Asghar told her excitedly that he was going to upload what he had filmed as soon as they got back to Granada.

'Why wait so long?' said Zahra. 'Why not tell the world now about the glorious reclaiming of Cordoba masjid?'

'I don't have data,' he said, missing her sarcasm.

'Just forget it. I'm going for a walk.'


She strode away and into town without turning back. Soon the sun gave her a headache. She bought a bottle of cold water from a shaded street vendor and drained the whole thing in one go. Feeling energised, she bought a map and walked down an elegant Moorish side street. She caught sight of Asghar – he had been following her from a distance.

'They're being punished for asking for their rights,' he said, continuing the conversation. 'I thought you would understand. Like Iraq and everything . . .'

'I'm not saying they're completely wrong but what will the papers say? It'll be, Muslims Go Crazy Again.'

'Well of course the newspapers hate us.'

'They're going to say we want to take over Europe, bring back the caliphate.'

'Are you embarrassed or something?'

'By stupid stunts, yeah maybe.'

Asghar turned round abruptly and marched back towards the *mesquita*. Zahra went further into the city. She thought about texting Asghar to tell him not to post the video on YouTube. Then she remembered that half-a-dozen people had filmed the protest; one way or another the confrontation would be shared round the world. Even if she had asked him, though, she wasn't sure he would have agreed. He had the forced determination of the naturally shy; he stuck stubbornly to the principles he had imbibed with his mother's milk. His view of history was unashamedly partial: when Muslims did well he was proud, and when they did badly he mourned.

She had surprised her family by choosing a community boy. When she told Mohsen, he had texted back: *He's a MUSLIM?* From then on, her reluctance to pray or wear hijab was less fraught; she had chosen sides – and that was enough. Even better, she had planned to guide Asghar into a new world. One where not everything was viewed through the lens of religious doctrine or cultural expectations; where it was not selling out to go to classical music concerts. (Not that she actually went to classical music concerts; but the important thing was that she wouldn't object on principle.) She wanted him to learn the lessons she had absorbed at Cambridge, where people floated freely above history and politics, and felt as though no era or culture was alien to their understanding.

She stumbled across an old synagogue. She ran her hands across the wall's Hebrew lettering and felt the grooves between her fingers. How had Jews felt about being caught between these two grand adversaries – Christians and Muslims? Religions that both paid homage to and repudiated their sacred texts. Stepping into the street, she found a statue of an Arab wearing a turban. Looking closer she noted it was the Jewish-Spanish philosopher Maimonides. A plaque erected by a Jewish organisation informed her that the great doctor had survived Muslim Spain to become a revered sage. Chased away by intolerance to Fez and then Cairo, he had become the personal physician to Saladin. The statue was not realistically carved, and the eyes looked blankly inert. She tried to imagine the life Maimonides had led: compromising with power; smoothing ruffled egos; making choices he could defend, and staying silent over those he could not.

After slowly retracing her steps – stopping only to admire some handmade silver jewellery and the local sombrero that resembled a boater – she found Asghar eating a sandwich on a bench near the *mesquita*. He looked forlorn.

'What are you eating?' she asked, sitting beside him.

'Try some,' he replied. She took a bite of cold tomato and tasteless cheese.

'Did you check the cheese?' she said.

'Not this time,' he said quietly. 'Benefit of the doubt.' She smiled at him. 'Do you want something else?' he asked. 'There's a man selling sweets.' They walked over to the stall where she had bought her bottle of water. Asghar gave her a packet of lime sweets that tasted surprisingly salty. She told him they were pretty good, and offered him a handful.

'A woman from Spanish radio was here,' he said, sucking in his cheeks. 'She wanted to interview me. She said it wasn't the first time Muslims had tried to pray in Cordoba. It happens every couple of years. They ask first but the Church always refuses them.'

'Did you talk to her?'

48

'The media only twist what you say, anyway. And I didn't want them thinking I was a fundo or anything.'

'Because you're not a fundo, are you?'

'How could you say that?'

'I said you're *not* a fundo. You should listen to what I actually say,' she said, playfully patting him on the head.

'I'm sorry,' he said, gripping her hand. 'Will you forgive me?'

'There's nothing to forgive,' she said, after a pause. 'You haven't done anything wrong. We just didn't communicate properly.'

'Yes,' said Asghar. 'Nothing really bad has happened, has it? No one's died or anything.'

'Forget about today.'

'Bus back to Granada?'

Zahra nodded with relief.


Back at Casa Benengeli, Ian made a fuss over them. He had heard about the incident on the radio and seen the murky phone footage posted by another tourist.

'When I saw Tariq dressed like that, I was so frightened,' he said. 'Anything could have happened.' He flapped his arms like a distressed bird.

'We're fine, Ian,' said Zahra. 'The media have blown it all out of proportion.'

'Alonso's a rogue,' he said. 'His parents will be devastated.'

'Won't the police just give him a caution?' asked Asghar.

'I heard one politician calling it cultural terrorism,' said Ian.

'That's ridiculous,' exclaimed Zahra.

'That cathedral is so enormous,' said Ian. 'I don't see why

they can't allow a corner for you people to say prayers – once a year, maybe. But then,' he said with a shake of his head, 'I don't understand this obsession with religion.'

'Isn't it more to do with globalisation—'

'I've made quite a study of Islamic culture,' Ian said, 'and there's plenty to admire. I adore the *Arabian Nights*, and those beautiful miniatures! But whenever I turn on the television, they all seem so . . . angry.'

'We might go to bed now, Ian,' said Asghar. 'We have to be up early tomorrow.'

'Of course, of course – I understand. But before you go I have something to show you both.' He looked at them with mischievous excitement. 'Since you arrived, I've been working on a special painting. I truly think it's my finest.' Zahra raised an eyebrow to Asghar as they followed Ian to his studio at the top of the house. Around the room were scattered attempts to capture the view from his balcony: canvases dotted with glowing houses and the Alhambra shining from its hilltop promontory. Ian led them to a corner, where a large painting was hidden beneath a paint-smirched white sheet.

'Take a look,' he invited. 'It's not finished, but I think you'll like it.'

Zahra bent down and slowly lifted the corner of the sheet.

'Look,' he insisted. 'I said you would inspire me!'

The painting showed Asghar and Zahra in full Moorish costume. Asghar was smoking a hookah pipe and wearing a gold turban; Zahra was dancing for him, about to cast off the first of what were presumably seven veils – each a deep green, the same colour as the cloak Tariq had lent her.

'I'm calling it: "The Muslim Bride". What do you think?'

'*Very* atmospheric,' said Asghar.

'It's the perfect memento to take back home to England – something to remember your time in Spain. I am loath to part with it.' He ran his hand down the side of the canvas. 'But I will do you a deal. This special painting is yours for only 300 euros.'

'Really?' said Asghar. Zahra shot him a pained look.

'Really,' said Ian. 'Do you like it?'

'Yes,' blurted out Asghar.

'Brilliant, I'll stick it on the bill when you leave.'

A week later, Zahra made Asghar carry the painting all the way back to London. He was already weighed down with her hand luggage – filled with pottery and clothes from Granada – but he said he didn't mind. He told her she looked very pretty in those seven veils.

# Chapter Five

Once a village outside the city, Kilburn was now a multi-cultural cluster close to more fashionable areas of north London. As Asghar had noted when they first visited the house that would become their married home, it had decent transport links both into town and back to the suburbs. There were plenty of Pakistani shops so there would be no problem buying chapatti flour or fresh-fried samosas. Walking through the high street, though, Asghar noticed less salubrious sights. Rastafarian tramps colonised the street benches, while Englishmen with tattoos peered at them from pubs draped with grubby St George flags. On their street, he was alarmed to see a police sign asking for witnesses to a stabbing. Zahra assured him this sort of thing happened all over London and that gangs only targeted other gang members. Asghar responded that he could easily be mistaken for an Asian gang member – especially walking home on a dark night.

When Zahra first viewed the house with him, she noted that although the area wasn't perfect – there were more betting shops and chicken houses than cafes and bookshops – the place was worth considering. For two bedrooms and a small garden it wasn't a bad deal. The spare room could double as a dressing room and study, she said – or even a nursery, added Asghar teasingly. She wanted to make an offer right away, but he was worried they were rushing. The Kilburn house was the first they had seen, and a more painstaking search might have found somewhere better and perhaps cheaper, not to mention closer to their parents. But Zahra said it was perfect, and that they needed to move quickly. Their short engagement did not allow the luxury of deliberation.

When Asghar told his parents that he would not be moving his new bride into their home, he faced a sustained attempt to dissuade him. His father played on Mrs Dhalani's recently diagnosed heart condition. But Asghar, bolstered by nightly encouragement on the phone from Zahra, remained resolute. He enjoyed the thrill of saying no to his parents, while feeling absolutely justified in doing so. He was not, after all, standing his ground for the sake of his own whims, but to fulfil his duty as a husband. His parents recognised his transformation from unmarried child to nearly married adult. They gave in. In fact, they made Asghar a generous offer. Mr Dhalani would help with the deposit and get his painting-and-decorating company to do up the house for free.

Asghar was delighted his parents had come round. When he told Zahra, though, she seemed oddly unenthusiastic.

'We don't need their help,' she said. 'I've worked it all out, and I can raise the deposit myself. My dad gave me some money for my eighteenth, and with my salary from the bank it should be enough.'

'They're being incredibly nice,' said Asghar, who as a student could contribute little except by proxy. 'They want to give us our inheritance in advance.'

'I'd prefer it if we were, you know, more independent.'

'What do you mean?' asked Asghar, genuinely puzzled.

'If we take the money it means we owe them something.'

'It's a gift, not a loan. We won't have to pay it back.'

'That's not what I meant. I don't know, it just makes me feel weird.'

'They're not making us live next door.'

'It *is* really kind, I know,' she admitted. 'It's just I've spent all my life trying to become independent, earning money, spending what I like. And now it'd feel like I'm back in debt.'

'It took me ages to win them over . . .' Asghar put on an injured, boyish tone. She eventually relented and they spent the weeks before the wedding arranging the mortgage with Mr Dhalani, and discussing with Mrs Dhalani exactly what the decorators would be doing to the house when the couple were on honeymoon in Spain.

Asghar had let his parents take the lead with the decorating. One of his strongest early memories was stumbling into the family garage and feeling light-headed with the paint fumes. His father had set up Dhalani Brothers before he was born. Its humble beginnings were a well-worn family legend. Mr Dhalani started out in the 1980s by knocking on doors and offering to paint peeling window frames and repair chipped doors. (He didn't have a brother, in fact, but felt that the name Dhalani Brothers gave the business an authoritative, family-friendly air.) He was sent packing many times and heard the

54

odd unpleasant comment, but he carried on undaunted. Soon he built a reputation for quality work, modestly priced. At this stage, boasted Mr Dhalani, he didn't own a single ladder. In those days it didn't matter because everyone had one in the garage.

After she married him, Asghar's mother joined the business. Back in East Africa, she had been a dressmaker and had a good eye for colours and patterns. She helped to expand the range of services offered by Dhalani Brothers beyond straight-forward repairs to wall-painting and -papering. Whenever she went to a henna party at a wealthy family's house, she picked up tips on the latest fashions. She knew when the Sachoos scrubbed out their dusty pink wallpaper and painted the walls a pale cream; she noted that the Ansaris had imported brown leather sofas from Singapore, and was not shy about asking for their contact. She set trends and created her own designs. Within a few years, nearly every kitchen in the community had a swirly ceiling, and every hallway a single horizontal band of wallpaper – the Dhalani signature. By the time Asghar was a teenager, the Dhalanis had a successful business with three vans and twelve employees. In the summer holidays, Asghar joined his father on different jobs, helping to lay down sticky protective strips round the skirting boards and light switches, and even doing some painting. Most of the houses they worked on were from within the community. Rather than having English- or Irishmen stomp round their homes blasting stereos and leaving copies of the *Sun* lying around for their children to pick up, they could be sure that Dhalani's boys would behave properly and complete the work on time – even if they were by now a bit expensive.

Unfortunately, when Asghar and Zahra arrived back from

honeymoon, they found the decorating job half-finished. The living room was covered with white sheets and the walls still needed a few more coats of paint. Asghar saw Zahra's frustrated expression and called his father straight away.

'He said his guys are at another job,' said Asghar, after a brief conversation in which he had said little. 'An emergency in Watford, some important guy at the mosque.'

'I see.'

'He says they'll be here as soon as possible. Tomorrow – maybe the day after?'

'What about the bedroom?' she asked, picking her way through the messy floor. Asghar ran up the stairs.

'Look,' he said. 'They've done the wallpaper band.' He ran his hand along the green and gold pattern that his mother had picked out.

'It's a bit brighter than I thought it would be,' she said.

'Yes, I told Dad to get the absolute best stuff. Maybe that's why they've taken so long to finish?' He poked his head into the bathroom and was pleasantly surprised: the new white tiles gleamed in the afternoon sun, and the windowsills were freshly painted. Once the sawdust peppering the floor had been cleaned up and the pungent smell had been dispelled, it would be ready to use. Their bedroom, on the other hand, was a catastrophe. Their bed lay in four stacked cardboard boxes; and the walls were still unpainted. By their feet lay an open-mouthed toolbox with hammers and screwdrivers sticking out like gargoyle tongues. He pushed them back in and closed the toolbox firmly.

'I wanted to have a lie down,' said Zahra impatiently.

'I've done these types of bed before. We order them all the time. They don't take that long to put together.'

'Where can I rest?'

'Put your bags down, and I'll sort out the sofa,' he said soothingly.

Downstairs, Asghar pulled the paint-spattered sheets angrily off the sofa. Why hadn't his dad got the place ready in time? It was typical of the business these days. Dhalani Brothers had been living off its reputation within the community for some time, and rarely ventured outside its circle of familiar clients. Sometimes Asghar wondered what would happen if they had to cater for English people as well; they wouldn't accept such shoddiness, he was sure. He opened the airing cupboard and pulled out the sheets and duvet his mother had thoughtfully left. She always did what she promised, he thought gratefully.

By the time Zahra came down, he had prepared a neat sofa bed and was making tea in the kitchen.

'I'm boiling the kettle,' he called out. 'Do you want the radio on?'

'I'd prefer quiet, if that's okay,' she said. Asghar switched on the radio and tuned it to football commentary.

'Just checking it works,' he said, turning the volume down to a barely audible, jagged hum. He poured the hot water into two mugs and added a dash of milk to both. He added two sugars to his own mug, and was about to do the same for Zahra's when he realised he didn't know how she took her tea. When she had visited his house, his mother prepared the hot drinks. She must have said something then, but he couldn't remember. He didn't feel he could ask – especially as she still seemed annoyed at the state of the house. Perhaps he could text his mother? She wouldn't reply quickly enough. He decided to add half a teaspoon and stir briskly. But she was already snoozing when he brought in her mug. He left it on the Moroccan side table she had brought from home, and went upstairs to construct the bed.

It was tough, tedious work, stripping the parts from their brown cardboard packaging and tight bubble wrapping. Once that was done he rewarded himself with popping some bubble wrap. For the next hour, he followed the instructions carefully, slotting together the frame and the planks and then hammering in the nails. The secret to making flat-pack furniture, his father told him, was to keep the screws loose until the whole object was in position. Tightening them too quickly would make it more difficult to correct mistakes later on. Sure enough, while putting the bed together, Asghar found that the wooden lip that was supposed to support the headboard was on the wrong side; he was forced to dismantle that whole section and start again. But the screws he had pushed in loosely seemed to have tightened of their own accord. They were a real pain to unwind and some had to be dug out with the forked backside of the hammer and fresh holes made beside them. When he had finished, there were ugly scars on the wood he hoped Zahra wouldn't notice.

Over the next few weeks, while Zahra was back at work and Asghar waited for his business course at Westminster to restart for the summer term, his father's workmen painted and repaired the whole house. In the early days, Dhalani Brothers hired family members or boys from the community wanting to earn extra money over the holidays. But the new generation spent their holidays broadening their minds with travel or taking up high-powered internships, and most were unwilling to stoop to a decorating job. And so Mr Dhalani hired young Muslim men from Kosovo or Hazaras from Afghanistan, who worked hard and were happy to be paid in cash. Asghar found them pleasingly deferential to the boss's son. They took their shoes off before entering the house and refused his offers of tea, claiming they wanted to complete the job as quickly as possible.

When it was done, the Kilburn house resembled the wealthy suburban homes his father specialised in: lots of cream and brown with the odd dash of green. In the corridor, the workmen had hung Mr Dhalani's wedding gift: a Quranic verse stitched in golden thread. Below that they set up a carved wooden dresser from Kenya, and placed on it a tooting elephant with real ivory tusks, and a skinny tribesman looking nobly towards the kitchen. At the same time, nearly every morning the deliveryman rang the bell and Asghar had to sign for another of Zahra's seemingly random online purchases: Indonesian tea sets, Iraqi lamps, Turkish tiles. When he asked how they would fit everything in, she told him they could take turns with what to display. After two months they could remove the tooting elephant, whose ivory tusks she disapproved of, and put in its place the Iraqi lamp. The rest could be kept in the attic. Asghar had to lug to the top of the house a Persian carpet that was too large for any of their floor spaces. Their biggest headache, though, was Ian's painting. Asghar suggested they display it in the living room above the blocked fireplace. It would be better than the mirror currently in place. She hadn't seemed very enthusiastic about such a public display. Perhaps the bedroom, he ventured shyly?

'Let's wait until we find the right place for it,' she said, hoping in time he would forget about it.

Not prepared to banish it to the attic, Asghar left it unwrapped under the bed, hoping, for his part, that she would come round.

When Zahra left for the bank early in the morning, Asghar was usually still sleeping. When he woke up, he took a long shower and mucked around online until midday, when he opened his business management textbooks. He really needed to get down to some serious studying. During his first year at Westminster, he had found the work confusing and hard to handle. Revising for his exams before the wedding, he found he didn't understand his chaotic lecture notes and had to read the primary texts on his own, trying to discern each phrase and paragraph, each formula and diagram, and in the end he'd almost failed. His mother sympathised; his father didn't. For Zahra he massaged the truth, claiming he had done 'pretty okay'.

He was also still struggling to adjust to university life. From the start, he had lived at home with his parents and travelled to and fro by train. This meant that, unlike the other students, he didn't have the chance to socialise much with his classmates during the evenings. Every lecture had been charged with social anxiety, especially when he tried to talk to girls. Entering the lecture theatre, he had searched out the most attractive and interesting-looking and tried to imagine striking up a conversation. One who caught his eye early on was a pretty Muslim girl who tucked her hair into a sleek black beret; like him she seemed not to know many people. He manoeuvred behind her during a lecture and smiled when she got up to leave. After two weeks, he plucked up the courage to say hello. Wishing to maintain a plausible deniability of romantic interest, he asked whether they could go over the lecture notes from the previous week. His were in a bit of a mess. (He didn't mention that the reason they were in such a mess was because he had been too distracted by her.) Did she have time to discuss the lecture over a canteen lunch? Somewhat to his surprise she said yes, gladly.

Over a microwaved vegetarian lasagne, she went over the history of double-entry bookkeeping and its modern application in business. His attempts to steer the conversation towards more personal matters, like hobbies or favourite films – the kind of things he imagined people talked to girls about – were met with friendly evasion. Then he noticed she was wearing a wedding band. He was destroyed for two days. He had invested so much in this girl; she had seemed like a perfect match. Looking back, Asghar could be wistful about his own naivety. Now he was married he could speak to this girl – Mona, Mina, her name now eluded him – on an equal footing, knowing that nothing was on the cards. He took out his phone and looked at the wedding pictures. Zahra looked so beautiful.

That Friday night, Zahra returned late from work. Asghar had been listening out, and when he heard her key slotting in the lock, he stopped playing *FIFA* on his Xbox, and started to clear away the stained teacups and bowls of hardened cereal that littered the lounge. She greeted him with a smart kiss on the cheek. He defrosted one of his mother's curries in the microwave and listened to her complain about a work colleague. Technically this guy Dave wasn't in charge of her, but he was always dropping by near the end of the day, asking her to do things that weren't actually her responsibility.

'He sounds horrible,' said Asghar.

'Dave's all right actually. He says he's looking out for me.'

'Maybe he's nice then?' he said, putting the frozen chapattis into a plastic bag and blasting them for thirty seconds. 'Give him a chance.'

'Anyway,' she said. 'How was your day? Busy, busy?'

'Something else came for you in the post. It's the big box – I haven't opened it.' He pointed with the dishcloth to where the box was standing. She ripped it open and lifted out a delicate red glass.

'Aren't they beautiful? They're Venetian.'

'They look a bit like wine glasses,' said Asghar, tentatively.

'You don't *have* to drink wine from them, you know,' she said teasingly. 'They come with a lovely decanter. Don't worry, I got a really good deal on eBay.'

'I don't know how much room we have . . .'

'That's why I'm going to order a new cabinet,' she said. He couldn't help smiling as he dished out the green-pepper lamb curry on two plates, and opened the steaming plastic chapatti bag. They carried their food through to the table in the living room and Zahra flicked through the TV channels as they ate.

'Oh, go back one,' Asghar said, through a mouthful of lamb. Zahra obeyed and found that his eye had been caught by a romantic comedy.

'Oh no, not this. I saw it at the cinema and it was rubbish.'

'When did you see it?'

'At Cambridge,' she said, before adding quickly, 'with Andrea.' She stood up and started doing stretches. 'I went to the gym at lunch and I'm all aching. Why don't we finish up and go for a walk?'

'What, in Kilburn?' he asked cautiously. 'Where do you want to go?'

'There's a dessert place open late. I saw a sign for it the other day.'

They scoffed their curry and left the dirty dishes in the sink.

The last remnants of sun filtered through the street's rustling trees. They walked to the end of the High Road where the old Irish pubs and modern bars jostled for attention. He put a protective arm round her shoulder as they walked past the tipsy crowd, which seemed to consist of people either uncontrollably happy or desolately sad. Then they reached the loan shops, betting shops and pound shops.

'I tell you how people live round here,' he said, trying out a joke. 'They borrow money from the loan shop, lose it at the betting shop and then have to use the pound shop!'

'Hilarious, Asghar. Did you make that up yourself?'

'I did indeed,' he said proudly.

The brightly lit dessert shop was called 'Cakes and Sheikhs'. He pointed at the name and she smiled. Inside were a couple of hijabi girls drinking strawberry milkshakes, and a black guy playing with a banana split while texting vehemently. Apart from them the place was empty. Behind the glass counter was an assortment of English cakes and Arabic sweets. Serving them was a middle-aged woman keen to chat. Zahra asked where she was from, and she said Basra in Iraq. Were there any specialities she could recommend, Asghar followed up. She showed them a syrupy, pastry confection that looked like baklava. They ordered a batch with two sides of vanilla ice cream and found an empty booth. The hijabis looked up. From their faces, Asghar guessed they were Malaysian. They turned back to their milkshakes and carried on speaking in low, quick murmurs.

'Do you think they're comparing boyfriends?' asked Zahra.

Asghar gave her a look. 'You think you can shock me,' he said, 'but I'm not as innocent as you think.'

'Oh, dark secrets!' she exclaimed. 'There must have been someone before me,' she said. 'There's always someone.'

63

'I've never had a girlfriend,' he said simply.

'You've been a good boy,' she said, in a mock-Indian accent. 'But,' she said, determined now, 'I want to know about your first crush.'

'There was you, of course.' He recalled her long hair, tossed back in slow waves.

'I'm boring. Anyone else?'

'My first school was all boys. But there was my friend's sister . . .'

'Here we go!'

'It was innocent, totally innocent,' said Asghar, pleased at the interest Zahra was showing in him. 'It's got a sad ending, though.'

'Aw, now I have to know.'

'My mate Danny had a sister called Sarah. I'd never met her before. And then one day he gave me this letter.' He put down his spoon and sat upright in his chair before continuing the story.


When he was twelve years old, Asghar joined a small prep school in Ealing called Enfield House. The owner-headmaster, Mr Powell, was a tall, hunched figure with a thick ginger beard and penetrating blue eyes. He had created the school by buying two large Victorian houses either side of his own and knocking all three together. He turned his old master bedroom at the top of the middle house into a study. He was a terrifying figure, sauntering round the school wearing his Cambridge gown, swishing the metal ruler he was now forbidden from using on his pupils.

A few weeks into his first term, Asghar recalled, Mr Powell

had called him upstairs to his study. Since he had failed a maths test the previous week, he was terrified that his measly scholarship would be withdrawn. But Mr Powell wanted to talk to him alongside Danny Seeley. His classmate was sitting on the leather sofa facing the headmaster; Asghar slid in beside him.

Mr Powell leant back on his plush bed covered with an oriental rug. 'Gentlemen' – he always referred to his boys as gentlemen – 'I've called you together because I want you to present a Scripture class next week.' Scripture was what they called religious studies at Enfield House. Mr Powell bobbed his crossed legs and carried on. 'Seeley, as a Jew, and Dhalani, as a Muslim, you are in a better position to teach this class on "other faiths", which I am compelled by the syllabus to cover.'

'What do you want us to talk about, sir?' Danny asked.

'Introduction to the religion; rundown of basic beliefs; differences from Christianity,' he replied. 'Fifteen minutes per faith, allow five minutes for questions. All square?' He fixed Asghar with his stare. 'All square, Dhalani?'

'Yes sir, that's fine, sir,' he said, his voice trembling.

'Thank you, gentlemen,' he said, and nodded to them to leave.

Outside, Asghar and Danny walked back to class down the spiral stairs. Though they had been classmates since the start of term, they had hardly spoken to each other. Danny was in the sporty set, while Asghar wasn't in any set at all. But Danny was happy to chat now. He had been born in Belize. His parents were from Manchester, but his father was in the army and had been stationed in Central America soon after getting married. Danny didn't remember much about the place because he

65

moved to London when he was a baby. His older sister, Sarah, who had gone to school in Belize, still spoke Spanish. Danny said he was at Enfield House on an army scholarship, and that his father now worked at the Northwood NATO base. His voice, Asghar noticed, wasn't nearly as posh as those of the other boys at Enfield. Though he was talkative, he took only a polite interest when Asghar told him about his own family background. Still, the next time they played football at lunchtime, Danny, the team captain, made sure he picked Asghar, if not first then certainly not last.

Later that week, they met during break to discuss the presentation. Danny told him he was surprised Mr Powell had picked him to represent the Jewish faith; his father wasn't even Jewish and his mother wasn't that religious. They were planning his bar mitzvah but only for his grandmother's sake. (Asghar thought a bar mitzvah was a circumcision ceremony – like the one his grandfather had been through in Zanzibar when he was eight years old. He had looked at Danny with awe that he could speak about it so calmly.) His sister Sarah would help him prepare for the ceremony, Danny said, because she knew quite a lot about Judaism. In fact, she had helped him write his presentation.

Asghar was intrigued by this family. He had never met anyone Jewish before Danny, and his knowledge had been shaped by the stories he had heard in Scripture classes. His illustrated Bible showed the Old Testament patriarchs with long beards and flowing robes, looking uncannily like the photographs of ayatollahs pinned to the walls of his Sunday madressa. Fair-haired and English, Danny looked very different. During assembly, he sang the hymns lustily, even those lines about Jesus being our Lord and Saviour, which

Asghar quietly mouthed, hoping Mr Powell wouldn't notice. The headmaster didn't like boys who didn't 'join in'. After they had planned their presentations, the boys ate their packed lunches. Eating his buttery cheese sandwich on crumbling white bread, Asghar saw that Danny's sandwich had a pink layer of ham cutting through it.

'My religion says I can't eat ham,' Asghar said.

'Ham's delicious,' he said, wiping his lips. 'Sorry,' he said, and put the sandwich respectfully back in his lunch box. 'Dad buys the ham, and I make the sandwiches. Mum won't do it. She doesn't eat sausages and bacon either, but I think that's because she's dieting. Dad takes me for a full English on Saturday mornings. Mum says she won't kiss me until I've brushed my teeth.'

'But it's against your religion,' Asghar said.

'It doesn't bother me but Sarah's pretty strict,' he admitted. 'She reads books and goes to synagogue.'

Asghar liked what he was hearing about Sarah.

In Scripture class the next week Danny, wearing a black skullcap and striped shawl, read out a short history of the Jewish people. He started with Abraham and Moses and carried on with Joseph and King David. He stumbled over some of the Hebrew words, but when he was done, Mr Powell praised him for doing an excellent job. Asghar stood up wearing a red-checked scarf his father had brought back from Makkah. Using notes culled from madressa, he outlined the basic tenets of Islamic belief. He stressed the closeness between Islam, Judaism and Christianity. Did they know, Asghar said, that the Torah, the Psalms and the Gospel were all revered in the Quran as holy books? Did they know that the prophets Danny had mentioned were all in the Quran with Arabic names – Ibrahim and Musa, Yusuf and Dawood?

'In fact,' he added, reading from his sheet, 'we consider all these prophets to be Muslims!'

'Dhalani, I have a question,' Mr Powell called out from the back of the class. Asghar looked up nervously. 'Seeley has just told us these prophets were of Israel. So how were they Muslims?'

Asghar went over what he had read out. Whoever had written the worksheet was obviously delighted to allow these prophets the privilege of being Muslim. Seeing Mr Powell's expression and that of his classmates, though, Asghar realised that outsiders might see such relabelling not as generous acceptance, but staking an unfair claim.

'When we say these prophets are Muslim, we don't mean they're, you know, actual Muslims,' he stumbled. 'They believed in Allah, who is the same as God, and they have a holy book. That's like being a Muslim.'

'Doesn't it say in the Quran,' asked Mr Powell, with a small smile playing on his lips, 'that Abraham and Moses were from the tribe of Israel?'

'Does it?' said Asghar, scrambling through his notes.

'Isn't it odd that I seem to know more about your religion than you do?' asked Mr Powell. The class tittered.

'Sir,' said Danny, 'isn't it true that Christians say the Torah predicted Jesus?'

'Passages in the Old Testament do predict the Messiah,' he said. 'Nothing, as far as I know, mentions the Muslim prophet. Speaking of which, why don't you take us on a journey through the Arabian sands, Dhalani?'

Asghar rushed through an account of the Prophet's achievements.

After class, Danny shrugged his shoulders and said Mr Powell was trying to mess with him; he shouldn't worry about it. After this they became friends. At morning registration, Asghar joined Danny and his mates as they repeated their favourite lines from *The Simpsons* and discussed strategies for the football-manager games they all played. At first, his other friends were wary of the newcomer but, with Danny's approval, they gradually began to indulge his presence – as long as he never challenged the established wisdoms over who were the best footballers in the league, and which girls from other schools were the most fanciable. It was easy for Asghar to keep quiet about the girls from other schools because he didn't know any.

One morning, Danny held him back, saying he needed to speak to him.

'Could you do us a favour?'

'Sure thing!' said Asghar.

'My sister Sarah's doing her RE coursework on religions of the world. She's got some questions about Islam. Could you help?'

'What kind of questions?'

'She's written them in a letter. Wait a second.' He rummaged in his satchel and brought out a fancy envelope with Asghar's name written in girlish, looping letters. Putting it carefully in his jacket pocket, Asghar assured Danny that he would work on it overnight. For the rest of the day, he walked round school quietly excited that he had a letter from a girl – an older English girl, no less – in his pocket. He checked regularly that it was still in place, fingering its edges through his jacket. Even Mr Powell swishing his metal ruler behind him could not crush his inner smile.

When he got home, he went straight to his room and closed the door. He took out the envelope and put it under the bright scrutiny of the desk lamp. He had left the door ajar; his parents never knocked before entering, and he would rather hear them coming. Not that he was doing anything wrong by reading the letter: in fact, by replying to Sarah he would be serving the faith by informing a non-believer – a Jewish girl, no less – about the principles of Islam. Had the Prophet not sent a similar letter to the Byzantine emperor inviting him to the true faith? And had not the emperor converted before he was forced to change his mind by his Christian subjects? Still, he wanted to keep Sarah's letter private. If his parents found out, his father would spoil everything by dictating the reply himself. He relished the secrecy. Picking up the letter, he tried to guess what was inside. Were these straightforward questions or was there perhaps a personal message? Had Danny spoken to Sarah about him, praised his qualities, said what a great guy he was? Did she think about him? As long as he didn't open the letter, it remained charged with possibility. Eventually, unable to hold back any longer, he withdrew a sheet of heavy art paper and started reading.

*Dear Asghar,*
*I'm sorry to disturb you like this but I'm Sarah, Danny's*
*sister. I'm doing a GCSE project on the different*
*religions. I know about Christianity and Judaism (I'm*
*actually Jewish) but I'm not so clued up on Islam! I*
*really understand if you're too busy or you don't want to*
*but these are some questions I would love you to help*
*me with.*

*1. Explain why Muslims pray five times a day.*

*2. According to Islam what are the benefits of fasting?*

*3. Why can men marry more than one wife?*

*4. Do all Muslims have to perform Jihad (Holy War)?*

*5. Are Muslims allowed to charge/accept interest on
   loans?*

*My coursework is due in two weeks. It would be
really great if you could answer these by next weekend.
Thank you!
Sarah*

The letter did not disappoint. True, there was no personal
message; but she had written that she would 'love' him to help
her; he enjoyed the feeling of being needed. Most of the questions were pretty easy to answer: the number of prayers was
decreed when the Prophet flew to heaven on the winged horse
Buraq; fasting was about sympathising with the poor and
hungry; she had made a schoolgirl error over the word jihad,
which principally meant moral striving, not fighting; and
charging interest was not allowed, though accepting it was
something else. Like his father said: if a bank offers you free
money, why refuse? He paused over the third question about
the number of wives a Muslim man could have. Maulana
Haider sounded defensive when he discussed the Quranic
rules on polygamy. One needed to understand the customs of
the time, the maulana argued, and the constraints under which
the Prophet was working: four wives was a reasonable number
to the pagans, who married dozens of women. Asghar knew
the arguments by heart; but when it came to drafting a response
to Sarah, he found it hard to articulate both how the Quran

was perfect for eternity, yet subject to the customs of medieval Arabia. He was torn between staying truthful to what he had been taught and wanting Sarah to like him.

Helping his mother with the washing up that evening, Asghar asked her casually why the Prophet had married more than four women.

'He loved perfume and women,' she replied, handing him a soapy plate. 'Don't drop it!' she warned.

'I won't, I won't,' he protested.

She wiped her face with the back of her yellow rubber glove.

'The Prophet was a handsome man with many noble qualities. He was also the leader of the Muslim community with many responsibilities. For those women it was a blessing to marry him.'

'What if Dad wanted to marry another woman?'

'Why are you speaking like that?' she said, turning the hot tap on full blast.

'What about when I get married? Can I have four wives?'

'I'll find you a nice girl from a good family. You don't need to worry about anything.' She leaned over and kissed him on the head.

'What if I wanted to marry a Christian or a Jew? Like the Prophet did.'

'Always comparing yourself to the Prophet! You are not the Prophet – you are Asghar Dhalani, and you will always make your mother happy.'

After evening prayers, Asghar pulled out his biography of the Prophet from a drawer filled with computer-games magazines. He looked up his wives in the index. The name of his Jewish wife was Safiya, a young woman captured after a Muslim victory in battle. Safiya had been unhappily married to a non-believing Jew. From her earliest years, so the story went, her imagination was stirred by stories of the Prophet's spiritual power. When the Prophet learned of this, he gave her a choice between remaining a Jewess and returning to her tribe, or staying with him and becoming a Muslim. She chose to embrace the Prophet and his message.

Asghar wondered whether to include this story in his letter to Sarah. True, it was a moving example of why the Prophet had been allowed more than four wives; but he was slightly uneasy about this tale of battles and captures – no matter how generous the Prophet's offer in the end. His own faith in the Prophet's intentions remained secure; yet others with no instinctive sense of his goodness – who were perhaps even suspicious of him – might react badly to parts of the story. He stayed up late to write his letter. Eventually, he did include an account of the Prophet's marriage to Safiya, but downplayed the military context and emphasised the free choice the Prophet had offered. He had not made anything up or put words into the Prophet's mouth; he had simply presented the story in a way that would appeal to the person reading it, to make them think well of Islam. At the end, he added a post-script that he hoped would show Sarah his gentler side.

*I hope you find these answers useful. I'm no expert! My thoughts on marriage are that you have to choose one person you grow to love through the years. Islam allows four wives, yes, but no one I know from my generation or my father or his father has ever had more than one wife. My mum would kill my dad if he married another woman! Anyway I hope you do well in your coursework,*

*and if you want any more help just speak to Danny and*
*he can pass on another letter.*
    *Yours truly,*
    *Asghar*

He wrote quickly and without reading over his words. The
flimsy white paper he had pinched from his father's study
lacked the charm of Sarah's thick art paper; yet it seemed more
businesslike – more masculine. Just before sealing the letter,
he spontaneously drew a smiley face next to his name.

The next morning, Asghar handed over the letter. Danny
thanked him for the speed of his response, and Asghar said
that it was nothing.

'It's good her school is making them study all religions,' said
Asghar, not daring to even say Sarah's name; for him just
saying 'her' was sufficiently erotic. 'Which school is it, by the
way?' he asked casually.

'A secondary school a bit far from here – where all her
primary school mates went.'

'Mixed, is it?'

'Yeah, it is.'

'Does she like sports or anything like that?'

'She's pretty good at tennis, though I can beat her most
days.'

'Acting and stuff?'

'Yeah, but she hates singing.'

Asghar left his questions there. He had plenty to feed his
imagination. Danny was fair-haired and so she must be too.
She was sporty and therefore slim and a tennis player and so
surely pretty. Her school was mixed so she must get attention

from boys – maybe she even had a boyfriend. That was accept-able for English people so he shouldn't judge her too harshly. She was interested in Islam but would Sarah, like Safiya, really go as far as converting?

He came to school the next day hoping she would have replied. But Danny said nothing. Surely there would be some-thing on the second day? Still nothing. By the third day Asghar was in despair: what he had written must have annoyed or repulsed her; he shouldn't have been so forward. He was tempted to ask Danny whether his sister was busy with her studies that week or perhaps away from home on a school trip or even – he feared and hoped – too ill to reply? He needed something to end his torture. After two weeks, when, save for the odd spasm of hope as he walked into registration each morning, he had totally given up, Danny finally handed over a letter with his name on, once more written in a girlish loop on thick art paper. This time he couldn't bear to wait until he got home, and at lunchtime practically ran to the library. It was empty apart from the friendly librarian re-shelving the books. She smiled at Asghar as he sat down, looking pleased to have pinched a reader from the football-obsessed boys. He opened the letter.

*Dear Asghar,*
*Thanks so much for all your help. It was all really interesting stuff, which I've put in my answers! And thanks for clearing up all the marriage stuff. I now understand all that much better.*
*Yours,*
*Sarah xx*

He read the letter three times before putting it back inside the envelope. Then he took it out again, trying to imagine he was opening it for the first time and had no idea what was inside. He noticed that Sarah thanked him twice, and that she had signed herself not 'yours faithfully' or 'yours sincerely' but simply 'yours'. Was this just courtesy or something more? Unlike the first letter, there were two – two! – kissing-crosses at the end. Were these kisses, Asghar wondered, like the ones ladies blew insouciantly across the room in black-and-white films? Or did they offer the prospect of real lips touching lips, kisses that could be redeemed in person? Or was she, he thought darkly, just being a flirt? He put such creeping doubts out of his mind and began composing a passionate reply. He began by saying how much he liked communicating with someone so interested in Islam. She was clearly an open-hearted young lady. He quoted a rabbi who had spoken at a pro-Palestine demonstration in Trafalgar Square last Ramzan. The rabbi, wearing an orthodox black hat with curling locks, had declared that Israel oppressed both Jews and Palestinians. Such people, wrote Asghar, were beacons of inter-faith hope during these troubled times. He added how pleased he was to be contacted by her, Sarah, a girl who was surely as beautiful as her handwriting. His fingers gripped the pen painfully as he filled up the page – if he stopped for even a second his nerve would vanish. He confessed that he was attracted to her; he repeated that she was beautiful and elaborated the virtues – modesty, elegance and intelligence – that he found in her personality. By now the ink in his pen was failing and his final sentence came out barely legible, a mere impressed shape: 'All my love, Asghar.'

Before he could reconsider what he had written, he asked

the librarian – a woman with dyed red hair and a patterned scarf that went down to her waist – for an envelope and sealed the letter. She looked at him with a benevolent eye.

'Is that for a friend of yours?' she asked.

'Yes,' he said, wanting to get out and give the letter to Danny as soon as possible.

'It's so lovely that boys are still writing letters. These days it's all chatting on the telephone.'

'I don't use the telephone.'

'Do you need a stamp?'

'No, thanks,' he said, turning away before she could ask any more embarrassing questions. He went looking for Danny but he wasn't in the playground or the lunchroom; he found him downing a carton of milk near the lockers, sweating after lunchtime football. After he handed over the letter, a cautious expression clouded Danny's face.

'She wanted some more information,' explained Asghar; 'she said it was urgent, for her exams.' Licking his white lips, Danny promised to hand the letter to his sister.

'Thanks,' said Asghar, relieved.

'Is it maths now?' Danny asked, playfully thwacking him on the chest. 'Come on, we'll be late.' He crushed the empty milk carton and threw it towards the bin; it bounced off the rim and fell down. Asghar swooped and swiftly canned it. Walking to class with his new friend beside him, he had never felt so at home in the outside world.

# Chapter Six

'So what happened?' asked Zahra, stealing some of Asghar's uneaten baklava. 'Did Sarah write back? Did you ever meet her?'

'She never replied.'

'Maybe Danny didn't give her the letter?'

'Maybe. All I know is we didn't speak much for a while.'

A loud bang interrupted them. The Iraqi lady had begun putting the chairs on the empty tables. A teenage girl – her daughter, no doubt – began mopping the floor under their feet. Everyone else had left and it was clearly closing time. Zahra walked down the High Road with her husband, feeling grateful he had taken her into his confidence. She felt bad that all he had to show for his teenage years was a crush he had never even met. She glanced at Asghar, walking quietly beside her – his lower lip jutting; his small ears rounded with fuzz – and felt a surge of affection. She took his hand and squeezed tightly.

'Thanks for telling me all that,' she said.

'I wanted you to know the story,' he said. 'Nothing really happened, but I don't want us to have secrets from each other. None at all.'

At home, Zahra, who felt she had got closer to him than ever that evening, tried to coax him into sex. She changed into her blue bra and pants that had recently arrived from an online lingerie store. Asghar came to bed in his usual red-checked pyjamas. He turned out his light and lay down to sleep.

'Do you mind if I use your light,' she asked. 'My bulb's gone and I want to read my book.'

'Okay,' said Asghar, drowsily. She put her hand on his shoulder and leaned across his body, brushing his chest with her blue bra, lingering against his body. 'Or maybe,' she said, 'we could stay up a little while longer?' Asghar, though, was already fast asleep.

Summer fitfully became autumn. The streets were carpeted with golden-brown leaves; rapacious squirrels began hoarding nuts. Asghar scraped through his course; Zahra felt overlooked at the bank.

Then Zahra got an email from Andrea. She complained playfully that since the wedding she had barely seen her – and hadn't even been properly introduced to Asghar. She suggested dinner at her place in south London with her boyfriend, Carl. It would be a good chance for them to catch up.

Andrea had not been especially supportive when Zahra told her she was engaged. 'How long have you known this guy?' she had asked. 'You only just broke up with Krish.'

Zahra told her that a proper friend would have backed her decision and helped soothe her doubts. They had a massive argument and for a while Zahra was adamant she would not invite Andrea to the wedding. Only when her mother said how much she was looking forward to seeing the polite young black girl she had met at graduation did Zahra put her back on the invitation list – she didn't want to provoke awkward questions about why they had fallen out. On her wedding day, she had spoken briefly to Andrea at the mosque when she had come to offer her congratulations. Zahra complimented her stunning pink sari – 'it was professionally wrapped,' Andrea boasted, before leaning in to say, 'I'm happy you've made your own decision.'

Andrea had always known her own mind; it was one of the things Zahra liked best about her. They had met in the parlour on their first night at college. As part of the freshers' initiation, a boy and girl were tied together at the legs and supposed to hop round the city going from pub to pub. Zahra didn't want to take part but was feeling the collective pressure of the rowdy organisers, when she overheard Andrea informing her prospective pub-crawl partner that she would not be shackled to anyone. Catching Zahra's eye, she strode towards her in her high heels, and said they should ditch this farce. They left the cheering, febrile parlour and went for a coffee in town.

Andrea told her she had been brought up by her mother in a roughish part of south London, but had been sponsored by her church to go to a private school. The school might have softened her accent but her attitude remained spiky and self-reliant. Like Zahra, she was reading economics but, unlike her, she had no idealistic ambitions about solving world hunger or working at the UN; she had already arranged a summer internship at one of the big investment banks. Once she was earning proper money, she would buy a place in Brixton near her childhood home and send her mother on a cruise round her home island, Barbados – something her mother had always dreamed about. Zahra had been impressed by Andrea's mercenary confidence. When she ventured that she would like to live abroad one day, maybe in India or Africa, Andrea dismissed her with impatient tongue-clicks. 'What's the point of living in some third-world country?' she asked; these were exactly the places their parents had moved to England to escape. Zahra had missed her friend's forthrightness, and she was looking forward to hearing Andrea's booming laugh once more.

They fixed a date for dinner, which Zahra then checked with Asghar.

'Where's Brixton exactly?' he asked.

'It's south London,' she said.

'Is it near the south mosque?'

'I don't know – I haven't been there in ages.'

'It's the only place round there I know,' said Asghar. 'I never go south otherwise.'

'Well, now's the chance to go south of the river in a city you've lived in all your life. And before you ask, no, it's not full of scary black people.'

'Did I say that?' he said.

Zahra was only teasing, but felt it had come out wrong. With Andrea she made all sorts of racial jokes and jokes about racism; but they fell flat with Asghar. He always took everything she said so seriously.

Instead of wine they bought posh juices and arrived early at the flat, which was in one of the beige-coloured blocks that had recently sprung up round the station. Zahra pressed the buzzer and through the intercom Andrea said she was coming to get them. She heard her clomping along the corridor in her heavy heels. The door opened and her old friend, dressed in a short black dress with bright, dangly earrings, immediately hugged her and said how good she looked.

'And how are *you*?' asked Zahra.

'Not too bad, you know,' she said with an enormous smile. Putting her left hand on her cheek, she struck an innocent face. The diamond glint was impossible to miss.

'Oh my God,' Zahra cried. 'You're engaged, you're engaged!' The girls hugged again, speaking, crying and laughing all at the same time.

'You're literally the first to know apart from the family,' said Andrea. 'I spent the whole day Skyping Barbados.'

'What did your mum say?'

'You know she loves Carl. She's happier for him than she is for me. But come in now, it's cold. And I'm forgetting my manners.'

Asghar was quietly holding the posh juices. Zahra beckoned him forward. 'Asghar meet Andrea, Andrea meet Asghar.' He thrust out a hand: 'Many congratulations.'

'And to you as well,' she said, pulling his handshake into a warm hug. 'Come up, the food will be here soon.'

Andrea's flat was larger than Zahra had expected: the living room had been combined with the kitchen to create one warm social space. The white walls were mostly plain except for a couple of modern African-style paintings: a black Jesus blessing a group of village children, and a dignified-looking Bajan in a green headdress selling fruit. By the shiny marble kitchen counters, Carl was grappling with an unruly kettle, from which steam was pouring in cloudy billows.

'I leave you alone for two minutes,' cried Andrea.

'Switch is buggered,' protested Carl, comically wafting his hand to disperse the steam. 'I've got to unplug it.'

'We know what to get you for a wedding present, then,' said Zahra.

'Great to see you,' said Carl, giving her a big hug. She felt oddly self-conscious having another man touch her in front of Asghar. He was a tall, skinny man, whose shaved head showed up healed scars under the kitchen spotlights. He stepped forward and took the juice bottles from Asghar's hands. 'Cheers, mate,' he said.

'No problem,' said Asghar, looking bereft now he was no longer designated juice-carrier. Carl poured some sticky apple and mango into two dainty wine glasses and invited the guests to settle down on the leather sofas. He poured himself and Andrea some white wine.

'Carl was going to steam these vegetables,' said Andrea, 'but as you can see . . .'

'We're ordering in,' said Carl, smiling. 'There's a Caribbean cafe that's just opened, Paradise Island. They deliver right to your front door.'

'Andrea doesn't believe in cooking,' said Zahra, turning to Asghar. 'It's against her principles.'

'My mum's a dinner lady: she's spent her whole life cooking for other people – at home for her family, at work for the schoolchildren,' said Andrea. 'Now I want to be cooked for.'

'She's just lazy,' said Carl. 'I try to teach her, but she never concentrates.'

'Hey, that's not fair!' said Andrea, slapping his thigh with the back of her hand. They knew each other so well it seemed to Zahra they were more like brother and sister than a romantic couple. They had started dating when she was fourteen and he was eighteen. Zahra had been shocked when Andrea told her this. But Andrea's mother liked having a man around the house and from the start had loved Carl like the son – or indeed loyal husband – she had never had.

Zahra couldn't imagine what her parents would have done if she had brought home a boy when she was fourteen. Checked her into a mental asylum? But perhaps, she reflected as she watched them quietly discuss the arrangements for dinner, her parents would have been as pragmatic as Andrea's mother. Carl was from the same Barbados community as Andrea and their mothers attended the same church on Sundays. Rather than letting her daughter loose on a world of troublesome men, she had subtly encouraged the relationship, even allowing him to sleep over when Andrea was sixteen. Mrs Amir would never have countenanced that, but Zahra did know a few teenage couples from the mosque who got engaged before university. Having someone to love kept you free from temptation, so the argument went. She glanced over at Asghar, who was sitting on the sofa gulping his juice.

'Andrea and I have been friends since university,' she said, trying to draw him into the conversation.

'We were quite a sight round college,' said Andrea. 'The only two dark girls.'

'They got a *lot* of attention from the boys,' said Carl with a sly smile.

'Just idiots messing round,' said Zahra. 'It wasn't anything serious.'

'I don't know,' he said. 'Remember, we were at Lighthouse that time . . .'

84

'We don't want to rake up old times now,' said Andrea lightly, 'it's so boring for Asghar. Now, tell me, Asghar, how was the honeymoon?'

'Oh really good – it's a really interesting place with lots of history. You know the Muslims ruled Spain for hundreds of years . . .' Zahra listened with relief as Asghar outlined the faded glories of the Andalusian Caliphate. (Thankfully he said nothing about Tariq.) At least Andrea had been alert enough to interrupt Carl, though she wished she had briefed him properly on what subjects to avoid round Asghar. Carl's boyish openness – one of his most attractive qualities – often led him to assume that everyone would be as relaxed about their wife going to clubs and meeting boys as he was. But dragging up old flirtations in front of a new partner was always impolite. That time at the club was when she had first met Krish. In all likelihood, Carl would not have mentioned his name; but she didn't want any hints carelessly dropped. She looked at Asghar, who had just finished describing the elegant structure of the Alhambra.

'For our honeymoon,' said Andrea, 'we were thinking of going on safari to Africa.'

'Africa isn't just one place,' said Zahra, who liked to tease her friend that she, Zahra, was more authentically African than she was.

'I know that,' said Andrea, annoyed.

'You want to see the elephants, don't you?' said Carl.

'I'm fed up of seeing them just on television. I want to see them in real life.'

'And the lions,' said Carl. 'Andrea loves lions as well. We saw them in London Zoo last week.'

'They looked so pathetic,' she said. 'Lions should be roaming round the savannah, sunning themselves in the open, chasing antelopes. Instead their manes were damp from the drizzle and feeding time was a bunch of dead rabbits chucked over the fence.'

'That's what happens when you take the animal out of his natural habitat,' said Asghar. 'He has his pride and his females, his way of doing things. Then these Europeans come along and kidnap him and put him in a cage. But I guess you guys know all about that.'

'It's not that easy for lions in Kenya,' said Zahra, wondering how Asghar had managed to bring up slavery within three sentences. 'They're an endangered species – poachers kill them for their skin. I saw a documentary about it once.'

'I don't understand,' said Asghar.

'What I'm saying, my dear,' said Zahra, tapping the side of his head with affectionate exasperation, 'is that it isn't as simple as evil Europeans stealing noble African lions. Scientists want to study the species and breed more of them.'

'Yeah,' Carl reflected, 'and some of them might not even like it in Africa. Maybe it's too hot for them.'

'What are you chatting about?' Andrea interjected.

'I'm serious! My uncle Stephen came over in the 1970s. He loved the weather here. Said it was so boring back home – hot every single day, always the same blue skies. He was a big man, you know, and he was always sweating in summer. His house was fitted up with air conditioning, and he loved blasting out freezing air, even when it was mild.'

'To be fair, your uncle Stephen was pretty strange. He was always going on about Queen and country, dressed in suits he couldn't afford. Not that there's anything wrong with being successful, but you can't totally forget who you are. He never once went back to Barbados – not even when his mother was ill. His funeral was rows and rows of white faces: work friends, wife's family. The only other black people were his kids.'

'Stephen had his own style, old-school, but he carried it,' said Carl.

Zahra admired a life lived according to your own choices; though she wondered how much damage Stephen had done to himself to be free of those ties – racial, cultural – that exerted such a pull.

The buzzer sounded loudly.

'About bloody time,' said Andrea, as Carl leapt from the sofa and rushed to collect the food.

'Don't forget the cash!' she called out. A sheepish Carl came back and raided her wallet for £20 notes. Zahra exchanged glances with her friend.

'Very well trained!' said Zahra.

'Like a lion-tamer, it takes years of practice,' she replied. Carl returned with two large plastic bags imprinted with the Paradise Island logo – two palm trees entwined like lovers. He unpacked the silver foil containers, which dripped oil on the spotless counter. Quickly, he realised the cafe had made a mistake with their order: there were four chicken dishes, but nothing vegetarian for Asghar and Zahra.

'Don't worry about it,' he told Andrea. 'I'll take the chicken pieces out.'

'Carl, what are you talking about,' she said. 'They can't touch anything non-halal.'

'I don't mind,' said Zahra.

'Don't let them get away with this,' said Andrea. 'That's terrible service – give me their card, let me ring them.' She punched the number into her phone and went next door. At first the others pretended not to overhear the loud argument filtering through the walls. Then a smile began to curl on Carl's lips and Zahra couldn't help giggling in response. When Andrea came back, she was in a cold fury.

'Typical Jamaicans,' she said, 'what can you expect? It's people like that who give us a bad name.'

'I'm sure they just made a mistake,' said Carl.

'Of course they made a mistake. That's the problem! And the guy on the phone was so rude. Can you imagine if they'd sent the wrong delivery to a white family? They'd be all over us, offering money back, free food for a month. He said *we* got the order wrong.'

'I don't think I did, sweetheart.'

'That's what I said. And even if you did, Carl, it doesn't matter, because they should know that when you're running a business, the customer is always right.' Andrea paced round the room in frustration. 'The deliveryman's in Tooting now,' she continued, 'he won't be back for an hour. I'm sorry, Zahra, we've paid for it now, and we can't go somewhere else.'

'Baby, let me go and pick it up,' said Carl. 'I'll get the bus. It'll take twenty minutes.' He gave her a comforting hug and she nodded, resting her head on his shoulder. This was a dynamic Zahra knew well: Andrea got upset, then gratefully submitted to Carl's attentions. Then Asghar piped up unexpectedly. 'I'll come with you on the bus,' he said. 'It's too much for you to carry.'

'Will you be all right?' said Zahra, slightly concerned at leaving Carl alone with him.

'We're only going down the road,' said Asghar.

'Great idea,' said Carl. 'Let's get going.' They put on their coats and left the flat.

88

'Everything goes wrong when people come over,' said Andrea, flopping on the sofa with her glass of wine.

'Come on. You don't have to be all posh round me.'

'What about Asghar?' Andrea asked. 'He's so intimidating.'

'Intimidating!'

'Like quiet. It's like he's silently judging me or something.'

'That's not fair, Andrea – you barely know him.'

'About as well as you did when you got engaged.'

Zahra was slightly taken aback; she hadn't expected her to leap into an argument.

'There are things you don't understand about my life – my family life, pressures I'm under, responsibilities I have . . .'

'So you got married because your parents told you?'

'Actually, his family doesn't like my family,' she said, not quite answering her question. 'But yes, I did want to marry somebody from inside the community, someone who would understand where I was coming from. Asghar liked me and I, well, it was an opportunity. He's a nice boy, really sweet. We love each other.'

'You sit like strangers.'

'So we're abnormal because we aren't throwing ourselves on each other in public?'

'You know I'll always give you my honest opinion, Zahra.'

'Don't worry, I know that.'

'Don't be offended, because I'm only saying what everyone at college was thinking. Why did you dump Krish?'

'You always go on about him.'

'I was there when you met him. I saw the whole relationship from start to finish. Krish was doolally for you. He treated you so well, proper respectful and kind – that's what you told me! Then one day you break up with him and two minutes later you're getting married to a guy I've never heard of.'

'I broke it off before things got too serious.'

'You never talk about it,' said Andrea. 'Don't you trust me?'

Zahra drained her juice; the inside of the wine glass was dirty with bits of mango and apple. She went to the kitchen sink and washed it, before filling it with clean water and taking two gulps. She felt the cold run down her chest. A sharp melancholy returned whenever she was reminded of how quickly she had been forced to make the decision that had shaped her life. There was no one she trusted to hear her story, or fully understand why she had taken the path she had. Andrea was a good friend in the world she had left behind; but there were limits to what she could understand.

'I'll say one thing,' she turned round and said, knowing that she needed to give Andrea something confidential. 'Krish was not . . . a perfect gentleman. He did things, well, he tried things I wasn't comfortable with. Pressured me into things . . .'

'How bad?'

'Bad enough to break up with someone.'

Andrea put down her glass and hugged her friend. 'Why didn't you say something?'

'It's not easy to talk about.'

'He forced you to do stuff?'

'I dealt with it before it got really bad. There's nothing more to say.'

'Oh Zahra, I'm sorry, I didn't know.'

Zahra was relieved to have turned the tables on Andrea. Soon Carl and Asghar came back with the food. The boys appeared to have got on well: a mutual interest in cricketing statistics had sustained them on the journey to and from Paradise Island. They unpacked the food and ate quickly; the trains north would soon be stopping. Andrea tried to make them stay longer with promises of coffee and a spare room for the night. But Zahra needed to be up early to finish some work. It took them so long to say goodbye they had to run for the last train, making it with only a minute to spare.

# Chapter Seven

Zahra's body tensed whenever Sally Webber walked past her desk. Sally was her boss, the woman who had plucked her from university to work in the new arm of a bank that dealt with ultra-high-net-worth clients – minimum £10 million in cash. Sally worked on the floor above and only rarely visited her junior staff. When she did appear, though, she was usually speaking to someone soon to be favoured with promotion. Zahra would stare straight at her central screen – it was flanked by two larger ones – and tap out an email energetically, listening out for what pearls Sally was dropping to others nearby. But she was often hard to hear because Dave, the guy sitting in the cubicle beside her, would be speaking loudly to a client on the phone, laughing uproari-ously, hoping Sally would overhear his convivial, sociable style. Dave, who had joined in the same cohort as Zahra, had also been to Cambridge, though at a larger and more prestigious college. 'Small world,' Zahra had exclaimed when they had met on their first day. Though within a week of meeting her other colleagues, nearly all of whom had been to the same three or four elite universities, she realised that the more appropriate reaction was not self-deprecating surprise but an assured sense that the system was working exactly as it should do.

On that same first day, Sally had stood in front of the young crowd and stated that they were the brightest and best of their generation. She was in her forties, neatly put together with short black hair; her sharp-edged face gave the impression she was keen on the gym. Zahra liked her easy self-confidence and lightly worn expertise. She had young twins but had barely taken any maternity leave, and apparently never mentioned them in the office. She outlined the way banking worked, stressing its role in keeping 'the economic wheels greased'. In these troubling times for the industry, she was proud of the bank's social responsibility programme. Not only did the bank pay vast amounts of cash for the Treasury to spend on schools and hospitals, it also sponsored art galleries and opera houses, and schemes for disadvantaged children to get access to the arts. That was part of the mission.

Sally seemed very down to earth to Zahra. Sometimes, when the team was working late to finish a report or project, Sally came round with the catering staff – middle-aged Mexican ladies wearing headphones, whether learning English or listening to music from back home Zahra never asked – and helped to hand out sandwiches and hot drinks. This was her way of saying she appreciated her staff's efforts.

During the interview for a permanent job, Sally told Zahra that she had performed excellently the previous summer during her internship; and that she knew Zahra was qualified for the job intellectually. What she wanted to know was how well she would fit in. Was she a people person?

Zahra said she was, and mentioned the community volunteering she did at the mosque. (Whenever she went to the old mosque, which was not very often, she always helped to serve the tea.) With people from all backgrounds, Sally asked? Sensing the implication of the question, she said that as someone with Indian and African backgrounds she was used to interacting with people from different cultures – her own family, for a start! She was pleased to see that Sally smiled at her joke.

Sally continued: would she be okay with entertaining potential investors and business partners? Zahra was slightly troubled by the word 'entertaining'; but she said she would happily take a client for a group dinner or a drink at the bar. Her answer seemed to satisfy Sally. She phoned her later that afternoon to say she had got the job.

Zahra started almost immediately after graduating. She had learned to create a professional persona that was tougher and more self-assured than she felt she actually was. She dressed like Sally and the other powerful women she saw in her office: black heels, black tights, black pencil skirt, white shirt, silver necklace with a flower pendant, foundation on her cheeks and a touch of lipstick, with her long dark hair tied back in a bun. She wore almost exactly the same outfit every day, varying only her heels and her pendant; it became a uniform, a way of keeping back her real self and creating another harder version to show the outside world. Her offices were in a large building not far from the Monument to the Great Fire of London. She found the newness of the city exhilarating: the fire had cleared away the slum streets and unsafe shacks, which had been gradually replaced with the reliable modernity that she saw today. One lunchtime she climbed the Monument and looked over London, its buildings shooting up like jagged metal plants. This was where she belonged, she told herself; this was where the future lay.

More than a year into the job, though, and Zahra had seen others, including Dave – thrusting young men with narrow ties and slicked-back hair – promoted far ahead of her. She worked hard but lacked the sureness of her more outgoing colleagues. As Sally had warned, the job involved socialising with clients at bars and restaurants, trying to charm middle-aged men into banking with them. She sometimes joined these occasions and was happy enough making small talk, sipping some sparkling water and going home early; but she found drunk men boring, sometimes over-friendly, and so she mostly avoided such gatherings. She couldn't care less if these men wanted to drown themselves in beer and make stupid jokes; she just didn't want to laugh along with them. There were also rumours, which she never properly verified, that after the pub they all went down to strip clubs where they spent thousands of pounds of company money entertaining the clients.

One day, not long after the dinner at Andrea's, Sally came over to see her in person. She perched on her desk and gave her an inviting smile.

'It's about time we had a catch-up,' she said. 'Lunch?' Her voice had a beguiling quality – like those BBC presenters who read the Shipping Forecast as she was dropping off to sleep. Zahra hadn't heard of anyone else she knew going for lunch with Sally – not even Dave. Maybe Sally was going to give her something better than a promotion; or maybe this was what you did before you fired someone. At one o'clock exactly,

Sally appeared at her desk. They walked to the cupboard in the corner and Zahra took out her long beige overcoat. She was rushing to put it on and got tangled up with the sleeves; Sally helped her out. She could feel the eyes of Dave and the others on her: suspicious and envious. Let them think what they want to think, thought Zahra, rather enjoying the attention.

Sally took her to a fancy fish restaurant in a covered market nearby; they sat at a wooden table without a cloth, the surface scored with scratches and burn marks that were supposed, Zahra imagined, to give the place a rustic, fishing village-like feel. Sally recommended she get the market fish, and could she be so bold as to order some wine? Zahra, presuming that she was asking permission to drink in her presence, nodded readily. Though she had never touched the stuff, she took pride in not being bothered by alcohol; at parties she had often encouraged others to drink and bought rounds of beers when she was having tap water. It was her way of deflecting questions about why she didn't join in. But when the waiter brought the white wine and after Sally dismissed his offers to test whether it was corked – 'I'm sure it's perfect,' she said – Zahra found that, before she could say anything, she had been poured a glass. The wine lay there in the large curved glass, resting elegantly, looking no more offensive than a light apple juice.

'I suppose you're wondering why Dave got a promotion but you didn't?' she asked, with surprising directness.

'I'm not saying anything against him,' Zahra said.

'He's a good worker; he does well for the company.'

'Yes, of course.'

'He's also completely ruthless.' She took a sip of her

wine and a conspiratorial smile played on her lips. 'Our business used to have some standards: you made money, yes, but you respected the people you did business with. Now it's all about the bottom line.' She looked at Zahra. 'Dave's going to join the eighteenth floor. He will make an awful lot of money for the bank. In two years' time, a bigger bank will poach him. For you, though, I have something different planned.'

The waiter brought over their food: they had both ordered the same thing, braised haddock with new potatoes and vegetables. Once he had dished out the carrots and peas, the waiter refilled Sally's empty wine glass. He then topped up Zahra's glass, even though she hadn't yet drunk from it. There was a pause in the conversation as they both set about their meals. Zahra cut into her haddock with a fish knife and began carefully removing the toothpick bones; Sally, she saw, was already taking big mouthfuls and pulling the bones from her mouth like a magician.

'One of the reasons I identified you early on,' she said, 'was because there's a particular market we would love to invest with us. And it's a market you could be of great help with. I'm talking of the Muslim pound.'

'Okay.'

'There's a lot of entrepreneurship in your community. All those Indian food companies, cash-and-carry empires – we're losing out to other high street banks because we don't have the same connections. Which is why I want you to join a new team I'm setting up that will pay special attention to ethnic-minority customers. You can be the Muslim representative.'

'What will I be expected to do?'

'Exploit your contacts. Talk to your father's friends at the mosque. Certain overseas clients from the Middle East. Tell them we can make the accounts compliant with sharia – that we promise not to invest their money in Israel, that kind of thing.' She took another gulp of wine.

'Think about it,' she said, calling the waiter for the bill.

'I'll do it,' she said quickly. 'Of course, I would be delighted to join the team.'

'Excellent,' said Sally, who didn't look the slightest bit surprised. 'Shall we toast?' She raised her wine glass. Zahra looked down: on the table she was confronted by the overfilled wine glass and the mineral water she had been drinking through the meal. 'Cheers?' said Sally expectantly. Zahra raised the heavy wine glass. 'Cheers,' she said and clinked Sally's glass a little too hard. She let the wine wash over her carefully sealed lips. 'Cheers,' she said while lowering her glass, to draw attention to her choice, but Sally was too busy paying the bill with the company card to notice.

As she was walking home from the Tube that evening, she was still light-headed from her encounter with Sally. Should she be pleased by her boss's offer, or should she be affronted? Pleased probably: take every opportunity you can get, that was her father's mantra. But she couldn't help thinking back over the successes of her life so far – being accepted by the bank, getting into Cambridge – and wondering how much had depended on the liberal sympathies of her interviewers, and her playing up to that liberalism. (Within limits she told herself: she hadn't, after all, drunk the wine, and back at the office had washed her mouth thoroughly.) At school, when she got the letter offering her a place, one of her friends had said, of course they want you – a Muslim *and* a woman, *and* one who didn't wear hijab. She meant it as a joke but Zahra had been upset; she always liked to think she achieved everything on her own terms.

Her phone buzzed and she found a WhatsApp message from her mum telling her not to forget it was one of the big nights at the mosque – some imam or other's birthday, one of the later ones she didn't know much about. 'If you cannot come to mosque, listen to the livestream. Good reports about the maulana.'

Zahra messaged back saying she would phone the next day. She ignored the bit about the maulana. This was one of her mother's regular attempts to resurrect her fading – but not yet extinguished – religious observance. As a young teenager driven home from mosque by her parents, she had been the clever girl in the back seat telling them exactly what she thought of the lecture. University had changed her perspective. A professor lecturing on his prize-winning economic theory was naturally more impressive than the type of preacher they got at the old mosque – a young bloke from Leicester with a couple of years in Iran under his belt. Someone like Sally, with all her intelligence and achievement, was ten times the person Maulana Haider was. That old world could not have seemed more irrelevant. Religion was a genre she felt she had outgrown – like teenage romance or fantasy fiction. She texted again saying she couldn't make the mosque because she needed to spend the evening with Asghar – the perfect community alibi.

Yet when she got home something held her back from telling Asghar about her promotion.

The next morning was Saturday and Zahra woke up early, leaving Asghar snoozing comfortably in bed. She knew he wouldn't be awake for another couple of hours. Downstairs she boiled the kettle, toasted some bread and fired up her

laptop. Sitting at the kitchen table, she idly scrolled on
Facebook. She hovered over Sally, wondering whether she
should offer to be friends with her. She decided not. Then
she looked up Krish to see whether he had posted anything
new. But he was still keeping his profile private. She still
thought of him sometimes – more often recently. Closing her
laptop, she drank her tea quickly, made herself another cup
and toasted more bread. She hadn't had a headache like this
for a long while.

Back during her final year at Cambridge, Zahra was leaning
out of her college window, retrieving the milk carton frosting
on the sill, when Andrea knocked at her door.

'Wow,' she said. 'This place looks awesome.' Zahra had redec-
orated her room that morning. During her first year, she had
put a *Titanic* poster up on her wall. But having absorbed the
traditional aesthetic of the college – its dark old paintings of
pale old men – she wanted something a bit classier. Googling
round she discovered that the actress in *Titanic* had also played
Ophelia in *Hamlet*. The Millais painting came up on the search
and, after clicking on the Tate's website, she fell in love with
the beautiful drowning girl. She had also covered her room
with eastern carpets and cushions from a hippy shop on King's
Parade. Hung across the walls were decorative blue-green head-
scarves her mother had optimistically brought back for her
from Dubai when she was a teenager, which had lain unloved
in her cupboard for years until Zahra had the idea to repurpose
them. The room smelled of sweetly burning joss sticks.

'I was going to make some tea,' said Zahra.

'No time,' said Andrea. 'We must go shopping right now.'

'Andrea!'

'You've got nothing to wear tonight,' she said, flicking dismissively through the clothes in her wardrobe.

'What's wrong with this?' said Zahra, who was wearing a black skirt and red cardigan over a white-frilled shirt. Andrea looked at her pitifully.

'I'm not sure I want to go then,' said Zahra. 'I need to read for this essay.'

'You promised!' cried Andrea. 'Carl really wants to see you. We'll make it fun, I promise.'

By the end of her first year, she had struggled to make many friends. Early on she had received a visit from a hijabi girl from the Islamic Society who asked her to come along to the meetings. She had agreed for politeness sake but had no intention of hanging round with other Muslims at Cambridge – the whole point of moving away was to escape all that. In any case, she told herself, she was too busy with work.

Luckily she had Andrea. They read over one another's essays and alternated going to lectures. Gradually they opened up about their home lives. Andrea told her about Carl, who she visited in south London every other weekend. He was coming up for a rare visit that weekend and wanted to go clubbing. Andrea was adamant Zahra should come along. Cambridge was dead for decent music, Andrea said, apart from a club near Sainsbury's where they did an R&B night every month. Reluctant at first, Zahra came round after a bit of persuasion. It felt like something she should try before she left. And it was all pretty innocent: she would go to the club, drink her soft drink and laugh at everyone dancing drunk. There wouldn't be much difference, she told herself, between being at the club and watching a reality show.

Andrea took her to Tribe, according to Andrea the only half-way decent clothes shop in the city. The shop name was spelled out in bulbs that flashed in time to loud pop music.

'I might find something for myself,' said Andrea, picking three dresses from the rack. She couldn't decide between a tight red number and a green one split down the side clasped with white hoops. Zahra thought they were both a bit much but didn't say anything. In the end Andrea bought both. 'One can be a present from Carl,' she said defensively.

'Now what about you,' said the sales assistant, a freckled girl with a Fens accent dressed in orange hot pants and black tights. Zahra didn't think anything on the racks suited her style. Since starting university, she had progressed from wearing flat shoes to knee-length boots and instead of trousers now wore skirts above the knee. But these dresses were a step too far. Andrea told her she had a lovely figure that she shouldn't be shy about showing off. She and the assistant chose six or seven outfits for her to try on in the changing room. After a delicate struggle getting it over her head, Zahra emerged wearing a dark blue dress that reached her neck but barely stretched to her thighs. Andrea loved it.

'It's so sexy,' she said.

'You really pull it off,' added the freckled assistant. Zahra bent down awkwardly, trying to pull the dress further over her legs. 'It's too short,' she said.

'Just be confident – feel free,' said Andrea.

'You can almost see my knickers, Andrea,' she said, disappearing into the changing room. None of the other outfits seemed right either, but whenever she complained Andrea and the assistant – quite a double act by now – repeated the mantra that she should be more confident. By the time Zahra reached the final outfit, the other two had become impatient. It was a long pink ruffled skirt matched with a corset-style jewelled top that exposed the shoulders. Zahra liked the colours and the fact that her legs were covered. It felt weird because you weren't supposed to wear it with a bra; but Zahra had never been top-heavy, so the danger of a wardrobe malfunction was somewhat reduced. Not that it mattered anyway, Andrea reminded her, because everyone at the club would be a stranger anyway.

After formal hall that evening, they set off for the club. Andrea's heels scraped across the stone path while Zahra, for whom walking in heels was as scary as ice-skating, had settled instead for her new silver ballet pumps. Andrea was kept warm by Carl. Since he had arrived that afternoon, he hadn't stopped touching her – linking hands, kissing her neck, brushing her bum. They whispered conversations and exchanged lovers' banter, from which Zahra was excluded.

The club was about twenty minutes from college. Andrea told them that on most evenings the Lighthouse catered to townies who liked chart music. They had a student night on Thursdays when they played indie. But tonight they had an R&B night that attracted the city's ethnic minorities including, Andrea claimed, African-American soldiers from the nearby US army base.

'We'll probably be the only students,' she added, handing her coat to the attendant. She had gone for the green dress with white hoops.

Zahra took off her coat but kept her cardigan wrapped round her shoulders. She tugged up the front of her bodice, uncomfortably aware that it kept on slipping down. Andrea had equipped her with tape which should have tacked the dress in place, but it kept on coming unstuck from the lining. She couldn't help feeling that saris, although equally revealing in their own way, were more elusively elegant. But at least she looked like she fitted in.

The club was heaving. On the ceiling, a rotating white light flashed in imitation of a lighthouse. Apart from a white girl working at the bar, everyone else was dark-skinned, either sitting in a booth or drinking at one of the high tables that sprouted from the floor. A guy in a tight white T-shirt approached Zahra, asking if he could buy her a drink. He smiled so expectantly she almost agreed. Before she could reply, Carl stepped forward protectively. The man raised his hands in mock surrender and walked away.

'He's just trying it on,' said Carl. 'Stay close and you'll be fine.' He asked what she wanted to drink.

'Lemonade,' said Zahra.

'Just lemonade, nothing to mix with it?' he asked.

'Oh, no, thanks. Not tonight. I don't need to – I can dance whenever. Don't need to drink.'

Carl had heard of the DJs from the London club scene. They were called the Scarlett Pimps, and their speciality was remixing classic soul tracks. Andrea wanted to dance right away. Carl claimed the music wasn't heavy enough for his tastes, and said he didn't mind saving some seats on his own. Zahra, who wanted to show off the moves she had been earnestly practising in front of the mirror that afternoon, handed Carl her cardigan and said she would join Andrea. Both girls ventured on to the floor. Andrea danced coolly with rolling shoulders and a swaying head, while Zahra snaked her body to the music. After a couple of songs, Zahra noticed an Asian boy looking at her from the bar. Suddenly she felt a bit weird, and was about to move away when she saw him down his drink and dance over with an unthreatening shuffle. He greeted Zahra with a closed-palm namaste; she replied with a smile and an ironic side-to-side Indian nod. This cultural connection established, they began dancing together. Andrea caught her eye and winked. Zahra ignored her, concentrating instead on keeping up with the guy's smooth movements, which she would have described as Bhangra moves, if she could remember what the hell Bhangra actually was.

As always with guys, she first checked out his shoes, which were shiny brown and curved at the tip. He wore black jeans and a white shirt with the top three buttons undone, exposing a light cushion of chest hair. His careful stubble and gelled hair disguised an angular face (large nose, jutting chin) but it had strong personality and his eyes seemed warm. The music changed gear to something more hardcore, and all three looked quizzically at one another. After briefly trying to keep up, they left the dance floor.

'Nice to see a familiar face,' the boy said to Zahra.

'What, do we know each other?' she replied archly, though inwardly panicking as Andrea retreated back to where Carl was sitting.

'You know what I'm saying – just a friendly face,' he said. 'It's great music here, but some of the girls can be a bit funny.'

'I wouldn't know – it's my first time.'

'Really? I must buy you a welcome drink!'

'Oh no, I should get back to my friends. They might be worried.'

'Are they your chaperones? No problem, we'll keep safely in sight.' He led her to a table from where they could be seen by them both. He waved to Andrea and Carl, and then mimed a sequence of actions: first he pointed to himself and then to Zahra, signalling a drink with his hands, and offering a quizzical shrug. Andrea replied with a double thumbs-up.

'See?' he said. 'Now I've got your friend's permission, you *can't* refuse.'

'Go on then,' said Zahra laughing. 'I'll have a lemonade.'

He bought the drink without asking why she wasn't drinking – she liked that – and a bottle of beer for himself. He told her his name was Krish and that he was a third year reading law. He was originally from Manchester, and wanted to move to London – he had a placement at a magic-circle law firm that summer. He loved the capital, and visited most weekends during term time.

'Easier with a car,' said Krish. 'Don't have to schlep to the station.'

'You've got a car?' said Zahra, impressed. Few undergraduates drove.

'It's an old BMW. The porter lets me keep it in the college car park. Really cool guy actually – he was born in India, army-type. I told him I needed it to drive back to my parents on the weekends.'

'My parents wanted me to go home every weekend. I told them college rules didn't let you.'

'You're meant to get a chit from your tutor,' he told her. She knew this but didn't mind him telling her as though she didn't. 'When I did that first term, my tutor looked surprised I'd bothered. Like it's one of those rules they don't expect you to keep.'

'It's hard to work out what they do care about and what they don't,' she said. 'But lucky they do have that rule, because

I could tell my mum I couldn't come home every weekend. Or right now I'd be watching crap telly.'

'That *would* be a shame,' said Krish, grinning.

They both sipped their drinks.

'Parents don't understand,' he continued. 'It's not like we're running round taking drugs or getting girls pregnant, is it?'

'I've definitely not got a girl pregnant,' said Zahra. 'And,' she pointed to the lemonade, 'I don't drink.' Something about Krish made her want to prove her respectability.

'You're Muslim, right?' He nodded in answer to his own question with an almost anthropological air. 'Hindus aren't supposed to drink either – I don't hardly ever – but my family doesn't care that much.'

'My parents worry my friends will be a bad influence. They don't consider that *I* could be a good influence on *them*.'

'They always expect the worst. As if their generation was perfect. The things the men in my family got up to back then – my uncles and that – I can't even say.'

'Oh really?' said Zahra, eager not to seem too innocent. 'I've got an uncle who got drunk and punched a British soldier. He ran away to Congo and came back with a second wife, an African.'

'Scandalous!'

'He died soon after. But his second wife stayed with the first and they brought up the kids together. Sort of sweet.'

They continued swapping family stories – stories they would have felt uncomfortable telling their white friends but which they trusted each other to appreciate in the right way. One of Krish's uncles had laced the family chai-pot with whisky, and the pundit had performed the puja drunk. Krish, who appeared to have little affection for Hindu priests, told the story with amused relish. Zahra laughed with him.

'Your family aren't Indian-Indian, then?' asked Krish.

'East African.'

'I knew you weren't Pakistani,' he said. 'Don't get me wrong, all those Pakis in Manchester – fresh off the boat or what?'

'They're not all like that,' said Zahra, feeling an odd solidarity with the Pakistanis she had scrupulously avoided at school.

'Yeah, but whenever you hear about some girl who's had her throat slit for chatting with a white boy, guaranteed it's some illiterate cab driver.'

'Not being able to read and write doesn't mean you can't tell right from wrong.'

'True, too true,' said Krish, sounding a bit out of his depth. He asked how she liked university.

'It's fine. But it's such a bubble. And so *white*.' She whispered the last word as though it were taboo.

'*So* white,' said Krish. 'I can't wait to move to London.'

'I know some cool places,' she said, hoping her fibbing didn't show in her expression.

'Maybe you could show me?'

'I don't know – they're pretty exclusive.'

'I'll leave me flat cap behind, I promise,' he said, exaggerating his Manchester accent. 'And once they see my moves . . .'

'You have *more* moves?' said Zahra.

'Don't mock the moves till you've seen them.'

She looked instinctively over to Andrea and Carl.

'I'm not saying you have to dance,' he said with mock-solemnity. 'You can look at me making a fool of myself.'

'How could I say no to that?' she said, surprised at how easy this was. He pulled her to the dance floor and showed off some comedy dance moves – twisting on the ball of his foot, flapping his arms like a chicken, hopping on one leg. Zahra couldn't stop laughing and even allowed him to pull her into a ballroom twirl.

After five songs, Zahra returned to her friends flushed with defiant excitement. She knew they must be dying to ask about the guy she had been talking with for the last hour; but she wanted to confide in Andrea alone, without Carl's inevitable wisecracks. So she avoided the subject for a few minutes and instead sized up the other girls' dresses with Andrea, distinguishing the flamboyant from the gaudy, the pretty from the showy. When Carl went to get more drinks, Zahra expected Andrea to ask about Krish immediately. But she didn't. When Andrea carried on the same conversation for two or three minutes, her friend became faintly irritated.

'Don't you want to know who I was talking to?' asked Zahra finally.

'Some guy from back home?' suggested Andrea.

'I don't know any guys from back home. He's from Manchester and his name's Krish.'

'Did you snog him?'

'Andrea! We just chatted, okay?'

'Trust me, if he hasn't made the lunge then he isn't serious.' Zahra rolled her eyes. 'I know more about this kind of thing than you,' said her friend, with a cynical air. 'Don't think because he's danced with you once, that he wants to marry you.'

Carl returned with the drinks. For a while they let the loud music fill the silence. Carl said he approved of Zahra's man. 'You suit each other,' he said.

'Just because they're Asian?' snapped Andrea.

'They've probably got more in common being from the same background – like you and me.'

'So you're saying if I was white you wouldn't go out with me?'

'No baby, if you was white I'd love you just the same.'

'Well, the way you stare at white girls.'

'Oh baby, you know I love you the best . . .'

Zahra smoothed her ruffled skirt and looked round the club. What happened now? Where was Krish? Would he come and find her? Scanning the dance floor, she couldn't see him – nor at the bar or cloakroom. Perhaps he was in the toilet, she told herself, but it had been ages since they had talked. Admittedly the queues were long in clubs. Surely he wouldn't leave without saying goodbye? He knew her name and, she supposed, could put a note in her pigeonhole the next morning. It wasn't like she was a Sarah or a Kate: Cambridge hardly teemed with Zahras. But by then the moment might have passed. She was sick of her watery lemonade but still drank more, nearly dropping the slippery glass. Her worry turned to sobering embarrassment: it was one thing to risk your reputation and be successful; quite another to dance with a man you barely knew, only to be abandoned. She felt the terrible vulnerability of really liking a boy. It was danger-ously vertiginous – no wonder they called it falling for someone.

As the strong pulse of one song faded, a soul classic slowed the beat. Andrea grabbed Carl's hand and Zahra's.

'Come on,' she said. 'We can't miss this.'

Andrea and Carl entwined themselves in an old-fashioned clinch, leaning on one another, her head on his shoulder. Zahra, feeling like the whole room's eyes were on her, danced alone.

'Nice to see you back,' said a voice behind her. She turned to see Krish smiling.

'I was sitting with my friends,' said Zahra.

'I know, I saw you from the decks. The DJ's a friend of a friend, and I had a go. Did you hear me?'

'Yeah, it was a great mix!'

By now they were dancing closely; nothing seemed more natural.

'All the time I was thinking, "What song could get Zahra back out dancing?" So I asked for Otis.' She listened to the singer's desperate words – calling for his lover to come home. Krish placed a warm hand on her hip and drew her closer; gently cupping her face, he kissed her lightly on the cheek. Zahra nuzzled his neck. She stopped for a moment and breathed in his aftershave. His hands drifted gently to her hips – so lightly that the slightest recoil from her could have dislodged them. He did not move them lower and she did not flinch. His restraint pleased her. But at some more private moment in the future his hands might creep a little lower, and that thought excited her. Her body felt light and unreal, flushed with the warmth of breast against chest, hand against hip. She wondered if this was what it was like to be drunk. She imagined her skin as a thin membrane stretched tight, which could burst at any moment.

Then the lights came up, and they broke apart.

Queuing for their coats, they exchanged their full names – his was Krishna Mehta – and phone numbers. Zahra had a new phone that she didn't know how to programme, so he did it for her. Naughtily, he also opened her Facebook, found his profile, and added himself as her friend.

'You've got a missed call from your mum.'

'It can wait till morning.'

'Send her a text when you get back. You never know how important it might be.'

'I'll do that,' she promised, as they stepped into the street. She liked that he cared about her mother.

'I'll call you tomorrow,' he said.

She nodded and quickly kissed his stubbled cheek, before running into the midnight air to catch up with Andrea and Carl.

She was brushing her teeth in her room, still buzzing from the night's adventures, when her phone rang.

'Hello?'

'Salaam aleikum, how are you?' asked her mother.

'Fine, fine, aleikum salaam,' replied Zahra, already irritated.

'We were calling and calling – where were you? How was your Saturday night? Was there something special on?'

'Yeah, it was great,' she said and started giggling.

'What's wrong?' said her mother.

'I'm fine, it was just some dinner thing,' said Zahra, trying to pull herself together; her head ached. 'Stop hassling me.'

'Are you drunk?' accused her father, who was listening in on another line.

'No! What are you talking about? What do you take me for?' she said, with genuine outrage. 'I would never do something like that. Mummy, tell him to say sorry to me.'

'But Zahra . . .' said her mother.

'No,' she insisted, 'I want him to apologise for saying something so horrible.' She had put on her best Cambridge voice.

'I'm sorry for saying that,' said Dr Amir. 'I apologise.'

'Go to sleep now,' said Mrs Amir. 'You must be tired, and you have lots of work to do.'

'I know I have work, Mum. I do take this seriously, you know.'

Her parents said a chastened goodnight. After that small victory, Zahra fell into bed and slept soundly.

# Chapter Eight

Asghar walked downstairs wrapped in the spongy white dressing gown Zahra's parents had bought him as a wedding present. His parents had bought her a sheer silk gown, but it hung in her cupboard clean and untouched. Sometimes, when she wasn't around, he rubbed his face against the silk gown, imagining it was her skin he was touching. Their intimacy was still at an impasse: he too afraid to make a move, she too proud. He wiped away the sleep in his eyes with his sleeve. Even though he'd been in bed for ten hours, he found it hard to chase away tiredness. He felt ashamed for staying in bed until mid-morning. It wasn't like he could plead the excuse of early starts during the week, given that he often stayed in bed until 10 or 10.30 when he had afternoon classes. Zahra, by contrast, was up at 6 every weekday to miss the rush hour, and only slept in another hour at weekends. Asghar felt sad they never slept in together. Just like before he was married, he always woke up alone.

He found Zahra on the sofa, quietly leafing through a magazine.

'Any tea?' he asked hopefully.

'There was a pot two hours ago. You'll have to refill the kettle.'

'Maybe later,' he said, plonking himself down next to her. 'What are you reading?' he asked, leaning over her shoulder.

'Nothing important,' she said.

'It looks interesting.'

'My old college magazine, if you must know,' she said.

'Any pictures of you?'

'Look, here's the old Dean. He's posing in his study with new students, the same way he did with us.' The students, Asghar noticed, were mostly women and ethnic minorities.

'Reminds me of Mr Powell's study.'

'It's funny, the people change but the types don't.'

'Was it hard to get in?' he asked.

'I almost didn't make it,' she said.

'Tell me about it?' he asked. He had heard legendary stories of Oxbridge interviews – the professor setting fire to a piece of paper and watching your reaction, that kind of thing – and wanted to know how Zahra had beaten the system.

Her first interview had gone badly, she told him. Asked by a shy, stiff professor hiding behind his thick black glasses who her favourite nineteenth-century economist was, she had replied Adam Smith – on whom she had written an A level essay. A sentence into her explanation of the market's invisible hand, she was cheerfully interrupted by the professor: she was in the wrong century. What did she make of David Ricardo? She had never heard of him. Walter Bagehot and *Lombard Street*? Her mind went blank. Leaving the interview, she hobbled down the winding stone steps in her uncomfortable new shoes and had a little weep. ('Oh I wish I could have been there!' cried Asghar.) By the time she reached the Dean's rooms, she was more composed.

This interview was not academically focused; rather, it was to decide whether Zahra would be a suitable addition to the college family, as the Dean said. An avuncular man with a soufflé of white hair, the Dean, rising from his dark blue armchair wearing a stained black frock coat, put his palm to his chest and gently bowed his head.

'Zahra – now, I wonder, could you help me, is it za-ra or zah-ra?' he asked. Zahra said she didn't mind.

'Let me see, you say here that your ethnic origin is East African Indian. Your parents must have had a tough time, Idi Amin and all that?'

'Yes, it was very difficult for my dad, very difficult.' Dr Amir had never talked about what had happened to him in Uganda and rarely mentioned his efforts to reclaim his lost house on the banks of Lake Victoria. Such was the silence he maintained about 1973, Zahra had never considered herself the child of refugees before; but she supposed that was what she was. She sensed that in the Dean's eyes she was not only exactly the kind of middle-class girl from the suburbs who would naturally suit Cambridge – she also had the intriguing aura of legitimate victimhood. For her family had been persecuted by a crazed African dictator, the kind of man made possible by the British withdrawal of protection from the Asians. The Dean could indulge in a more comfortable kind of colonial guilt than the one left-wing academics were always harping on: not guilt over the empire itself, but that it had ended too soon.

He asked Zahra about growing up in London. He sincerely

hoped she had never experienced any unpleasantness. 'I know it can be difficult these days, though of course it must be easier without the . . .' – he mimed the shape of a head-covering.

'Everyone at school was fine,' she said, trying to sway the subject back to why she had chosen the college. 'In fact, it was my economics teacher who told me to apply here. He went to Cambridge.'

'A college old boy?' the Dean asked, his voice quickening.

'No, he went to Jesus. But he said I'd do better here. He was worried I'd be offended by the Christian name.'

A brief smile played on the Dean's lips. 'Well, in origin we all *are* Christian colleges, and I like to think we still are in some sense. But I wouldn't take the names too literally,' he said.

'I'm *not* offended, of course. I chose this college for its academic record but Jesus shouldn't take that as a snub. The college, I mean.'

He looked pleased by her little joke. 'Underneath we're all the same, aren't we?'

'Absolutely, in fact,' she said, driving swiftly on to a pre-prepared topic, 'one of the reasons I love Shakespeare so much is because he was so wise about these things.'

'Oh yes,' said the Dean, 'tell me more.'

Playing Jessica in her school production of *The Merchant of Venice*, she had got to know most of the play almost by heart. Before her interview she had gone over the famous speech. 'As Shylock says, "Hath not a Jew eyes? Hath not a Jew hands, organs, dimensions, senses, affections, passions . . ."'

She recited nearly all of it, and when she faltered the Dean completed her words: '"If you prick us, do we not bleed? If you tickle us, do we not laugh?"'

'I always thought you could do the speech again, with Muslim instead of Jew,' she said. 'Hath not a Muslim hands, organs, dimensions, senses, affections, passions . . .'

As she left, the Dean shook Zahra's hand firmly. 'We'll be seeing each other again, I'm sure,' he said. Later in the day she did a short test which, her confidence recovered, she aced.

'Wow, he really said it was better you didn't wear hijab?' asked Asghar.

'Sort of. Guys like the Dean aren't racist; they don't say because you're brown you can't come here. But you have to prove you aren't an imposter: that you can adjust to their ways; admire the culture you want to be a part of. If you challenge them a bit, you do it with the help of Shakespeare – not, you know, the way your friend Tariq does. Give them something they can trust.'

'Shakespeare's their Quran,' said Asghar solemnly. 'Their holy text.'

Zahra looked pointedly at her watch. 'Aren't we meant to be visiting your family this afternoon?'

'You know, I completely forgot. Let me check my phone.' He dashed upstairs to find it and came back looking pained. 'Mum texted two hours ago: she wants us to come to Southall for lunch, and then wander round the shops.'

'So we'll be there all afternoon?' she asked. Asghar caught her sharp tone. Between visiting her family and his own they rarely had a weekend to themselves to visit art galleries, as they had done on their second date, or to go for a walk in Regent's Park and explore the mosque – something they had always talked about but hadn't yet got round to doing. But maybe he was reading too much into her words; she could have been annoyed at him for waking up so late. He looked at his wife's impenetrable expression – her mouth slightly curved, her eyes looking levelly at him – and, not for the first time, wondered what she was really thinking.

The train was the usual multi-ethnic west London mix. Approaching Southall, though, the black people and Chinese people and white people all got out and only the Asians remained. The atmosphere changed. The men in trouser shirts and the women in Punjabi dresses relaxed into conversing in a variety of dialects. A young man with sculptured facial hair started playing Bollywood music through his phone, while some aunties cracked open their Tupperware and offered Bombay mix round the carriage. With one stop to go, the skies opened and the windows were swiftly streaked with rain. Asghar hadn't brought an umbrella – he lost them so often they weren't worth buying. As the train slowed, Zahra searched her handbag and drew out her small, yellow umbrella. She unfurled it on the drenched platform and hugged Asghar close. It was only designed for one person and water still struck Asghar forcefully in the face. He stumbled into dirty puddles that sullied his upturned trousers. Through the misty rain, he could see the other passengers running for cover – flip-flops slapping the ground, wet saris clinging to the ladies' arms – and for a moment he imagined they were not in rainy west London, but in the middle of an Indian monsoon.

They reached the shelter of the ticket barriers totally soaked. Zahra's wet clothes weighed heavily and Asghar's drowned socks squelched. They could only laugh at the absurdity of their appearance.

'I did my hair especially to impress your mum,' said Zahra, pulling at the stringy strands trailing down her cheeks. 'Now it looks a mess.'

'I look as bad as you,' he assured her.

'No one's looking at you,' she retorted, pulling out her hair-clips. Just then Asghar got a text from his sister: the family were in the Light of Lahore, a few minutes from the station. He wiped his fingers on his trousers and typed a reply.

'They're already at the restaurant. I told them not to wait. Shall we stay here until the rain stops?'

'It doesn't look like it will,' she said. 'There's no point drying off, only to get wet again.'

'You keep your umbrella,' said Asghar. 'I'll improvise.' He went to the news kiosk and bought a copy of the *Daily Telegraph* – the newspaper with the widest pages he could find – and fashioned himself a paper hat.

'How do I look?' he said, modelling for her.

'Like a prat.'

'But a dry prat.'

The Dhalanis were at their usual spot at a long Formica table in the middle of the restaurant. On Sunday evenings, when Asghar was a boy, Mr Dhalani would burst into the living room while the family were watching television – a biblical epic, *Samson and Delilah* perhaps – and announce that Mrs Dhalani shouldn't bother preparing dinner because they were going to Southall. This happened about once a month – it was his father's one predictably spontaneous gesture. He would drive them towards Southall, get frustrated when they got stuck in a tailback, and curse those bloody Sikhs with their Gurdwara traffic. At the Light of Lahore, ordering was chaotic. They would pick fights over who would get what they wanted, and someone would always feel aggrieved that their tastes hadn't been accommodated. In the end Mr Dhalani would imperiously dictate the order for them.

120

Leading Zahra towards their special table – dodging the waiters in dirty aprons balancing trays of smoky meat – Asghar saw Fatima snatching the laminated menu from her mother. He prayed they would be on their best behaviour for Zahra.

'Asghar, salaam aleikum, come, come,' his father called out. 'And daughter, my other daughter, come over, please.'

Asghar tried to sit at the far end of the table. But Mr Dhalani insisted that they come closer, opposite one another, Asghar beside his father and Zahra next to her mother-in-law.

'So nice to see you, Zahra,' said Mrs Dhalani, kissing her on both cheeks. 'Oh, you're so wet!'

'I'm sorry, auntie, we got caught in the rain from the station.'

'No auntie please: call me mum. Asghar,' she said, turning to her son. 'You made her walk from the station?' She tutted. 'We could have collected you in the car. She'll catch death in this weather.'

'Don't worry,' said Zahra, 'I'm warming up now.' The tandoor ovens made the restaurant a furnace.

'You need to buy a car,' said Mr Dhalani to his son. 'None of this struggling by train business.'

'He hasn't passed his driving test,' piped up Fatima, annoyed at having been banished to the end of the table. Asghar looked at her testily. He had spent six months learning to drive but failed his test, twice. He drove fine with his instructor, but when it came to performing under pressure, he made silly mistakes. After the second failure – his major error was stalling at a junction – he gave up trying. That had been a year earlier. He found the prospect of relearning what he had already learnt exhausting.

'I passed first time – lucky me,' said Zahra. 'Why don't I take you out for a refresher?'

'Yes,' said Fatima, 'let her teach you to drive.'

'I don't think that's a good idea,' said Asghar, glancing uncomfortably at his parents.

'Why not?' said his mother, joining in the teasing fun. 'Women are better drivers than men. They're more careful.'

'If you drove the car as much as me, you would have some bumps and scratches, too,' said Mr Dhalani touchily. He had reversed their Mercedes into a bollard a week before the wedding and his wife had not let him forget it. 'But Zahra,' he continued, turning to his daughter-in-law, 'if you want to teach our boy, go ahead. Third-time lucky, eh?'

The waiter – short, rotund and with a moustache of uneven thickness – arrived to take their order. Mr Dhalani asked for final requests. 'Is there anything you wanted?' Asghar asked his wife.

'Could we get a veg dish, maybe?' she asked.

'The mixed grill comes with onions and peppers,' said Mr Dhalani. 'The vegetables are always left over.' Zahra, wedged between Asghar's mother and sister, nodded and smiled tightly.

'You must have been here before?' asked Asghar.

'When I was young, I think. Somebody had a wedding reception here.'

'We came here every week, pretty much. They get you in and out quickly, but it's fantastic food.'

When the food arrived – sizzling hot kebabs and spicy chicken, naan breads, mango lassis – Asghar piled Zahra's plate with onions and peppers.

'That's what you wanted, isn't it?' he said, smiling.

'What are you doing, Asghar?' said his mother aghast. 'Give her some proper meat first. Here let me.' She speared two tandoori chicken breasts and thrust them on to Zahra's plate.

'That's more than enough,' she protested.

'No, you must be hungry after your week's work,' said Mr Dhalani, offering her a long, wobbling kebab. 'How's the job?'

'Hard work, but I'm enjoying it. My manager called me in for a chat the other day. She said I was doing well. I could be in for a promotion, maybe a bonus.' She hadn't meant to show off so baldly, but figured that the Dhalanis wouldn't get self-deprecation.

'Wow,' said Mrs Dhalani. 'Well done!'

'You must always keep your manager happy,' said Mr Dhalani. 'As the manager of my own business, I know that.'

'Sounds like she likes you,' said Asghar, not wishing to let on that this was the first he had heard about a promotion.

'She's been at the bank for, like, fifteen years. Pretty impressive. Especially with two kids – twins.'

'My grandfather was a twin,' said Mrs Dhalani. 'Not identical. He and his brother were like chalk and cheese. Uncle was always laughing and joking, but my grandfather, you couldn't even sneeze in his presence. Zahra, you'd better be careful . . .'

She pointed at Zahra's stomach and gave a sympathetic shake of the head, as though imagining a pair of twins perhaps – who knew? – already battling it out in her womb.

'With English people you have to make them think they're cleverer than you, even if you're cleverer than them,' said Mr Dhalani, swallowing a mouthful of red chicken before pronouncing: 'Your cleverness is showing you are just clever enough.'

'Things have all changed now,' said Zahra. 'The canteen even serves halal food.'

Coos of amazed appreciation went round the table.

'You know better than I do about offices,' acknowledged her father-in-law, 'but be careful of English people. They say one thing on the face and another behind your back.'

The rain had stopped and after lunch the family walked round the shops and stalls of Southall. First they stopped at an ice-cream vendor and bought frozen pistachio kulfi in conical tubs; then they went to House of Paan, where Mr Dhalani got everyone a triangular green leaf wrapped in foil and dripping with betel juice. Asghar stuffed the whole thing in his mouth. He loved the sweet seediness of paan, the way its aftertaste lingered pleasantly in your throat. Zahra nibbled at the edges of hers. She often did this with food she wanted to savour. She never devoured chocolate at speed, like Asghar did, but instead carefully broke up the segments to eat over an hour or so.

Zahra and Mrs Dhalani stopped to inspect a fabric shop run by an Indian tailor sitting at his sewing machine. Asghar hovered behind, watching the tailor's powerful feminine hands manipulate the cloth, pressing the machine pedal with a pianist's acute attention. Mrs Dhalani said something to him in Hindi, and the tailor stopped working to show her the material. Asghar carried on walking. Further ahead, his dad and sister were picking up Hindu trinkets spread out at a pavement stall; he caught up and found Fatima waving a plastic Hanuman with wind-up monkey arms. Asghar left them to their fun.

Bubbling up from the flooded drains was the oily stench of curry the restaurants had poured out. Distracted by the smell, he walked straight into a pile of bin bags. Behind him a gang of boys laughed. He turned round as the gang pushed past him. They were dressed in baggy trousers and bomber jackets, their hair was gelled into bristling ridges, and their pierced ears showed off gleaming studs. Rude boys. It was an appropriate name, he thought. They catcalled two girls crossing the road. The girls, whom the boys seemed to know, were dressed in white tracksuits with the designer's initials emblazoned in large letters. One boy began dancing round the older girl, while his mates cheered from the sidelines. She flicked her hair at him to show she wasn't playing.

'Come on, why won't you dance with me? Why?' he pleaded.

'Have some respect, man!' she shot back, with not a little theatrical outrage.

'Burn! Burn!' cried one of his boys.

'It's nothing,' the dancing boy assured his crew. 'My dad knows her dad. If I wanted, I could marry her like that.' He snapped his fingers.

'Shut up!' the girl said. Asghar felt like helping but there was nothing he could say; besides, he didn't want to interfere with another community's cultural mores – for all he knew, this was an accepted dating ritual in the world of Southall Sikhs. He walked quickly onwards.

It began raining again. Asghar spotted the Medina Islamic bookshop and took refuge inside. The shop was empty apart from a man at the counter sorting through a large pile of Arabic books. He was dressed in a dirty off-white gown that rippled round his bulging waist. He wore a full beard except for his smoothly shaven upper lip. He looked up from his task and offered a muttered salaam before returning to his books. Asghar replied gratefully, relieved to be in a familiar – and dry – place. He glanced at his watch. His mum and Zahra would probably be ages in the fabric shop; right now, they would be getting the tailor to take down those holders that looked like enormous rolling pins and unfurl the material, before carefully fingering its quality. Those Indian shops had a strong joss-stick smell in honour of their multiple gods. He preferred the singular Arabian scent in the bookshop, where a silver oud burner smoked in the corner. The perfume wafted over the books of history and theology and law.

The shelves were packed with thick brown tomes whose Arabic titles were printed in golden letters. The only other bookshop he used was WHSmiths, where he had bought study guides and his GCSE set texts. He plucked down a biography of the Prophet that ran to nearly a thousand pages. The book's heft lent it an intimidating feel, especially compared with the Karen Armstrong biography he had borrowed from Zahra but not yet opened. He looked at the title: *The Sira of Ibn Ishaq*. Who on earth was this? He had never heard Ibn Ishaq mentioned by Maulana Haider. But then the maulana never said from where exactly he got the stories he told on the minbar. He always referred to 'the most reliable sources' or 'the best eyewitnesses'. Beside the biographies and hadith collections were a number of Qurans translated into English. They didn't have the navy blue and gold Yusuf Ali translation that he had used at madressa; neither did they have the sun-yellow N. J. Dawood Penguin version his father kept in his study drawer. They had all been printed in Saudi Arabia, and did not name translators.

He opened a Quran and turned to the short, intense verses at the back. These were his favourites. At madressa he had memorised them for an end-of-year competition. He read the translation of 'Mankind', the last verse, mouthing the Arabic at the same time. 'Say: I seek refuge in the Lord of mankind – the King of mankind, the God of mankind – from the evil of a sneaking whisperer, who whispers in the heart of man, one who could be a demon or a man.'

His eyes were turning to the commentary on the facing page when the bookseller shouted a welcoming salaam to the man coming through the door. The new arrival shook out his umbrella and handed it to the bookseller. When he removed his damp white turban Asghar recognised with a jolt of surprise that it was Tariq, the man he had last seen being forcibly removed from the Cordoba mosque. Tariq wore a striped cloak down to his ankles; his head was shaved and his once wispy ginger beard was now fulsome and thick. He looked older than he had only months earlier. He recognised Asghar straight away, and greeted him with open arms.

'Brother, where have you been?' he asked, pressing his cheeks on Asghar's. He smelt powerfully of musk.

'You know Tariq al-Andalusi?' asked the bookseller, sounding impressed.

'We've met a couple of times,' Asghar said casually.

'Brother Asghar visited our mosque in Granada. He was present for Friday prayers at Qurtuba mosque. He was about to join us, I believe, when the Pope's guards arrested us.'

'We were going to help, but didn't realise what was happening. It was so confusing.'

'No need to worry, Brother Asghar,' he said, inclining his head, 'I know your heart was with us.'

'What happened?'

'They took me to prison and taunted me with names – *morisco*, *marrano*, troublemaker, terrorist, you know.'

'Did they torture you?' asked the bookseller, his voice trembling.

Tariq did not answer directly. 'Thanks to Allah, I stayed

loyal to my fellow brothers. Unfortunately others were not so strong.'

'Sheikh Tariq is spreading the word about the bad situation in Spain,' the bookseller told Asghar. 'He's going to reclaim al-Andalus for Islam. Invite back the Muslims who were kicked out by the Christians. Just like the Palestinians will reclaim their homeland from the Jews.'

'One step at a time, Brother Umar, one step at a time,' said Tariq with a smile. His accent sounded less Spanish now and more generically Middle Eastern. 'But yes, we are on the march in Europe. The anti-Muslim hatred has become too much to bear. We are strangers who will soon be in the Abode of Islam. I ask you, though, brothers, why take yourself to the Abode of Islam when you can bring the Abode of Islam over here?'

'I could listen to this man all day,' said a beaming Umar.

'You must come to our meeting next week,' said Tariq. 'Brother Umar is making the arrangements.'

'My place in Willesden.'

'Alhamdulillah,' said Tariq. 'This is a discussion group for curious individuals.' He turned his piercing grey eyes to Asghar. 'We would be honoured if you could join us.'

'I'll have to check the dates but . . .' In his excitement he almost dropped his Quran.

'Brother Asghar, don't let the Holy Quran slip. We must treat the words of Allah with respect.' He took the Quran from Asghar, kissed it, placed it on his own forehead, and then kissed it again.

'Leave your wife at home. Come alone.'

# Chapter Nine

That evening Asghar found one of Tariq's speeches on YouTube. Speaking on the BBC, he said that by praying in the Cordoba mosque he was simply exercising the freedom of worship enshrined by the United Nations Declaration of Human Rights. How could the Spanish authorities deny his right to pray in a mosque? This was another example of Western double standards, he railed, from the war on terror to the treatment of the Palestinians. Asghar shared the clip on Facebook and it got nearly twenty likes mainly from mosque friends – the most he had ever got from anything he had posted.

Zahra, however, did not like the video. Instead, the next morning, she posted a newspaper article by a Muslim journalist condemning violence done in the name of Islam, and calling on 'moderate Muslims' to unite against the fanatics. The article annoyed Asghar. Why, he wondered, should Muslims apologise for every bad apple in their barrel? English people never apologised for invading other people's countries – let alone for the crimes of other white people. The term 'moderate Muslim' sounded so watery and weak. In response, he posted articles highlighting attacks on mosques and discrimination against Muslims; and one from a well-known foreign correspondent that argued it was pure hypocrisy to allow Israel nuclear weapons, but not Iran. More likes accrued. Zahra did not comment on these articles, and they never raised the subject in real life.

On the evening of Tariq's meeting, Asghar told Zahra he was going to a careers talk at college. Feeling pleasurably conspiratorial, he left the house and turned right as though walking to Queen's Park; but instead, he walked round the block to Kilburn High Road, from where he caught the bus to Willesden. On Umar's street, dusk was encroaching on the narrow houses separated by low brick walls. Through the exposed windows he saw English families watching television, stupefied by the images flashing across their faces. Unlike them, Asghar thought, he was doing something important with his evening.

Umar's house was not numbered but he knew it was the right place from the holographic Allah sticker on the glass side panel. As he had been instructed, he knocked three times. Umar opened the door and invited him to remove his shoes. Asghar slipped off his black Clarks and set them on a wooden shoe rack beside a pungent collection of brown sandals and white trainers. On the wall there was a framed photograph of the bookseller, his niqab-wearing wife and their five children – the boys in smart blue suits, the girls in frilly pink dresses. Above that was a black-and-white photograph of a middle-aged man with a large beard and pockmarked cheeks; in the corner was a diagonal black mourning strip.

Asghar followed Umar past the eerily empty kitchen – usually an area of bustling female activity at Muslim gatherings – and towards the back of the house. The living room was bare of furniture and covered with an austere white sheet. There was no sign of Tariq but six or seven men sat silently with their backs against the walls. Oddly no one was checking their phone. Most had North African profiles or the blunt features of a Somali or Sudanese – Asghar always confused the two. Their uniform was a dish-dash (white or blue) with a cheap leather jacket and white gym socks. Everyone wore a beard of some sort – either clipped or furry. Asghar rubbed his face self-consciously, wondering if his two-day stubble – the longest he could go without irritating Zahra – was sufficient to blend in. He sat in a corner. No one spoke to him or to each other.

Tariq walked in wearing a smart suit and open-necked shirt matched with a white skullcap. He apologised for being late. He had come straight from a university Islamic Society talk in East London, and so many people wanted to ask him questions that he had been delayed. He sat cross-legged on the floor, like a businessman about to start a yoga class.

'Sitting on the floor has health benefits for posture, breathing and digestion – there has been scientific research about this,' he said. 'Chairs are an unnatural innovation. Did the Prophet – peace and blessings be upon him – sit on chairs? No, he did not. And we should emulate him in all our behaviours. You know,' he said, leaning forward, 'there is a theory that the Ottoman Empire began to decline when the Sultans stopped using cushions, and began sitting upright at tables.'

Umar welcomed in a teenage boy Asghar recognised from the hallway photograph. Tariq beckoned him and the others forward.

'Come, let's sit in a circle together. Yes, like the Sufis do – but don't worry, I won't make you kiss the Prophet's toenails!' The group shuffled into a rough oval. Asghar ended up beside Umar's son. Tariq continued: 'Brothers, many of you don't know one another except by emailing or messaging. We have brought you together because we have a common cause: to analyse the bad situation of Muslims in the world today – especially in Europe, especially in London – and to plan some remedies. At the university this afternoon, I met a brother who had experienced discrimination and Islamophobia, but was too shy to speak in a large group. I'm pleased he has accepted my invitation to come along this evening. Welcome, Akbar.' An earnest-looking, glasses-wearing young man raised his palm in response. Then Tariq turned to Asghar. 'And this is the bold young man involved in our operation at Qurtuba masjid. He witnessed personally our struggle for equal rights.'

Asghar acknowledged Tariq's praise, enjoying the admiration emanating from the circle.

'But let me first invite our gracious host Umar to start proceedings by introducing himself,' said Tariq. The bookseller adjusted his large body and began telling his story in lightly accented English.

Umar had been born in Egypt in 1967, the year of the fateful capture of Jerusalem, into a prominent Muslim Brotherhood family. 'When Anwar Sadat flew to the enemy's lair and made peace with the devil,' said Umar, 'he brought upon himself the righteous anger of the Muslims. He was sent to meet the judgment of Almighty Allah.'

Following Sadat's assassination, Umar and his father were arrested and taken to a Cairo jail, where they shared a cell with four other men.

'We coped with the bad conditions,' said Umar, 'through reciting the Holy Quran. The guards did not allow copies in our cell, but my father knew the whole book by heart – he was a hafiz.'

Asghar was impressed: he could never remember more than those short verses.

Umar continued: 'Other prisoners asked him to recite their favourite verses. Many, who suffered at the hands of this *Firawn*, chose the miracles of Musa. They had had a terrible time. One man had his nails ripped out; another was whipped with chains. My father comforted them. He himself was questioned many times. And me? I was a child, the same age as Sayyid' – he put a hand on his son's shoulder – 'and I could not tell the interrogators anything. After some months, my father and I were separated. My cell was cleaner, the guards were not so harsh and there was cool running water to perform wudhu. Within weeks, I was told I would be released; I didn't believe them, but then I was given a confession to sign. Brothers, I refused until I knew my father would be released with me. They told me he was a serious criminal siding with enemies of the regime. I protested that he was simply reciting the Holy Quran to the other prisoners but these godless servants of *Firawn* – may Allah curse them – did not listen. My poor mother came and told me to sign the confession; she couldn't be deprived of a husband *and* a son. That night I prayed and prayed for Allah to give me a signal. When I slept, the Prophet himself came to me in a dream and told me to sign. Three days later I was released, without being allowed to say farewell to my father.'

'What happened to him?' Tariq prompted. 'Tell them.'

'Two months later my father's death certificate arrived in

the post. They said he had hanged himself in prison. This was a lie: *Firawn* ordered his death. My mother collapsed but I remained strong. It was a privilege to be the son of a martyr. I envied him.'

His voice wobbled briefly. Shortly after his father's death, he had claimed asylum in the UK. He married the British-born daughter of a Muslim Brotherhood leader.

'At the time, the West was helping our mujahideen brothers in Afghanistan. Now they only support dictators. We are living in bad times, my brothers. Alhamdulillah we have wise reverts such as Sheikh Tariq al-Andalusi, who can raise our conscious-ness – and communicate with the Europeans in a way they understand.'

'Humbled, I'm humbled,' said Tariq. He turned to the circle. 'Brother Umar has welcomed me here in London. I must commend his son Sayyid as well for taking me to the top tourist sites. I had always wanted to see the Tower of London. It was where King Henry beheaded that fanatic Thomas More – the defender of Katharine, daughter of Ferdinand and Isabella, destroyers of al-Andalus. Sayyid – a thousand thanks.' He winked at him.

Sayyid, like his father, was overweight. His wrinkled forehead belied his youth and his beard was made up of coarse black hairs with rust-coloured stragglers. Asghar wondered what it must have been like for him growing up in the shadow of a martyred grandfather, the one whose photograph loomed so large in the corridor. Sayyid had sat calmly through his father's speech, marking the moments of high drama – Sadat's assas-sination, his grandfather's murder – with a muttered curse or low cry of compassion. There was a grave authority about his manner. He was the kind of Muslim friend Asghar would have liked while growing up, but at the new mosque all the boys wanted to talk about was exam results and football, which was a problem because Asghar didn't do well in exams and could never pick a favourite team. For the mosque boys, Islam was a set of rituals to be rushed through without leaving any deeper impression. No one teased out the meaning of faith or fundamentally questioned the values of the society in which they lived. Their parallel selves never crossed. To satisfy his hunger for seriousness, Asghar thought many times about approaching Maulana Haider after the majlis or piping up during the times he came to their house for dinner. But he was always too busy with more important people, notably Mr Dhalani. Tariq was much more welcoming. Instead of preaching, he allowed them to speak first. It made a refreshing change.

Tariq invited the others to share their stories. After a short pause, one man wearing a long green shirt, his age difficult to tell, began describing how the mosque he had been planning to build had been turned down for planning permission multiple times by the council – they always cited health and safety concerns, but never specified what these might be. They were forced to perform Friday prayers above his halal meat shop. Attendance was poor because of the terrible smell. Another man, Somali and slightly older, said the police accused him of dealing drugs on his estate. They harassed him so much he was afraid of leaving his flat. A thin-faced Pakistani guy with a reedy voice described how one day, he was walking home from an ice-cream parlour with his wife when some drunks spilling out from a pub began abusing them; one thug, he said, had approached his wife and taunted her to show them her hair. When she shouted back, they poured a glass of beer over her hijab. She stood there dripping as the white men ran off laughing.

Tariq clicked his tongue. 'They shall find their punishment in the world to come and, God willing, in this one also.' He turned to the student he had brought along from his university talk. 'Why don't you tell us your story?'

The bespectacled Akbar had organised a debate about Israel on campus. One speaker was a Gazan who worked for a Palestinian charity. He had been difficult to get hold of, said Akbar, and he was going to draw a big crowd. But the Jewish Society protested, saying he was an anti-Semite – 'You know,' said Akbar, 'the usual stuff about how anyone criticising Jews *must* be racist.' At the last minute, the Palestinian was banned from entering the country. 'I was genuinely shocked,' said Akbar. 'I didn't know Britain could be so two-faced over freedom of speech.'

'There is a depth to their hatred that cannot be measured,' said Tariq. 'We remind them of the moral standards they have thrown away.'

'Last year the history department had this conference on Islamic history, where they invited this Danish woman who said, I heard at least, that there was no evidence the Prophet even existed!'

'Such insults are normal these days,' said Tariq, shaking his head wearily.

Akbar said he had organised a demonstration to protest against the ban. 'Loads of white people came to support us waving their rainbow CND flags,' he said. 'It was pretty cool. But I was called into the vice-chancellor's office and told to stop "making trouble" because I was a good student and shouldn't jeopardise my future. None of the anti-war guys were called in – only me.'

'There are no white leftists in Guantanamo,' said Umar darkly.

136

'Thank you, Akbar. Okay, perhaps time for a break? Brother Umar, what's for dinner?'

Umar explained that, out of respect for Tariq, he had told his wife and daughters to spend the night with his sister. They would send the boys out to get kebab and chips. Umar whispered in his son's ear. Sayyid pulled himself up nimbly and tapped Akbar's shoulder, and then Asghar's.

'Let's get the kebabs,' he said. 'It's round the corner.'

Walking out together, Asghar got chatting to Akbar. He spoke to him about studying in London; like Asghar, he was from the suburbs, though from the east rather than the west. He lived with his parents in Ilford and commuted every day. Asghar said his journey was easier now he had moved to Kilburn with his wife.

'You're married!' said Akbar, whistling in admiration.

'Yeah,' said Asghar shyly. 'We got married in the spring.'

'No kids coming or nothing?'

'God no,' said Asghar. The thought of him and Zahra having children seemed absurd when they still hadn't even slept together. 'What I meant to say was that Zahra, that's my wife, wants to get to a better stage in her career before taking maternity leave.'

Sayyid broke in: 'She works? That's not Islamic.'

'Didn't Bibi Khadija work?' said Asghar cautiously. 'The Prophet didn't mind that.'

'Not *after* she married him,' said Sayyid.

'He's right,' said Akbar solemnly. 'I've told my mother to find me a proper home girl. I don't care if we earn less money. I'm not materialistic like that.'

'Sheikh Tariq says there shouldn't be an imbalance between male and female,' said Sayyid. 'If a woman earns more than a man, he won't feel man enough. His wife no longer finds him attractive. Women hate wimps.'

'No offence, Asghar,' said Akbar, 'but he's right. You should be looking after your wife, not the other way round.'

Asghar stayed quiet until they reached the takeaway joint.

'Chicken or meat?' Sayyid asked Asghar.

'Meat,' he said, though secretly he preferred chicken. Too much spiced meat gave him a stomach upset.

The man at the counter, who seemed to know Sayyid, skewered a dozen kebabs and prepared flat naan bread with onion, salad and a lathering of chilli and garlic sauce. He then slapped thick, oily chips into yellow polystyrene packets and stuffed them in a white plastic bag. Asghar carried the chips. As the bags swayed in his hands, the vinegar smell rose to his nostrils. On the way back, he listened to Sayyid telling Akbar about Tariq's new group: 'Strangers of Europe'. It was based at the Medina bookshop in Southall. He told Akbar he should forget his Islamic Society at university, where he did not have the freedom to speak his mind.

'And you, Asghar,' said Sayyid, 'you've been on our radar a long time.'

'Really?' said Asghar. By now they were about to re-enter the house.

'Take this kebab to Sheikh Tariq,' said Sayyid. 'He wants to speak to you.'

As soon as he saw him enter the living room, Tariq invited Asghar to sit down with an elaborate sweep of his arm. Asghar poured his chips on to his plate and unwrapped his kebab roll. Tariq took a bent chip and began chewing.

'You've been quiet so far,' he said, in a tone of gentle reproach. 'I hope you also have a story to share. You wouldn't

138

be here unless you felt the same as my other boys.' Asghar ate his chips slowly. He had found it a comfort listening to the boys' complaints without the fear of Zahra's voice always piping up, 'Yes, but on the other hand . . .' When he complained to her about anti-Muslim bias in the media, for example, she would say, 'You should blame those idiots for giving them the ammunition,' or 'Britain's the best place in the world to be a Muslim.' There were things about his child-hood – secret things, painful things – he was nervous about telling her.

'I have something,' Asghar admitted. 'I have a story from school days, about my old headmaster. It was a strange time.'

'We're ready to listen,' said Tariq. 'For now, eat in peace.'

Asghar unrolled his kebab and began scraping off the hot chilli sauce. Sayyid and Akbar, he saw, were devouring their portions with wolfish speed. He took a small bite of kebab and let the hot taste fill his mouth. He knew he would prob-ably feel ill later that evening but for now, among friends, he tried not to think too hard about the consequences.


Once they had finished the food and put the rubbish in the kitchen, Asghar began speaking – at first nervously, and then with more fluency – about an incident from his schooldays.

One Thursday evening at the new mosque, Maulana Haider launched a 'freedom to practise your faith' campaign. The idea was originally Mr Dhalani's. Asghar's father had been roused by complaints from people at the new mosque that their work-places and their children's schools were not allowing them to pray at lunchtime. 'No more missing prayers,' thundered the maulana from the polished wooden pulpit. 'Your boss must provide a suitable room to perform noonday namaaz. This has been our right since the days of empire.'

After the lecture, Mr Dhalani announced that the new mosque had drafted a standard letter explaining the Islamic necessity of praying at appointed times, and the moral obligation on workplaces and schools to provide places to pray. A queue of men lined up outside his office afterwards to get their copy. They filled in their bosses' names and addresses above where Maulana Haider had signed with a flourish. Asghar stuffed and sealed the envelopes. Some men tried to take the letters home, but Mr Dhalani stopped them.

'Don't worry about it,' he said, sliding the letters out of their hands and putting them back in the pile. 'We'll post it on your behalf, free of charge.' Asghar caught a few worried looks. After everyone had gone, Asghar filled in a letter for himself. 'Dear Mr Powell,' he wrote in his neatest handwriting, before the printed letter began: 'We are asking to worship our Lord in the way we are compelled. As a Christian I'm sure you understand . . .' Once he was done, he sealed the letter and put it on the posting pile.

'Just give him the letter in person. Saves on postage,' said Mr Dhalani, tickling his son's chin. In the last few weeks Asghar had sprouted a few wispy hairs. 'Look at you!' he said. 'Not even a teenager and you're already on the path to a full beard, masha-allah – like your father.' He stroked his own rough goatee with fine appreciation. 'You are baligh now,' he said softly, conferring upon his son the sacred status of a mature moral agent. 'No more shilly-shallying: you must be a proper Muslim now.'

The problem was that Asghar's budding facial hair violated the strict rules of Enfield House. Mr Powell had already hauled him into his study and told him to come back the next day clean-shaven; back at home, though, his father told him to say the beard was part of his religious observance. It was not merely about imitating the Holy Prophet (though that was important): it signified the threshold of adulthood. All this didn't stop the greasy hairs irritating his skin. He tried to compromise by reducing the hairs to a few millimetres – barely a beard, more a beard-shaped shadow. He hoped both his father and Mr Powell could be fooled. But his trimming satisfied nobody.

It was the autumn term during his second year at the school. The boys at Enfield House trampled the last flowers in the headmaster's garden searching for their lost footballs. Asghar, on the other hand, spent his lunchtimes alone on the cloak-room benches concealed among the coats and satchels. He was hiding from Mr Powell: more specifically, he was hiding his beard from Mr Powell. (This year he wasn't taking him for Scripture.) The headmaster stalked the grounds at lunch-time looking for litterers, and so the safest place was inside. Just in case he did come past, though, Asghar always held a can of coke which he could put to his lips to obscure his face. He ended up drinking two or three cokes a day, which drained his lunch money and made his teeth buzz.

The Monday after the maulana's campaign began, Asghar sat in the cloakroom nibbling a soggy samosa, armed, for variety's sake, with a full can of fizzy orange. The mosque's letter lay crumpled inside his jacket pocket. He was wondering about how to pass it to Mr Powell when his illegal beard made speaking to him impossible. Just then, his nemesis swooped down the corridor. Asghar put the soda can to his lips. The headmaster stopped in front of him and waited while he drank. Asghar's chest felt like it was going to explode. Still Mr Powell waited. The bubbly drink slid down Asghar's windpipe, setting off a coughing fit.

'Dhalani,' he said wearily, 'I've turned a blind eye until now but this is getting silly.' Asghar was too busy coughing to respond. 'School rules state that every boy should be clean-shaven. It's a part of school discipline and there can be no exceptions. Do you think the rules don't apply to you? That you're special for some reason? Come here,' said the head-master in exasperation, pulling Asghar by the arm and marching him up the spiral stairs towards his study-bedroom. Asghar steeled himself for a severe telling-off; but that was okay, he could deal with words.

Instead of the study, though, Mr Powell led him to a dingy side corridor with a cracked wooden door. He took out a key and unlocked a toilet cubicle. The place was freezing. A small frosted window was jammed open. Above it, a patient spider danced on a single strand of web. Mr Powell opened the cabinet above the sink and took out a soap bar, a shaggy shaving brush and a cut-throat razor.

'During national service we were all taught to shave,' said Mr Powell, 'no matter what our background. There were work-ing-class lads just like you – no clue how to clean themselves. Since your father clearly has no interest in hygiene, I suppose it's up to me.'

He flicked open the razor with a smile, showing his yellow tombstone teeth amid a forest of beard.

'I don't know how to shave with a razor,' ventured Asghar, 'I borrow my dad's electric trimmer.'

'If you won't shave yourself,' he said, 'I'll do it for you.' The plughole gulped as he sealed the sink. He turned on both taps: the freezing and boiling water rushed together in a foaming mass. He took the soap bar and lathered the brush before applying the white cream roughly on Asghar's face. The brush tickled his lips and nostrils. Mr Powell pressed the blade to his chin and began scraping his skin. Asghar flinched at each burning stroke, but Mr Powell didn't stop until every hair was removed.

'There you go,' he said jovially. 'That's better.' Before he left, he threw him a towel and told him to clean up and get to class. Wiping his naked face in front of the mirror, Asghar saw dozens of bloody nicks on his neck, chin and upper lip; he staunched them with torn bits of toilet paper. When the blood dried, he peeled off the stained confetti and washed his face in cold water. His face was hot with shame and anger. After leaving the toilet, he slipped the mosque letter under Mr Powell's study door before walking slowly down the stairs and hiding by the cloakroom benches until his wounds healed.

At dinner, his father didn't mention his newly shaven appearance; he was more worried about whether the head-master had received the letter. Had he handed it over? Yes, replied Asghar, bewildered that he had gone through such a humiliation for something his father seemed not to have even noticed was missing.

'Have you prayed this evening?' he asked.

'Yes.'

'Both Maghrib and Isha.'

'Yes!'

'Good,' he said. 'I want you praying on time from now on – right on the minute. That is what a baligh boy does.'

It seemed like his father only ever addressed him to ask whether he had fulfilled his old instructions or to give him new ones. He felt he was never listened to.

143

One benefit of being beardless was that there was no need to hide from Mr Powell, so he ventured to the fields where the other boys played football at lunchtime. Danny spotted him and found a position for him in defence. Asghar was pleased they seemed to be friends again and the awkwardness over Sarah had been forgotten. He was the first to admit he wasn't an outstanding player, but he could make himself useful. He thrived on confidence: if his first moments went well so would the rest of his game. Playing that lunchtime, his touch was solid and his lay-offs accurate. He hassled the opposition vigorously and bravely dived in front of hard shots. When cleverer players tricked him, he quickly recovered. When his team piled forward, he held the defensive line. Danny praised him loudly for that most rare quality in schoolboy football: unselfishness. Asghar passed the ball to Danny every chance he had, hitting long balls into the opposition's penalty area for him to chase. When one of his passes sailed into the head-master's garden, his teammates berated him as he ran to collect it. But Danny shouted encouragement.

'Good idea,' he said, clapping his hands above his head.

After a week or so of consistent performances, Asghar and Danny found themselves queuing together at the water fountain. Danny mentioned the House football tournament coming up and told Asghar he needed him in defence. 'The way you've been playing no one could deny you a place. And you're bigger than you used to be.' He tested Asghar's toughening biceps. Asghar drank his water, imagining making a saving tackle and lifting the cup with Danny by his side. Maybe Sarah would be there to cheer them on, her blonde hair curling under a pink bobble hat.

'The tournament starts in two weeks,' said Danny.

'Great,' said Asghar. 'I'll get in training.' As he walked to class a vague feeling came over him. What was happening in two weeks? He couldn't remember, but it felt like something important.

After school that evening, Asghar knocked cautiously on the living room door. He was wary of disturbing his mother's special time. Since they had got cable television she had been glued to Indian soap operas – clapping the hero, booing the villain, scolding the matriarch who crushed the daughter-in-law. She complained grumpily about English soaps; this boy got Aids or that girl fell pregnant, scandals so distant from her own world they could have been taking place on another planet. Indian soaps were a bit over-the-top, she admitted, but the dilemmas they tackled – the poor girl resisting the advances of a rich relative, the mixed-caste couple trying to gain their parents' approval – were ones with which she could identify. Mr Dhalani never watched them with her and she liked it that way. Once she had cleared the dishes and made the tea she settled down with a chocolate bar to enjoy – as her husband described it – being agitated by other people's problems.

'Come, behta,' she said. 'Come next to me.' He sat down awkwardly. Not so long ago he would have lain down on the sofa tucked close to her warm body; now he was too tall to fit comfortably. She rubbed his chin. 'Nice and clean and smooth. Keep it like that.'

His mother had never liked beards, and was always encouraging her husband to shave his off.

'Mummy, I've had some good news at school,' he said, feeling pleased she had noticed his shaved face.

'What?' she asked excitedly.

'I've been selected to play for my House football team – in the five-a-side competition.'

'Oh, very good,' she said.

'I'll have to stay late after school that day. It's okay, though, I'll get the train.'

'Is it happening soon?'

'Actually, I was going to ask you. Are we doing anything in two weeks?'

'Two weeks, two weeks . . . nothing, no.'

'Oh, that's okay then, because I thought—'

'Only Ramzan might have started by then. Let's look at the calendar.' She walked to the kitchen noticeboard where a purple poster showed where the Gregorian and Hijri dates overlapped.

'Fasting starts on the twenty-fourth or twenty-fifth October, depending on the sighting of the moon. When is your match?'

'I'm not sure – I'll have to check,' said Asghar. But he didn't have to: he already knew the match would fall on the third or fourth day of the fasting month.

'Are we going to mosque right from the start?'

'You and Fatima can't miss Quran. If you don't go every day, they won't ask you to recite.'

Back in his room he made some quick calculations. The tournament ended about an hour before sunset, which was around the time they set up the low wooden benches for Quran. Then came prayers, followed by breaking the fast with sweet tea, soft dates and hot curry. If his team were knocked out early he might make it for Quran – but if they got to the final, he would barely be back in time for food. How he would cope with fasting and playing at the same time was a more serious problem. Taking no food or drink from sunrise to sunset was hard enough when

146

lazing at home on a Saturday; playing an intense football tournament might be too much. Not for the first time, Asghar cursed his luck that just as something exciting was happening in the outside world, he was being dragged back home.

Then a tempting thought occurred. Could he miss one fast? Watching cricket with his father, he had seen the Pakistani team drink gallons of juice during Ramzan. His father told him that since cricket was their livelihood, they had permission to miss fasts and make them up later. Participating in a school tournament was a bit like his profession, he told himself – so couldn't he miss one day? But he knew what his father's answer would be.

'You're now a baligh boy. Everything is compulsory: prayers, fasting, everything. No more messing around like a child.'

When he was eight or nine years old and struggling with a fast, Asghar's mother quietly sent him to bed with milk and toast. Yet now that Asghar was shaving, he was, Islamically speaking, a responsible agent. Fasts had to be observed except for illness, pregnancy or travel – none of which applied. So he had to fast.

On match day, Asghar woke up an hour before sunrise and stuffed himself with food. He requested a three-egg omelette from his mother. After devouring the cheesy mess and four thick slices of toast, he went to the sink and filled a large glass of water. Usually he had two large glasses but this morning he had four. It was strange that something so tasteless was so difficult to swallow; still he forced himself, feeling his stomach fill up, like a camel about to embark on a desert journey. Knowing that his mother would forbid him from strenuous exercise while fasting, Asghar had not mentioned the football tournament again. Instead, the night before, he had told her he would be staying late at the library and going to mosque on his own by train. While she was driving him to the station that morning, Asghar was relieved she did not question him about his evening plans: a lie would have broken his fast.

He had eaten enough food to last until lunchtime without a stomach rumble, but he was soon desperately thirsty. The water he had drunk that morning had dried up by the time of the first match. Each match lasted twenty minutes with a two-minute break at halftime. Soon after kick-off his House, the Crows, scored – Danny's diving header – but their opponents, the Storks, equalised when their striker slammed home a loose ball in the penalty area. Asghar had made two or three decisive interceptions by then so could not be blamed for this one slip. The game was drawn. The Crows stayed on and the Peacocks lined up to face them. The Peacocks were a poor team but Danny warned them not to take it easy. Within five minutes, the Crows were two goals up and even Asghar was venturing forward for corners, hoping to get an assist. They were attacking so much that when the Peacocks did get the ball, Asghar had to run back hard to protect his goalkeeper. His team won 3–0 in the end, but the game had taken a physical toll.

Playing back-to-back games, Asghar hadn't felt thirsty; afterwards, though, spit filled his mouth and swallowing felt like gurgling hot sand. He concentrated on breathing deeply. Woozy thoughts floated across his mind. Wasn't it lucky that you were allowed to breathe during fasting? Holding your breath for fourteen hours would be a tough ask. Maulana Haider preached that fasting made you think about the plight of the poor; but fasting only made Asghar think about pink sherbet and samosas. He had no mental space to think of anyone else. The dinner ladies brought round trays of roughly sliced oranges and packets of bottled water. Danny slipped an orange slice between his teeth like a mouth-guard. Sticky juice rolled down his chin and on to his shirt. After throwing his desiccated peel in the bin, Danny passed the orange tray to Asghar.

'You've got to rehydrate,' he said. Asghar shook his head. 'I'm fasting.'

'Oranges are practically water,' he urged.

'I can't have water either,' said Asghar, now feeling really sick.

Danny swigged from his bottle and turned to find Mr Powell standing beside them in a green mackintosh and bowler hat.

'What's happening here?'

'Sir, he says he won't drink,' said Danny. 'But I don't think he's feeling well.'

'I told you, Danny, I'm fasting,' said Asghar, his head between his legs.

'Fasting?' Mr Powell rasped.

'It's part of my religion,' said Asghar. 'It's the fasting month.'

'Can't you break the fast if you're not feeling well?'

'That's only if you're ill. I chose to play football.'

'Look,' said Mr Powell, losing patience, 'I don't want you collapsing: surely this religion of yours isn't so intransigent. Drink some water.'

He gave him a bottle. Asghar unscrewed it. As the cap gave way, water droplets splashed on his hand. He brought the bottle slowly to his lips, waiting for Mr Powell to move. When it was clear that the headmaster wanted to see him drink the water, Asghar paused – and then poured the bottle's contents over his head, letting the water streak past his sealed lips.

'This is pure defiance,' said Mr Powell, his face purpling with anger.

'You can't force me to break my fast!' cried Asghar, summoning up the last of his energy.

'Get out,' he replied with quiet fury. 'Go home right now.'

Collapsed on the train, Asghar saw the sun unwinding in the grey-pink sky. He would miss Quran but with luck might make the food: he hoped it would be chicken curry and yellow naan. A few stops from his destination, he felt the carriage trundle to a halt. From the window, he saw gardens behind the rows of semi-detached houses with drying clothes flapping in the wind and rusty bikes latched together next to the sheds. Flowery net curtains cast a milky shadow over their windows. He checked his watch: ten minutes before he could break his fast. Right now at the mosque the men would be queuing behind the new stainless-steel sinks Mr Dhalani had installed, pulling off their socks and rolling up their sleeves, soothing their dry mouths with water before spitting it out and readying themselves for prayer and then breaking their fasts. It was now dusk and someone in one of the houses switched on their kitchen lights. He could see an English family setting the table for dinner. The mum was serving lasagne, which right then looked like the most delicious meal in the world. The sky dimmed and the sun disappeared. It was surely time to break his fast. He fished in his pocket for anything edible: some stray nuts or jelly babies, perhaps. He found nothing except a half-eaten chocolate bar covered in fluff. The English mum dug into the steaming lasagne and served her two boys; he saw the cheesy strings stretch, then break. It was dark enough now. Cleaning the chocolate with his fingers he said a quick prayer and took a bite of Bounty. The train began to move.

*

150

'He refused the water?' said the head of science, Miss Harris, with the iron hair curls.

'He tipped the water *over* his head,' replied Mr Powell.

'He did what?'

The headmaster mimed tipping a bottle of water over his head.

'Does that mean something – you know, culturally?'

'If it does, Miss Harris, I've never heard of it.'

'Refuses to drink water, but happy to waste it,' she said. 'Can't break the fast even though he made himself ill. That's religious sophistry at its worst.'

Asghar was spying on this conversation from his hideaway on the benches behind the coats. The day after the football tournament disaster, he had been banished to his old position once more – for once he had left, the Crows had been knocked out in the semi-final, leaking four goals.

Mr Powell and Miss Harris were standing in what they thought was an empty corridor.

'In some ways it's quite admirable,' said Mr Powell. 'The other boys couldn't handle half an hour without pizza and chips or a burger.'

Asghar's mouth began to water.

'Their performance drops off in Ramadan,' said Miss Harris. 'We should tell the parents the boys should only fast at week-ends. If they want to be active members of the school community they can't be fainting from hunger.'

'And have you noticed,' said Mr Powell, lowering his voice, 'when they're on Ramadan their breath doesn't half pong.'

Asghar held his breath.

'What are you going to do with the boy?' asked Miss Harris.

'We have to tread carefully, if you know what I mean. They

pay regularly. And if they like the school, they always tell their cousins.'

'We have to keep the school's culture intact, headmaster.'

'I've got a letter from his mosque asking for a prayer room at lunchtime.'

'Give them an inch and they'll take a mile.'

'I'm inclined to grant his wish,' said Mr Powell. 'We can't be too narrow-minded about such things.'

'That's very generous of you, headmaster.'

Asghar couldn't work out Mr Powell's tone: he didn't seem upset or angry; in fact, he sounded quite sympathetic. Just then he heard Mr Powell's loud voice. 'Dhalani!' he called from the far end of the corridor. 'I can see you skulking, come over here.'

Asghar rubbed his chin – luckily he had shaved that morning – and emerged from the coats.

'Still fasting?' asked Mr Powell. Asghar nodded. 'Well, each to his own. I've got this letter you pushed under my door.' Asghar felt as though he were about to start an exam or a cross-country run.

'I've considered this request and, I can tell you, I've decided to allow it,' said Mr Powell coolly. 'I've found you a place to pray. Do you have some sort of rug? Run and get it.'

Asghar opened his rucksack and found the blue prayer mat his mother had thoughtfully packed for him, still wrapped in its plastic covering.

'Follow me,' said Mr Powell. Asghar walked up the school's narrow spiral staircase. They approached the first-floor art studio that was always empty at lunchtimes; it seemed a decent enough place, but Mr Powell carried on up the stairs. The studio smelled of dried glue anyway, thought Asghar, and he didn't want paint on his prayer mat. On the next floor up was a supplies cupboard where chalk, dusters, pens and old textbooks were stored. It was quite small but would be acceptable. Again, though, they walked straight past it. Perhaps the headmaster didn't want to risk him pocketing the coloured pens – fair enough. They reached the school's top floor and Mr Powell's study. It had a lovely oriental carpet and a skylight window through which sunshine streamed; it was perfect. He was just wondering how to say thanks when Mr Powell opened the toilet cubicle door, the same place where he had shaved him.

'Here you are,' he said, smiling, 'this is the perfect place for you.'

The toilet smelled strongly of disinfectant. 'I've had the cleaners give it a once over,' said Mr Powell. 'You can do your washing in the sink.' Asghar saw the spider was building a web on the outside of the window.

'Carry on then,' said the headmaster. 'You don't want prayer time to end.' Asghar mechanically turned on the taps and let the water run. 'I'll leave you to it,' said Mr Powell and shut him in. Asghar locked the door. He rolled up his sleeves and performed a quick ablution in the icy water. He unfurled his prayer mat and laid it on the wet floor. The space was tight and the edges curled over the toilet's base. He found Makkah with a compass and said his prayers as fast as he could – careful not to bang his head on the sink bowl when he stood up straight. When he was done, he saw that the spider had spun a web across the width of the window. He jammed open the window, crushed the spider and web in his hands and flushed them down the toilet.

*

'The weakest of homes is the home of the spider – if only they knew,' said Tariq. Asghar looked up. He had not expected to carry on so long or confess so much; but he felt relieved. When he had told his parents what had happened, they removed him from Enfield House. They enrolled him in the local state school where he had to deal with exhausted teachers and chaotic students – stopping Muslim children praying was the least of the head's worries. He withdrew from social life outside the mosque: his world contracted. Danny and Sarah became distant figures in his memory. Mr Powell was a charismatic ogre who reared his head only in nightmares.

Tariq embraced Asghar and held him against his tense, muscular chest. A weeping Umar gave him a powerful bear hug. Sayyid and Akbar shook his hand. Asghar suppressed a tearful tremor rising in his throat. When everyone had hugged everyone else, Tariq caught Asghar's sleeve and led him to one side. He took out a brown envelope and handed it to him.

'I have specially chosen this for you from Umar's bookshop,' he told him in a low voice. 'Go home and read it.' He looked at Asghar intently with his grey eyes. 'Read it properly.' Riding the bus home, he took out the black and green pamphlet. Its title was *Western Sexual Revolution: A New Slavery*.

# Chapter Ten

While Asghar was out at his careers event, or whatever it was – Zahra couldn't exactly recall – she decided to Skype Andrea. Sitting on her old red armchair with her laptop on her cushioned lap, she chatted about the wedding arrangements. Zahra would be the maid of honour – 'It shouldn't really be "maid", though, should it?' said Andrea, laughing. Zahra forced a smile. They spent an hour sending each other possible designs for Andrea's dress: sleek dresses, lacy dresses, puffy dresses that would never do but were good for a laugh.

'Count yourself lucky,' said Zahra. 'You can choose what to wear for your own bloody wedding.'

'I thought you did choose?'

'Well, technically yes, but Asghar's mum was really interfering. It was like I had a choice, but didn't really.'

'I'm not being mean or anything but Carl's parents are dirt

poor. They can't afford to pay for anything, and neither can he. Because I'm paying, I choose what I want.'

'I wish I could have paid for mine!'

'I saw how your mum was really pressuring you that day.'

'Actually,' she said, changing tack as soon as she felt Andrea was taking advantage of her honesty, 'actually, I accepted that; I even liked going ultra-traditional.'

'Really?'

'There's something cool about rebelling against the rebellion everyone expects—'

'I saw Krish the other day,' interrupted Andrea.

'Right.' Zahra felt her voice tighten. She tried to compose her reactions.

'Sorry, I didn't know if you knew he was around.'

'We don't speak now. I mean, we don't "not speak", just that we haven't spoken recently.'

'It was at Adam's party,' said Andrea. 'He's moved to east London. Massive place, totally dodgy area.'

'How was he?'

'Krish? Didn't speak to him but he wasn't with anybody – a girl, I mean – and he didn't go home with anyone either. I told Carl to monitor his movements.'

'He can do what he wants. It's been ages now. I'm married, for God's sake!' Still she was grateful for the news.

'For what it's worth, Asghar's a really nice boy,' said Andrea in her magnanimous voice. 'He's quieter than Krish, but every-one's different.'

'Yes, everyone is different.'

Carl came into shot behind Andrea, wearing boxer shorts and a T-shirt; he put his finger to his lips. He surprised Andrea by putting his hands on her sides and tickling her. She squealed with delight.

'Bye, Zahra, text you soon,' she said, snapping shut her laptop.

And so married life continued. When they first moved in together Zahra had grand cooking plans and firmly refused her mother's neatly labelled curry boxes; but whenever she tried cooking it turned out either burned or bland. There was no point remaining proud. Usually, after she let him know she was leaving work, Asghar texted her the evening's food options. If she did not fancy anything from either of their mother's kitchens – the freezer was by now packed with plastic tubs of daal and rice – would she pick up something from the Pakistani cafe on the way home from the station? When they were bored of curry, it was fish and chips or Chinese. They always sat at the table to eat and rarely in front of the television. But gradually they would position their chairs in such a way as to be able to see the screen, or eat with both their laptops open in front of them.

Zahra had planned to put a framed print of Van Gogh's *Sunflowers* above the blocked fireplace. But Mrs Amir inadvertently stymied the plan with her wedding present: a 38-inch flat-screen television, which for reasons involving plugs and aerials was best mounted above the old fireplace. Zahra would have preferred something subtler, but her mother had paid so much for the set – as much as the Persian carpet that didn't fit, thought Zahra ruefully – that they could hardly leave it languishing in its box.

In the evenings Zahra controlled the remote. She liked

police procedurals and quizzes. Asghar's favourite programmes were the ones that filmed strikingly different families – black evangelicals and white liberals; poor scruffs and perfidious aristocrats – living together for a week.

'It shows people are naturally good-hearted,' he told Zahra. 'No matter how much they argue, at the end they always understand each other.'

'After shouting their heads off for an hour.'

'Okay, but then they come together.'

'Maybe it helps that they never see each other again,' said Zahra.

Zahra made periodic efforts to revive their relationship. They both liked walking and, while the weather was still bearable, they took the overground to Hampstead Heath. Asghar had never been there before: he knew the heath only through the schoolboy cracks about the men who hung round there at night. But as they started tramping through the grass he guessed that Zahra would not appreciate a joke about who might be rustling in the bushes. The couple walked quietly except to speculate on the name of a beautiful flower, or to comment on how English families no longer went to church on Sundays.

In her own way, Zahra was equally withdrawn. With Krish she liked making funny remarks about people's appearances – especially Indians. Walking in a Cambridge shopping centre once, she had spied a middle-aged woman whose sari was flapping round her bulging stomach. Zahra had turned to Krish and whispered 'for shame, for shame' in an Indian accent. He laughed so hard he had to bury his face in her shoulder. But on Hampstead Heath when Zahra passed an Indian family ripe for mockery – father with moustache and greasy hair, mother clutching crinkled carrier bags from the cash and carry, children in matching purple jump suits – Zahra held back. Her guardedness did nothing for their relationship, for there was no quicker route to intimacy than having your worst instincts indulged – and then forgiven. As she trudged over the grassy tussocks, she reflected that while the outside world might regard them as a properly married couple, the reality was that they were just two virgins holding hands.

She took to visiting the local library. It lacked the wood-panelled calm of her college library; with its hard plastic chairs and multilingual drug awareness posters, the local library resembled a doctor's surgery more than a haven for readers. She did find, however, a stack of golden-age detective novels that nobody had borrowed in years. Every Saturday morning, while Asghar snoozed till noon, she discovered a newish mystery. She spent two hours at the newish Starbucks – packed with other middle-class people escaping the high street – sipping hot chocolate and reading Agatha Christie and Dorothy L. Sayers. She found suspense annoying, and preferred to begin these books by flicking through to the back pages to learn who the murderer was, after which she would try to pick up the clues the author had planted.

Walking home from the library one Saturday before Christmas, she saw three Muslims handing out flyers. Their leader, a short man with a full beard and shaved upper lip, warned the present-buyers via megaphone that Western civilisation was teetering on collapse because of such rapacious consumerism. When Zahra walked past he lowered his gaze to the dropping-stained pavement. She sailed past holding her uncovered head high. The next week she saw they had set up a trestle table draped with a green cloth stitched with the sign: *Muhammad, heir to Jesus.* This time the men had brought their wives, who were sitting on plastic stools and chatting behind their niqabs. Zahra examined some of the multi-coloured pamphlets spread on the table. Glancing up, she noticed a woman rubbing the legs of a placid little girl wearing a frilly blue dress. The woman dipped into a black handbag and took out some cream – the same brand Zahra used. She applied the cream to the girl's legs – which, Zahra saw, were dotted with eczema patches – before rubbing the residue into her own hands and then putting her gloves back on.

'Sister,' the lady called out from behind her niqab, 'sister, come here.'

Zahra walked away, having little interest in being questioned by a bunch of fanatics.

Sometimes at night, after finishing her detective book, Zahra would lie face-down on the bed, her face pressed into her pillow. She wanted to be asleep, or at least plausibly so, before Asghar got home. (These days he was spending more time with his new friends.) Six months into the marriage and they had given up trying to have sex. As the cold weather swept in, their bedroom became difficult to heat so she went to bed wrapped in cosy pyjamas and thick socks. They grew comfortable with chaste cuddling and kissing on the forehead and shoulders but Asghar never pushed things any further. Zahra dropped hints – wearing make-up to bed, laying her legs over his – but he still did not respond. Sometimes, while he slept, she rubbed herself against his body and felt him slowly harden. There was nothing wrong with the mechanics; she could arouse him – but only when he was unconscious.

They didn't even speak about sex any more; their conversations were dominated by practical decisions such as who did the washing up or who would do the vacuuming. They were more like housemates, who tolerated each other so long as they didn't have to spend too much time together.

It had been so different with Krish, at least at first. A few days after she had met him at the Lighthouse, she was taken by him to a noodle bar that had only recently opened; it was packed so they sat at a table outside under a glowing heater shaped like a Chinese hat. They talked easily about their respective courses and their friends and laughed at silly Cambridge traditions. When he paid the bill it was still early. He told her he wanted to see a new American teen comedy, but that his friends only went to the pretentious arts cinema. He gave Zahra such an endearing look that she agreed to go with him to the multiplex in the shopping centre. They munched salty popcorn and slurped cartons of coke; it was like being back in the suburbs.

That weekend Krish had invited her to formal hall. The dinner turned out to be much grander than the one at Zahra's college: there were English waitresses instead of Polish ones, and the food was of better quality. After dinner, he took her to the Junior Parlour, which resembled a gentlemen's club with red leather armchairs and a roaring fire. He bought her an orange soda and himself a ginger beer. He had not drunk wine at dinner, only water. She knew he drank, of course, because he had been swigging a beer in the club when they met, but she liked that he was making an effort to be respectful. When she suggested she should go back to college, he invited her up to his rooms.

'I want you to meet Adam,' he said. 'Quite a character – he's a philosopher.'

'I should get home.'

'I'll walk you back afterwards,' he said, giving her a keen grin. He led her through the moonlit courtyards and up a stone staircase towards his rooms. A guy in a red dressing gown, carrying an un-plunged cafetière, welcomed her warmly. He turned down the lively jazz music and offered them some coffee.

'I'm about to grind more beans,' he said.

'Why are you playing this again?' asked Krish.

'We've gone over this so many times,' sighed Adam, a touch camply. '*Hot Fives & Sevens* was the best thing he ever did.'

'You can't beat "What a Wonderful World..."'

Zahra sensed they were performing a discussion they had had many times on their own. She tried to follow the argument closely, remembering the names of artists and albums – the only jazz she had heard was in films. But she grew restless as the two boys continued to talk without making any attempt to draw her into the conversation.

'So,' she said, pushing herself into a brief lull, 'you guys don't listen to modern stuff?'

'Jazz ended in 1970 with *Bitches Brew*,' proclaimed Adam.

'Bitches what?' said Zahra.

'Like witches. You know.'

'I get it.'

'Why don't we listen?' said Adam, leaping up to change the record player in the corner.

'You'll never convince me, Adam, no matter how many times you play it,' said Krish. 'I don't like wild Miles.'

Zahra sat on the inflatable orange sofa and tasted Adam's sugarless coffee. When Krish sat down beside her, the sofa deflated, leaning their bodies against one another. She adjusted her weight so he wouldn't think she was too heavy. Her skin warmed where his arm and leg pressed against her. They sat in silence listening to the album. There were bits she could bob her head to but mainly it sounded all over the place; and it went on for ages. Eventually Adam stopped the record.

'Was that the whole thing?' she asked.

'No, just the first track.'

'Bit self-indulgent?' she questioned.

'You have to follow the improvisatory wave . . .'

'Zahra's got a point,' said Krish. 'It never lets you settle into a comfortable rhythm.'

'It's superbly disturbing,' said Adam.

'What's so great about being disturbed?' asked Zahra, puzzled.

'What she means, I think,' said Krish, interjecting, 'is that if you're going to make great music, then make it for everyone.'

'What I meant was,' said Zahra, 'what's wrong with music you can nod your head to while you sip your coffee. Or even dance . . .'

'It's only fair,' said Adam, his coffee mug dangerously sloshing, 'that as the guest you pick something from the collection.'

'What if I don't find anything I like?'

'I would be mortally offended.'

Zahra flicked through his records searching for something unimpeachable.

'Here's another genius . . .' She handed Adam a Jackson Five record. As soon as the music started all three of them began singing along crazily. They got through the whole album. Around midnight, Krish walked her back to her college and waited chivalrously by the gate until she had entered her building. To her relief and regret, he hadn't tried to kiss her goodnight.

Zahra and Krish began having lunch together at the buttery on the lecture site. It was a cheap place that served hot soup and rolls but was usually quiet by the time morning lectures were over. Gradually they began to speak more seriously about their lives back home. Krish told her about his first 'sort-of-girlfriend' – Cathy from his sixth-form college – who had 'broken his heart' years earlier. Zahra wondered what this Cathy girl was like, whether she was good looking, whether she was the one who had introduced him to jazz. He asked her if there was a boy back home she had fallen for. She confessed she had never dated anyone else – how exciting to use the word 'else'! – apart from silly crushes on teachers. This was the truth. At her all-girls school, she had rarely come into contact with boys. It was one of the reasons she had applied to far-away Cambridge rather than a London university, which would have entailed the restrictions of living at home. Krish in turn complained about growing up in an Indian family.

'They're so hypocritical,' he said of the Hindu elders who urged charity at temple but only funded projects for fellow Hindus. Zahra said it was the same at her mosque. 'As if we weren't all equal!' he exclaimed.

'And the way they treat women as second-class citizens,' she said. 'They don't even let them vote in the mosque elections.'

After lunch, they were about to wander back to their respective libraries, when Zahra tugged Krish's plaid shirt. 'I thought I was the only person who felt this way about things,' she said softly. 'I'm glad I've got you to talk to.'

He drew her into a hug. 'I'm glad I've got you too,' he said. He bent forward to kiss her. She turned her face, allowing him only a peck on the cheek.

Looking back, Zahra never thought she was playing the

innocent. She liked to think all the physical stuff was a distraction – as though sexual feelings would debase the purity of their relationship. But she had seen enough romantic films and overheard enough at school to realise that a man might wait weeks or months but sooner or later he was going to try and take things further. She started to feel the hot pressure of desire urging her to lower her defences. Their fingers had brushed twice: once at the cinema and another time on a crisp sunny morning on Trinity Backs, but they never even held hands. The moral boundaries that had defined her from childhood had proved surprisingly durable: it was as though there were an involuntary force-field round her body repelling his approaches.

At the Marabar cafe, a new place serving Indian street food at extortionate prices, she tried to explain this to Andrea.

'He's fine with it,' she said. 'He sent me a wake-up text this morning,' she said, handing Andrea her phone: *I dreamt about you last night K x.*

'I know what he was dreaming about,' said Andrea.

'Don't say that,' said Zahra, pulling her phone from her friend's hand.

'Well, it wasn't walking you up the aisle.'

'We don't walk up the aisle, Andrea.'

'I never dream about Carl. I mean, properly at night, not daydream in lectures. I dream about my dad.'

'You said you don't remember him.'

'Mum still has photos from before he buggered off. But let's not talk about me: it's boring.'

Andrea often raised her own painful past only to deflect it straight away. It was as though she wanted Zahra to glimpse her deepest self, but no more.

'You're doing the right thing,' she continued. 'Keep pushing him away and he'll come back stronger. He's completely doo-lally.'

'I'm not trying to lead him on,' said Zahra in an injured tone. 'I just have strong views on such things.'

'Such things?'

Zahra lowered her voice: 'I think sex should be saved for marriage. It's not a Muslim thing. It's just better for society and better for the individual. Fewer broken homes, fewer unwanted children.'

'Oh, thanks.'

'I didn't mean you, I just meant in general.'

'I kept Carl waiting a year before I let him have me . . . properly. But he's only human so from time to time I did, you know, give him a helping hand.'

She made a crude gesture.

'Andrea, that's awful – what were you, fifteen!'

'It was like shaking a bottle of coke until the top burst.'

'I can't listen to this,' said Zahra, choking with laughter.

'It's quite cool actually, when it happens. You're the one in charge.' Andrea went on to describe various acts in the wise tone of the sexually experienced. 'Don't judge me, Zahra. Carl's the only man I've ever been with. I've never teased a guy.'

'I'm not teasing!' said Zahra. 'It's principles.'

'If you join the game, you have to play by the rules. Otherwise people get hurt.'

'Who says it's his rules and not my rules?'

'God, I thought church girls were bad with the "I'll kiss and cuddle but no stray hands" bullshit. You are seriously leading that boy on if you've been seeing him for what – how many weeks now? – and not let him touch you.'

166

'We have kissed,' she said brightly, 'just not on the lips.'

'Do you want to convert to Hinduism, marry this guy?'

'Hindus convert to Islam, not the other way round.'

'Would he want to?'

'He's not religious so he probably wouldn't care. What's the difference between a non-practising Hindu and a non-practising Muslim?'

'There's a big difference, actually.'

'Does Carl believe?'

'He likes the ritual, like me. Look – if you love him then make him happy. Unless,' she paused for a second, 'unless all this good-girl stuff is a cover.'

'What are you saying?'

'Maybe you're holding back because you don't see it going anywhere. But the only way you'll find out is if you try. Things change afterwards – believe me.'

Over the holidays, Zahra and Krish kept in touch via Facebook and text message: outside the house, on her way to work at the local library, she phoned him and they chatted about this and that and nothing at all. Sometimes they spoke late at night before going to sleep. It was strange being back at home, lying in her old bed, whispering to a boy. Her father suspected nothing. To him, she was the triumphant returning scholar who must be allowed to work in peace, uncompelled by housework. Her mother was more alert. During one of their whispered chats, Zahra froze in silence as a floorboard creaked gently under Mrs Amir's padded slippers. She assumed she was simply going to the bathroom. When it happened a second and a third time, though, she gave up calling him from inside the house.

A week before she was due to return to university, the family were having a takeaway dinner. When they were done, before Zahra could slip back to her revision, Mrs Amir asked her to clear the table and load the dishwasher. Dr Amir protested before Zahra could. 'She can't waste her time with dishes,' he said. 'She needs to rest before going back to work – not to be worn out with washing up.' Zahra looked gratefully at her father; he was the only one in the family who understood what academic success required. Her mother, a housewife since she got married, could not see why her daughter's studies should be privileged over her traditional duties.

'I don't know how her husband will cope with such a princess,' Mrs Amir grumbled.

'She's my princess,' said Dr Amir, rubbing his daughter's head. 'If our boys don't like that, she won't marry anyone: she'll stay here and look after Daddy.' Zahra wrapped her arms round her father's neck and kissed him three times on the cheek. 'You're the best dad in the world,' she said. As she escaped the kitchen, her mother crashed the dirty plates into the sink.

Back in her room, Zahra sat down at the desk her parents had bought for her when she was a child. It was too small now, really, and her massive folders and piles of books left little space to work comfortably. She retreated to her red armchair with a primer on *The Theory of Moral Sentiments*. 'Of the degrees of the different passions which are consistent with propriety . . .' she read.

Five minutes later she texted Krish, telling him her mother was being a total bore about the washing up. It felt good to vent. After a minute or so he hadn't replied. She checked her sent messages and, yes, it had gone through fine. She tried going back to work but kept the phone in her hand, occasionally waving it in the air, to better catch any new message flying

168

down from Manchester. When he didn't reply for ten minutes she started to get annoyed that he was ignoring her; another twenty minutes and she was in despair. Her mind veered towards the vile fantasy that he, Krish, had not replied because he was with another girl. Maybe his ex-girlfriend Cathy had dropped by; maybe she was, right at this moment, kissing him in his room, touching him, giving him all the physical pleasures she had denied him.

She resented the astonishing advantages English girls had over her. They could snare a man with sex and not worry about their parents finding out or the culture disapproving. At school, virgins were frozen out from the grown-up girls' conversations about how far they had gone with which guy, and how many times. For them sexual experience was the mark of adulthood, not ruinous shame. Sometimes she blamed her parents for moving to a country that had such astonishingly different sexual values – didn't they realise the problems they would cause their children? But it wasn't really their fault. How could they have known how things would change? When her parents arrived in the country all those years ago, English parents had in general frowned on permissive youngsters. But now those youngsters were parents, they could not deny their children the sexual freedom for which they had fought so hard – and which they continued to exploit in their affairs and second marriages. She wondered, though, whether they ever experienced a pang of atavistic nostalgia while making breakfast for their daughters' boyfriends.

Just then Krish texted back. He had been at temple running a children's sports club; slipping out for a break, he had looked at his phone and seen her message. He signed off with a postscript: *You're revising too hard. You need 2 have some fun.*

*I'm planning a special trip . . . xx.* Zahra was flooded with forgiveness. She felt slightly embarrassed by her judgmental thoughts about English girls. Who was she to be so self-righteous? She had done enough fantasising about boys to know how lonely it was to have no one care for you. Who said she couldn't have some fun? After all, Andrea had been with Carl since she was fourteen and the sky hadn't fallen in; she hadn't been struck by a thunderbolt. And Krish wasn't some random guy: they had been seeing each other for nearly three months. Perhaps her caution was becoming a kind of cruelty. And if she didn't give something of herself to Krish – meet him halfway at least – there was the risk he would abandon her for the ocean of sexual opportunity elsewhere.

She went back up a week before exam term started. Krish had also come up early and suggested they take that Friday off for the special trip he had mentioned in his text. He wanted to visit Grantchester, an idyllic village south of Cambridge that all the student couples visited.

'We can go to all the historic places: sit in the orchard, visit Byron's pool.'

'I'm not swimming in some filthy pool,' she said with mock-seriousness.

'It'll be beautiful, trust me.'

'Are we punting there?' she asked hopefully. She liked the thought of lying in a sunny boat as he acted the gondolier.

'It might be easier to drive. Punting's harder than it looks.'

'Okay then, driving.'

'We can take a picnic. Crisps and dips, bread and cheese and jams?'

'Yes,' said Zahra, smiling. 'Sounds perfect.'

On Friday morning, she dropped into the supermarket to

pick up the picnic food, and made her way to his college. Krish's black BMW was handsome but streaked with dirt. Zahra put the plastic shopping bags in a leaf-strewn boot and dusted off the crumb-filled seats, all with a relaxed good humour. She liked that she had the right to tick him off.

It was her job to navigate out of the city and towards the meadows. After some messing around with the one-way system they arrived fairly quickly. The weather was warm when the sun was out but cool when it slipped behind the clouds. They parked in a country lay-by and walked into the village, past some large houses with neat rose gardens. Wandering past the Old Vicarage and towards the river, Krish took Zahra's hand. They saw some backpackers and watched a troupe of proficient punters hurtle down the river. Soon they reached the place Krish had planned for the picnic: the poolside where the student Byron had stripped off and plunged into the water.

The pool was a touch murky and clotted with brambles and twigs. It didn't seem like anyone had swum there recently. Zahra laid out a red-checked picnic cloth and started unwrapping the plastic plates and cutlery, while Krish unpacked the food. They sliced the posh bread and dug into the dips; soon the picnic rug was pleasantly messy with their leftovers. They lay side by side on the dewy grass, leaving the open jam pots and soft cheeses for the wasps. By now the morning clouds had dissipated and the sky had cleared to a brilliant blue; the sun heated their bodies. Krish moved his hands towards her skirt and caressed the material between his fingers. She allowed his warm hands to rest on her body. He turned on his side to face her and she did the same. They were only a few inches away from each other. A rush of dangerous pleasure passed through Zahra's body; she knew this was what he had planned from the moment he proposed this trip. She had decided not to think about it too much and, as Andrea had advised, let her feelings guide her judgment. Krish tipped his head forward and kissed Zahra. She pulled back slightly; but he pressed on. They kissed again, this time with more urgency – lips moist, tongues touching. Krish pulled her towards him; when their chests touched Zahra put her own arms around him, pulling them closer together. He dotted little kisses on her forehead and then her cheeks. He caressed her long hair before pulling it aside and kissing her neck. Zahra had imagined what it might be like to be kissed on the lips, but no one had told her that being kissed on the neck could be so powerfully erotic. Every touch made her head swim. When he moved down from her neck to kiss her breasts, she resisted him. The grass underneath her prickled uncomfortably. She drew his head back towards her lips, where in recompense she kissed him more passionately.

When they stopped kissing they caressed each other with words, talking about when they first met.

'I thought you were really beautiful, but that you were out of my league,' said Krish.

'Oh, darling,' said Zahra, 'I was so upset when you disappeared. I thought I wouldn't see you again.' They cuddled closely and warmed each other up as the clouds returned. Zahra fell asleep in his embrace. When she woke up the sun had dipped beneath the trees and it was getting chilly. Reluctantly untwining herself from him, she stood up, stretched her constricted limbs and smoothed down her skirt. After packing the rubbish in the carrier bags, they walked back towards the car and dumped everything in the boot. On the way back, Zahra touched the back of Krish's head affectionately, and at the traffic lights he rubbed her thigh lightly before changing gear. By the time they arrived back at college it was nearly dark. He found his spot in the car park at the edge of the dark courtyard, lit by the windows of the hard-working dons. Before they knew it they were kissing again.

Soon he was running those hands up and down her black tights. He went further and further upwards with each stroke. Zahra concentrated on the kissing and ignored his hands, now not so much wandering as marching up her leg. As his warm fingers moved closer to her knickers her body convulsed. The word 'stop' rose in her throat but she could not utter it. She was being reckless, she knew that, but it felt so right she could not imagine how it could be wrong; besides, she had come so far that a few inches more would not make any difference. His hand was now firmly between her legs, gently rubbing her knickers, pushing into her pulsing softness. Heat flared throughout her body, she closed her eyes and held him tightly; heavy breathing became moaning and then a sudden yelp, and a shuddering.

Krish rolled down the window, letting in some cool air. 'How was that?' he asked.

'I don't know what happened,' said Zahra, covering her face with her hands.

'You seemed to enjoy it,' he said, sounding a little too proud of himself.

'I don't know . . . I don't know if I really . . . ?'

'Baby, it's nothing to be ashamed of.'

She peeped at him between her fingers.

'You don't have to reply, if you don't want to,' he said, 'but I'm in love with you.'

He gave her a quick hug. Zahra felt strange. He had said

he loved her. That gave everything that had just happened a respectable – even spiritual – dimension, didn't it? They had not jumped into bed at the first opportunity; they had waited months to be sure before even kissing; and if things had gone further than she had expected, then at least she could say that her first sexual experience was with a man she loved – and who loved her. Not that she had given him everything: she had not, after all, removed a stitch of clothing. And nothing truly scandalous could happen with your clothes on – could it?

He walked her back to college and, after kissing her good-night, told her he would come round the next evening. As soon as she shut the door she waited until his steps had faded from the corridor, and then she rushed into the shower. A wave of tight emotion made her throat itch. She felt a bit like she had done the first time she had stayed away from home, in a dormitory on the edge of Epping Forest. The foxes had kept her up all night with their screaming.

She stayed in the shower until the hot water ran out. Holding back had given her power; now she felt powerless, and it was frightening.

After a restless night, she woke early and dressed in her anonymous revision clothes: black jeans and a long baggy grey sweatshirt. Andrea had texted to ask how things had gone. Zahra knew her friend would wheedle the whole story out of her in five minutes. She could imagine what Andrea would say – the sordid details she would triumphantly pounce on. She ignored her.

Tucked away on the empty fourth floor of the university library, she felt protected from the outside world. For an hour she managed to read a popular critique of Adam Smith she was planning to crib for an essay. Rereading her notes, she found all she had written down were fierce slogans about exploitation and laissez-faire economics. She kept telling herself that nothing bad had happened. But then why, when she thought about it, did she feel a gripping tension in her stomach? Why did she feel so homesick? She knew she had behaved pretty respectably in comparison with most other girls. To those girls, she thought hopefully, I'm still the prude they always thought I was.

Zahra's parents had never explicitly warned her about boys. More powerful than an explicit argument – arguments can, after all, be countered – was the blanket atmosphere at home, at madressa and at the old mosque that implied she would remain pure until she made a respectable marriage. That atmosphere had diffused into her soul and become an essential part of her being. As long as she could tell herself that she and Krish were simply good friends, she could hold everything in balance. Now that she had done, well, *something* with him, she could not hold it all together. She felt ashamed of how much she had enjoyed him touching her; and then felt angry at herself for being so ashamed.

Her parents had drawn those lines but she had been free to reject them. So why the struggle? The sexual chaos she had seen at school made her see the value of uprightness. Intimidating sexual displays – year-eight girls showing off their chests with push-up bras; sixth-formers boasting about what they got up to with unknown men in pubs – had affected her more deeply than any sermon at the mosque. Such girls were said to have low self-esteem or affection issues; but the pale secular language of victimhood did not accord with the reality of girls gunning to lose their virginity, or coolly

175

comparing how many men they had slept with. In her own eyes, Zahra had become one of those girls. She had violated an essential part of her being. And boys? Give them an inch and they'll take a mile. She slammed her notebook shut.

How could she have allowed him to push her so far? She could not reconstruct what had happened in the car with much accuracy; but thinking back, was there a moment when he had actually asked, and she had actually said yes to him? Her phone vibrated. It was Krish texting. *Can't wait to see you later xxx* ☺. That smiling, triumphant face sickened her. She felt like vomiting. But not all was lost. She could stop things now; she could take control of her destiny. She texted back quickly before she could change her mind: *I'm in the UL. Would be good to meet for lunch in usual place. We should talk.*

# Chapter Eleven

Every other Sunday, Zahra and Asghar visited their families in the suburbs. The Dhalani residence was closer and they usually stopped there first. Zahra would disappear into the kitchen with her mother-in-law, while Asghar and his dad watched football or cricket on television. Father and son rarely spoke to one another, apart from occasionally yelping when someone scored or a wicket went down. Zahra prepared food and tea with Mrs Dhalani. Their interaction followed the same routine: her mother-in-law would always enquire if the fresh roundness in Zahra's face signalled the early stages of pregnancy – a question to which Zahra responded by self-consciously pinching her neck and vowing to give up chocolate croissants. Mrs Dhalani would drop them at the Amir family home. Zahra always invited her inside for a cup of tea but Mrs Dhalani insisted she had to rush away to do something important – set up an event at the mosque or visit an elderly lady who had just moved into the community's sheltered housing. Zahra was sad their families did not get on better; but she admired the tact with which Mrs Dhalani avoided meeting Mrs Amir.

Zahra returned home like a visiting celebrity, with cousins popping round to see her. She rushed upstairs with her mother to go through old dresses, leaving Asghar in the living room with Dr Amir. He greeted his son-in-law with a friendly series of shoulder punches before interrogating him on his career plans. Later, Zahra and Asghar would catch the Tube laden with frozen curries and Indian sweets. No matter how much they protested that they couldn't carry all this stuff, and didn't have enough space in their freezer, Mrs Amir never listened. It was her way of exercising loving control.

This routine was disturbed one weekend in the new year when Zahra went to see her parents without Asghar because he was hanging out with his new mates. She was surprised he had made new friends so fast – he was usually so awkward with people he didn't know. When she asked who these friends were, he was suspiciously evasive.

'Just some guys, you know, guys.'

'You sure these "guys" aren't some girl you've met?'

'Absolutely not,' he said. 'I'll swear on the Quran.'

'Don't worry,' she said with a low laugh, 'you really aren't the type.'

Zahra took the train home on her own. From the station she walked up the hill she had tackled for so many years as a teenager. She knew every bush, plant and flowerbed on the route – if not their proper names, then certainly their look and smell. Their next-door neighbour had beautifully tended pink flowers that Zahra had secretly plucked, dried and pressed into her diary. She had found that diary at the bottom of her clothes cupboard the last time she had been home. It was filled with

178

embarrassingly romantic thoughts about imaginary men and disturbingly hateful rants about her mother. Unwilling to take it to Kilburn in case Asghar stumbled across it, but also reluctant to throw it away, she had hidden it back in the cupboard.

She pressed the doorbell but no one answered. Her father's car wasn't in the driveway; he must be at the mosque, she thought, but where was her mother? She rang again but still no answer. Rummaging in her handbag, she found her house keys, still linked up with the old key ring she bought when she was fourteen; the plastic was so scratched you could barely see the Playboy bunny's ears. She let herself inside, where she found her mother in the living room watching television with the volume turned up loud.

'Hi, Mum,' said Zahra, but her mother didn't turn round. 'Hello, Mum!' she repeated, in a brasher tone.

'What? What's happened?' panicked Mrs Amir, as Zahra walked between her and the television.

'Nothing's happened. I told you I was coming.'

'Why didn't you ring the doorbell?' she said, scrambling for the remote control and pausing the programme.

'I did, Mum, I did. You had the television on really loud.'

'No, I didn't,' she said.

'You must be going deaf,' said Zahra, following this up with a reassuring kiss on the head. She breathed her mother's jasmine scent.

'Is that a new perfume?'

'It is,' she said grumpily. 'I suppose you want to take it.'

'I didn't say I wanted to take it. God, Mum, you're so on edge today. I just wanted to know the brand.'

This was how they talked these days: gentle bickering always on the verge of dangerous escalation.

'Have you eaten?' her mother asked.

'Just a cereal bar. I'm trying to keep my weight down,' Zahra said, sitting on the opposite sofa.

'Wait until you have kids: you'll find it impossible.' Her mother shifted her body self-consciously.

'What are you watching?' asked Zahra.

'It's just started,' she said. 'This famous chef is travelling to Iran. Watch it with me. You remember Iran, don't you?'

'I remember wearing your scratchy black scarf.'

'It's a Muslim country,' said Mrs Amir.

'I was ten years old!'

'That's the right age.'

'Let's just watch,' she said, trying to smooth things over.

An English chef, wearing a cream suit and hat, stood on a traffic-choked street in Tehran and declared that he wanted to explore the rich culinary history of Persia. The scene was intercut with images of Iranian women in bright chadors and puffed-up hair visible beneath their hijabs. Zahra watched as the chef waved at a street vendor selling kebabs, before he listened attentively to another chef making vermicelli soup. Leaving Tehran, he travelled to Mashhad, where the scene was introduced with images of tall men in flowing black robes walking along dusty roads. Mrs Amir reminded her daughter that they had visited the city when she was a child.

'Look!' exclaimed Mrs Amir, as the camera panned to the Imam Reza mosque with its golden dome and brilliantly patterned tiling. 'We were there, do you remember?' The scene shifted to the mosque's kitchens, where the chef sampled the food served to pilgrims. He made sweet rice with the bottom crisply done.

'That rice and curry was so delicious – and blessed by the Imam as well,' said Mrs Amir.

'All those poor people chased us around the courtyard,' said Zahra. 'I was scared they would steal my money, so I just gave it away.'

'You were always too kind-hearted,' said her mother ruefully.

In the second half of the show, the chef returned to London and interviewed the owner of an Iranian restaurant behind Edgware Road. Farhad told the presenter he had left Iran in 1980, just after the revolution. His mother, the only member of his family to come with him, had begun by cooking for other exiles. A poetry-lover by nature, Farhad was forced to run a restaurant. He couldn't have done it without his wife, Norma, he told the presenter, who had been taught to cook Persian cuisine by his mother, and his daughter, who worked as a waitress for him at weekends. Mother and daughter were filmed working in the kitchen and serving at table: Norma, an excitable Yorkshire woman wearing bright oriental prints, said she fell in love with Farhad because he, like her, was a foreigner in London.

'They're Shah's people,' said Mrs Amir suspiciously. This was her catch-all term for not-obviously-religious Iranians living in London, her logic being that if you had the perfect Islamic state to live in, why would you want to move away? 'Why don't they talk about how bad the Shah was?' she added.

'That man opposed the Shah,' said Zahra. 'He was attacked by Khomeini.'

'Imam Khomeini,' Mrs Amir corrected her.

'What about all those prison massacres? Wasn't he responsible?'

'If anything bad happened, I'm sure the Imam knew nothing about it.'

'Right, he was only the Supreme Leader, not important at all.'

'Why do you believe everything the media tells you? The West just wants Iran's oil. Like they had in the Shah's time.'

'That's so simplistic, Mum. Farhad is just like us – an immigrant who wants to make a better life.'

'I am *not* like him,' said her mother. 'I'm not an immigrant. I'm British through and through – born under British rule, with a British passport.' Zahra could not press the point; her essential Britishness was one of her mother's perennial fantasies, an unassailable part of her identity. The programme interviewed one of the Shah's old guard, who reminisced about Iran in the sixties and seventies. A snapshot of Tehran's upper classes wearing swimsuits by the pool was contrasted with a modern sea of veiled women.

'Look at those people,' Mrs Amir tutted. 'They had swimming pools, while the poor didn't even have water to drink.'

'Looked a bit more fun in those days . . .' Zahra muttered.

'What?'

'You have to admit bad stuff happens in Iran.'

'You don't know anything . . .' She went on to lecture Zahra about how Imam Khomeini was the most important figure in her Islamic development: she had started wearing hijab after Maulana Haider repeated the ayatollah's exhortations from the pulpit. Unlike the decadent Shah, she said, the Imam had lived modestly. When he found his house was being painted, he ordered the work to stop half-finished. He didn't want to live in luxury. 'You don't remember this, but the taxi driver in Tehran showed it to us – still half-painted! Why doesn't the programme say this?'

'You've been watching too much Press TV,' said Zahra.

'Like the BBC is so unbiased?' In this mood Mrs Amir couldn't be budged. In her mind Imam Khomeini – he was always Imam to her, like Imam Ali or Imam Hussein or Imam Reza – was an embodiment of holiness, not a flawed politician, let alone a tyrant.

'Where's Asghar then?' she asked, turning down the volume.

'He's gone out with his friends.'

'Muslim friends or English friends?' she asked.

'English friends, I think.'

'It's always good to have Muslim friends.' Her mother seemed unusually stuck on religion today.

'Like I said, I don't know. I don't check up on everything he does.'

'He could have phoned to say he wasn't coming. I'm like his mother.'

'He doesn't call his own mother, either,' said Zahra.

They watched the news together in silence. The football highlights came on – men running, screaming, spitting, seemingly at random. Zahra turned abruptly to her mother.

'Mummy, can I talk to you about something?' Her mother caught something in her tone and looked round worried. 'I don't know what to do. Asghar, he's just – he's not the person I expected to marry.'

'What are you saying – that you're unhappy?'

'I'm not, I don't know, I'm not the happiest I've been.'

'You walk into the house together like strangers. You don't speak to each other. With your father we laughed together so much. At least in the early days.'

'We did laugh, Mum, we did. When I first saw him for that coffee and at the art gallery, we had a really fun time.'

'You came home glowing . . .'

'It was my decision and no one else's. Not yours or Dad's or the community's or anyone's.'

'We raised you to be independent.'

'But he's changed. We don't laugh; we hardly speak. He doesn't pay attention to me, at night,' she said, her eyes imploring her mother to catch the implication. 'He lies in bed playing stupid games on his phone. If I try to say something we always end up arguing.'

'Did I tell you to marry him?' demanded Mrs Amir. 'Did I force you? I said you wouldn't respect him – and you rolled your eyes at me.' Zahra did not recall her mother saying any of those things. Clearly that's what she had been thinking, though. 'He's too young for you – he doesn't even have a job. A wife must feel she's being looked after.'

'It doesn't have to be like that,' said Zahra, her eyes glistening. 'Look at Andrea and Carl, she's the breadwinner and he's . . .'

'Andrea and Carl are not like you and Asghar. It's different for them.'

Zahra started crying. Mrs Amir softened immediately, and abruptly came over to hug her daughter.

'I'm sorry, Mummy,' said Zahra.

Mrs Amir murmured that everything would be okay in the end. 'Do you remember how me and your father used to always fight?' she asked.

Zahra nodded, wiping her tears on her mother's shoulder.

'You know your father lives in his own world: if it's not the mosque then it's the hospital, and if it's not the hospital then it's the mosque. Home is a place to relax between the two. He would sit in his armchair reading the paper, and I would ask what he was reading. He said he was reading about cricket. I said tell me about the cricket. He said I didn't know the players. He was right. But I didn't care about that – I just wanted him to talk to me. So I said things to get a reaction.'

'Like what?'

'I challenged him on everything: if he told me off for not cleaning the bathroom, I told him I had spent the day clearing the kitchen. If he wanted a maid, I said, then he should pay for one. That's what Islam says, I told him. That made him angry. The worst was when I told him not to waste his time at the old mosque because hardly anyone goes any more.'

Zahra's childhood memories were vividly punctuated by her parents' arguments. One time she remembered seeing her mother slumped on the kitchen floor, sobbing and with her hair dripping. Her father had thrown a glass of water over her in frustration and she was refusing to move until he apologised; he had called Zahra to talk some sense into her. She must have been twelve years old.

'You know when things got better? When I started leaving him alone. I stopped demanding attention, and so we lived comfortably,' she said.

'What are you saying?' her daughter said. 'That I should do like you did? Let him win the whole time?'

'Do you *ever* let him win?' Mrs Amir was interrupted by the growl of her husband's car in the drive. 'Your father's home,' she said, pulling on her slippers and relocating to the kitchen.

Dr Amir entered the house whistling a Motown song Zahra guessed had just been playing on the radio – his car was the one place he could indulge his musical tastes. He looked knackered: dark half-moon pouches had grown under his eyes, and silver stubble afflicted his neck and cheeks.

185

'Zahra,' he said in a playful tone, 'how is my stranger girl?'

'Don't call me that,' she said, giving her father a big hug. 'You never reply to my texts.'

'I can't read those tiny messages,' he said. 'I need to speak to my flesh-and-blood Zahra.' He caressed her cheek and patted her head. 'Where's Asghar?'

'He couldn't come.'

'What a shame,' he said, his voice noticeably brighter. 'The sun's out,' he said. 'Come into the garden.'

The pale winter sun hardly blunted the chilly wind that blew through the garden, rustling the bare apple trees. Zahra helped her father bring out the green garden furniture and laid it out on the brown stone patio. Dr Amir had only recently had the patio laid – he was sick of mowing the large lawn, and moved quickly when he had seen it recommended on some home improvement television show. Without checking with the rest of the family, he got the landscapers to tear up the old garden. Only Zahra's pleading had saved the apple trees.

'This mosque's giving me so much trouble,' said Dr Amir, fishing from his pocket a samosa wrapped in blue tissue paper. 'Leftovers from last night,' he said, breaking the triangular pastry in half, spilling the mince and offering it to his daughter. 'We've got fifty samosas left. Not enough people to take them.'

'Sorry I couldn't come last night,' said Zahra. 'I was so tired after work . . .'

'What can I expect? Now even your mother goes to the new mosque.'

'Mohsen will go when he's back from Edinburgh.'

'He's staying over the holidays to do extra work. He says it's too much trouble moving from his flat.'

Zahra looked at her father forlornly. As a teenager, she often helped him out at the mosque, sitting with him in his office and going through files and typing up his notes. She was the first audience for his latest scheme or plan; often she would end up curled asleep under a blanket in his armchair. She looked back fondly on those times.

On one of these nights at the old mosque, when the vote was held to decide on the move to Manor Grove, she had taken refuge from the arguments in the upstairs crèche. It was the first time she had met Asghar: he was nine and she was twelve. He was staring at her while she was combing out her tangled hair; and she had stood up and run after him. Once she had caught him, she carried him, gasping and giggling, back to the crèche. She knelt over him and stuck out her tongue. He smiled. She tickled his stomach and he laughed. She pursed her lips into a half-smile, as though unsure how to continue the fun. His hair had been combed into a neat side parting: she ruffled it up and moulded him two horns.

After her father had lost the vote and the mosque had been moved to Manor Grove, Dr Amir had stubbornly insisted that he would stay at the original site. But most of the congregation had obediently followed Mr Dhalani to Manor Grove. The new place was much bigger – and the journey from the congested bustle of the inner suburbs to the quasi-countryside suited the community's social aspirations: the move came when thriving businesses such as Dhalani Brothers allowed them to move to bigger houses in better areas.

Despite Dr Amir's entreaties, Maulana Haider moved to the new mosque as well. At Manor Grove, he stayed in the old cottage at the end of the gardens. Zahra had noticed the place on her wedding day. It was made of stone and had ivy creeping up the chimney, like something out of a fairy tale – apart from the children's toys littering the entrance and the enormous black cloaks drying on the washing line outside.

At first the traffic between the two mosques had been fluid; but gradually nearly everyone leaked away to the bigger premises. The new mosque innovated by handing out Friday prayer lunches in silver-foil takeaway packets. Soon every function – from seminars to funerals – was followed by a full meal of rice and curry; by comparison the old mosque's tea and biscuits seemed paltry.

By the time Zahra was at university, Dr Amir's plans for a multi-faith centre had stalled. The new mosque had already tapped up all the wealthiest community members. In theory, though, the new development was still in train and multiple dignitaries – an Iraqi ayatollah's son who could help with funding, a prospective MP feeling out local power bases – were shown round the broken sheds and weedy grounds and told about the site's impending transformation into badminton courts and a private cinema. Some came away impressed – at least according to Dr Amir. Zahra knew he could be very convincing. But no progress was made; the dignitaries began flocking to the new mosque, and the old remained as decrepit as it had always been.

'Maybe it was a mistake to let our mosque be called "old" and their mosque "new"', suggested Zahra.

'I started calling it the old mosque,' said Dr Amir, 'because our people like old things – old friends or old times or old traditions. For them new means strange, not authentic. But,' he added regretfully, 'Dhalani began saying we were old because our facilities were old-fashioned and our buildings rotting. They always get the biggest televisions, widescreen, high definition. But they don't even let women vote in the committee elections!'

'How's your building going?'

'Everywhere I look in that office, I see boxes – boxes of planning applications and boxes of fundraising schemes, all rejected. Your mother used to help me sort through them.'

'I'll talk to her,' promised Zahra.

'Do you know she sleeps in your old bedroom now? She says I snore and she can't get any rest . . .' He trailed off.

'Why don't we check out the apple trees?' she asked.

After Sunday madressa, in late autumn when the four trees finally bore ripe fruit, she and her father would collect the apples in black plastic bags and present them to Mrs Amir. She made apple crumble and apple juice and apple jams. There were far too many, though, and they had to dump all the sweet-smelling rotting apples in the bin.

'Every year you complained about the mess and said you would cut the trees down with a chainsaw,' said Zahra.

'I was only joking,' he protested. 'How could I cut down these wonderful specimens?'

'But you wanted to pave over them.'

'Never!' he insisted. He shook the tree closest to him, re-assuring her of its exemplary solidity. 'When we first came here this tree was the same size as you. And like you, it made a mess growing up. But I indulged you both.' He drifted to the tallest tree and pulled on the improvised swing hanging from its thickest branch. The swing was made from a single stretch of rope with a sanded plank of wood at the end; the rope had been hammered into the branch with a nail that had rusted reddish-brown, like the bark. He put his foot on the plank and turned to Zahra with a mischievous look.

189

'Give me a push up.'

'Dad, you're too heavy.'

'Nonsense,' he said, a foot wobbling on the plank.

'What if the neighbours see?' she asked.

'It's my garden and my tree. I swing where I want!' Zahra looked nervously at the apple tree's branch, which was bending ominously.

'Be careful up there,' she said as he hauled both feet on to the sanded plank.

He yodelled like Tarzan, knuckling his chest. She couldn't help smiling. He swayed for a bit and then looked at her.

'Help me down,' he said, slightly abashed. 'I'm dizzy.' She caught hold of her father's swaying legs; their bodies rocked together for a few moments, until he was perfectly still. He lowered himself on to the plank and jumped off. He dusted down his trousers fiercely, as though trying to wipe away his boyish exertion.

'Do you want to have a go?' he asked.

'I'm not dressed properly.'

'I forget you're not a little girl any more.'

'I am at heart, really.'

'There's something I need to tell you.' He stood upright. 'Since you got married your mother and I have been considering our future.'

'What? Like moving back to East Africa?' This was the long-mooted plan for their retirement.

'Not exactly. More like . . . a parting of the ways.' A chill passed through Zahra.

'What's happening? When?'

'We haven't loved each other for a long time.'

'So you're divorcing?'

'So many questions, Zahra, and I don't know the answers.'

She looked at her father's tired face. A pale thought dawned on her. 'About Asghar,' she said. 'Actually, things aren't that easy between us either.'

'Oh,' he said, looking worried. 'What's he done?'

'It's not what he's done exactly. I just didn't know him that well when I married him.'

'Your mother and I spent exactly six hours together before I sent a proposal on her.'

'It was about the same amount of time for us,' said Zahra with a hollow laugh. 'Two dates: one coffee, and one art gallery.'

'I've always supported you,' he said, 'even when that Dhalani is badmouthing me at the new mosque. Why blame the son for the father's sin? He's a shy boy, a simple boy – too simple, maybe.'

'I always liked that he was nothing like his father,' she said softly. 'He's not arrogant, or boastful . . .' She tried to enumerate his best qualities. 'He's honest, trustworthy, good-hearted.' She smiled. 'We'll make it work.'

'I'm glad,' said Dr Amir, kissing his daughter and walking back to the house. 'I'm happy that you're settled.' Zahra followed him over the grass and towards the patio doors. 'Be nice to Mum,' she said. 'Do something fun for her birthday – buy her a present, take her out for dinner.'

He shook his head sadly. 'No, you do something nice for Asghar.' She stopped on the steps and watched her father enter the house. When he closed the patio doors, a shimmery wave of light passed across the glass, banishing him to the dark interior.

The garden was full of memories. She remembered running away from a massive beetle processing slowly along the grass, then tripping and grazing her knee; she remembered the hours she spent trying to complete fifty hula-hoop circles, after which she collapsed on the grass, aching and sweating, with a deep sense of accomplishment. She looked up at her bedroom window. Her cuddly toys were huddled on the sill: Ali the lion and Pheel the elephant and Baa-Baa the sheep, a friendly menagerie waiting patiently for her return. As long as they were still there, this place felt like home and Kilburn merely the place she was staying temporarily – as though she were on a long holiday. But now her father wanted to break up her family. Had he found someone else? She shuddered at the thought.

# Chapter Twelve

After breaking up with Krish, Zahra had fallen into a funk for the rest of her time at Cambridge. She threw herself into work and got a decent 2:1 – about as much as she deserved, she thought. After graduation not even the excitement of her banking internship could break her morose mood. She went to the office early and mostly stayed late. One day, in late autumn after she got home at 10 p.m., she ignored her parents in the lounge and went straight to the kitchen, where she ladled dollops of curry from the covered saucepan on the cooker, took the plate to her room and ate slowly while blasting Elgar's Cello Concerto through her headphones. Growing up she had never listened much to classical music; but after watching a film about Jacqueline du Pré at the college cinema club, she had been gripped by this piece's exhilarating tragedy. Afterwards, to cheer herself up, she watched a couple of episodes of *Friends* on DVD, before rereading an old Harry Potter. The Polish films and South American novels she had bought from the charity shop in Cambridge lay untouched on her bedside table.

Still unable to sleep, she checked Facebook. At work she allowed herself to look at Krish's profile once – or maybe twice – a day, scanning his postings, photographs and friends' list for girls she didn't recognise. This wasn't healthy behaviour, she knew, but she didn't have the heart to exclude him fully from her world – not yet, at least. Clicking on his face – a cute picture of him in sunglasses she had taken on King's Parade – she hadn't found much to arouse suspicion so far. Until now, when she found she couldn't access his full profile. At first she assumed Facebook was playing up, so she logged out and then back in. Once again she was blocked: clearly she had been unfriended. What was he up to? Hadn't they agreed to remain friends after the break-up? There was only one explanation for Krish's sneakiness: he had a new girlfriend, and didn't want her to see their romantic photos and senti-mental messages. She felt like ringing him up and demanding answers; but that would give him the satisfaction of knowing he had upset her. She shut her laptop.

An hour later, still restless, she opened it again. In the time she had been offline, Krish had changed his profile picture to a sepia photograph of his shoes resting on a beach. This was the same pair he had worn all the time they had gone out; but now the brown leather looked creased and the crevices were dotted with grains of sand. Funny, he was usually so careful about keeping them spotlessly polished. She guessed this new girl, whoever the hell she was, was the type who went round taking arty photographs with a sepia filter. Wow, she thought, she must really have him under the thumb. He never even let Zahra persuade him to throw out that awful pink-striped shirt he wore to their lunches and to which, for some reason, he was sentimentally attached.

Just then a message alert popped up. She panicked. Could he know somehow that she was trying to access his profile? She hovered over the red dot: *Hi, salaams. It's Asghar, do you remember me?* the message read. She tried to place the name.

*Do we know each other?* she replied.

*Yes . . .* he typed back, *from the old mosque. Our dads worked together on the committee.* A vague memory stirred in her mind.

*Were you the boy who teased me in madressa?*

*No, no, I was the boy in the crèche. We messed around.*

Messed around? What was this guy talking about? She went on Asghar's profile – a silver hand engraved with Allah's name – and searched his pictures. There were a couple from when he was a boy – a faded image of him in a frilly shirt and purple bowtie, attending a wedding at the old mosque. Suddenly she remembered who he was.

*You're the kid I played with, we ran around the crèche?*

*Yes!* he responded. Then there was a pause. *What you up to these days?* he wrote eventually.

*Just done Cambridge. Economics. Pretty standard.*

*Wow! Cambridge, that's amazing!* he typed back quickly. *I'm doing business in London. It's really tiring. Things were easier when we were kids, right?*

His eagerness cheered her up. She typed back: *I'm just doing this bank thing. They're working us incredibly hard. Impressive people, though.*

He asked whether she had much free time at the weekends. Sometimes, she said. Would she like to have coffee, perhaps, near her house? Catch up on old times? She was intrigued but alarmed that someone from the community might see them and make assumptions. Weekends weren't good for her, she said, but a weekday in central London might work. They agreed to meet that Friday, at Verona, an Italian coffee shop near her office in the City.

Leaving the office that day, Zahra smoothed her black pencil skirt and walked briskly to Verona. Sally was off that day so she could be more relaxed about popping out for half an hour. She had said yes to Asghar because there was no reason to say no – and also because she was curious to see how the boy had turned out. She did worry slightly that he might be taking this coffee for more than it truly meant: according to community tradition, a boy and a girl could meet three or four times before the boy had to either break it off or send a proposal. Things were changing these days, though. Two madressa friends had dated quietly for six months before announcing their engagement. In any case, they wouldn't be meeting on the community's terms; they were simply two childhood acquaintances catching up on old times.

When she arrived he was already there sitting at a window seat reading the sugar packets carefully. He was wearing blue jeans and a brown jumper; to her pleasant surprise, he was perfectly clean-shaven.

'Zahra?' he called out.

'Asghar,' she said, striding towards him. 'How's it going?'

'Salaam aleikum!'

'Aleikum salaam,' she replied instinctively. She sat down opposite him.

'Do you want a coffee? Let me get you a coffee.'

'Cappuccino, with no sugar. Thanks.'

'*Cappuccino*,' he said, in an Italian accent. 'One *cappuccino* coming up.'

Asghar went to the counter and Zahra was left alone. She thought about getting out her phone and checking Facebook to see if Krish had re-friended her but she managed to resist. He came back with two delicious chocolate cappuccinos.

He asked what it was like studying at Cambridge. She took the chance to describe all the funny rituals, like wearing gowns at formal hall and saying Latin grace before dinner. By her third year at college she liked to argue that grace was too culturally exclusive. 'Why don't we do a bismillah before eating one day?' she asked her English friends at formal hall, enjoying their uncertainty over what a bismillah actually was. 'Don't worry, it's just like grace but in Arabic. Nothing to be scared of.'

But sitting here with Asghar she spoke of the ceremony fondly, even reverently, as an important part of the college's history. He seemed impressed. The only interesting thing about his university, he told her, was that it had the highest percentage of Muslims in the country – though they were mainly Sunnis from Bangladesh, which made Friday prayers difficult because he felt uncomfortable praying the Shia way with his hands by his sides instead of folded over his front. What he did now, he explained, was to curve his hands towards each other at the waist making sure his fingers didn't touch.

'So far I've got away with it,' he said, demonstrating his trick.

After an awkward pause, he asked about her commute from the suburbs into central London.

'It's not bad, actually,' said Zahra, 'as long as you have a book.'

197

'I love reading.'

'What's your favourite book then?'

'I've got this book on the Islamic conquests. It's amazing how far they reached.'

'Really?'

'Spain has just fallen and they're about to attack France.'

'I love Dorothy Sayers,' said Zahra. 'Do you know her?'

'Is she a jazz singer?'

They both sipped some coffee.

'Actually, I'm thinking of finding somewhere more central,' she said. 'Maybe move in with my friend Andrea.'

'Oh,' said Asghar. 'That would be very expensive, wouldn't it?'

'Once you've lived away from home, it's hard to go back. You need your freedom.'

The word freedom hung in the air, its meanings multiplying dangerously.

'What about you?' said Zahra. 'Don't you want to live with your mates?'

'Some guys I know at uni have a shared house. I went there once: the place is a complete tip – glasses on the dining table, bin bags lying around, and they never clean the toilet. Really rank.' He twitched his nose like a distressed rabbit. 'They invited me to share with them, but I said no. What's the point when I have a clean house and hot food back home?' Asghar took another sip of coffee and shyly poured in another packet of sugar. 'I was surprised when you agreed to meet,' he said.

'Why?'

'I don't know. I thought you'd be more aloof.'

'Is that my reputation? The girl who thinks she's above everyone else?'

198

'I've never heard anyone say that exactly. I thought because we haven't spoken for a long time—'

'What did your parents say – do they know you're here?'

'I don't tell them everything,' he said, with a mischievous look that made Zahra smile as well.

'My parents don't know I'm here either. That makes us both rebels.'

'I wasn't sure you'd remember me from the old mosque,' he added, 'but I remember. I've thought a lot about you over the years. Wondered what you were doing. Then you popped up on Facebook the other day – it was one of those, "You may know one of these people" things – and I thought I'd message you.' He stopped his tumbling confession and looked guiltily at her. 'My mum calls you the Cambridge girl.'

'It's funny because three other girls from the mosque also went to Cambridge. No one talks about them like that?'

'They're different,' he said. 'They came home every Ramzan, went to mosque during the holidays. Two were already engaged before they started university. They call you the Cambridge girl because you acted like a Cambridge girl.'

'Is that supposed to be flattering?'

'What?'

'Is it a positive thing to say?'

'I don't know. They just said it. But I always liked it – liked the idea of you.'

'Well,' she said, feeling flattered. 'I'm glad my reputation precedes me.'

'How's your cappuccino?' he asked. 'Do you want another one?'

'I probably have to get back to work,' she said.

'Of course, of course, that's fine.' He half stood up, as though expecting her to rush off immediately.

'But if you wanted we could meet again, whenever,' she said lightly.

When Zahra got home, she found Asghar had messaged her already saying how much he had enjoyed catching up. Could he see her again soon? She liked how openly keen he was; he probably didn't have much experience with girls. That was no bad thing: at least, unlike Krish, he wouldn't go on about his old girlfriend. And he was a sweet kid. She hadn't felt the spark of attraction she had with Krish at the club. But during their forty-five-minute coffee she had the feeling of being safe – of comfortable, rooted homeliness – which she had never really had with Krish. She felt like Asghar was welcoming her back to the community, but on different terms from those on which she had left. It was like the time she had visited her relations back in Nairobi. Her cousins asked so many questions about life in London, about the glamour and the wealth of the city, questions they could ask her because she was one of them, and yet not one of them.

She messaged Asghar asking whether he fancied the late opening at the National Gallery, and was pleased when he seemed so enthusiastic. Most community boys were proudly uncultured; the closest they came to artistic appreciation was cooing over the graphics in their computer games. If she and Asghar were to become friends, she needed to know whether her finely thought-through opinions could mean something to him.

She had planned to arrive ten minutes after the agreed time, but because of work she ended up twenty minutes late. The weather had turned and the grey sky matched the pallor of

Trafalgar Square's stone. Rushing to the entrance she found Asghar wasn't there. 'He must have gone to the bloody British Museum,' she thought. She considered texting him but what if he had gone home already – or even stood her up? She scanned the square fruitlessly before entering the portico. The lady at the counter suggested she try the side entrance. She walked round the building to the glass-fronted lobby where she found Asghar sitting passively on a bench. When he saw her, he jumped up and smiled broadly.

'I was waiting for you at the main entrance,' she said.

'Oh no, so sorry,' said Asghar. His mortification made Zahra feel guilty.

'Don't worry. I got lost when I came here the first time.'


Shuttling through the medieval galleries, they barely stopped to glance at the paintings: the cartoonish figures and bloody crucifixions were incomprehensibly alien. Arriving at the Renaissance, she slowed down and began praising the humanity of the portraits.

'Is there any Islamic art?' asked Asghar.

'I don't think so. Just Western.'

'I like those Turkish tiles. Nice patterns.'

'There are some in the British Museum,' she replied airily. It crossed her mind that he might disapprove of paintings of people. 'We have a long tradition of portraiture in Islam, too,' she added. 'There are some beautiful Persian miniatures – not here, but I've seen them on the internet.'

'In Iran, we saw these amazing pictures of Imam Hussein,' said Asghar. 'Really detailed: almost like photos. We brought one home, and I copied it for my GCSE Art.'

She led him to the non-figurative safety of Van Gogh's *Sunflowers*. The couple in front of them – an Asian man in a light blue jumper, and his English girlfriend in a green and white dress – quietly stared at the painting and then moved away. Imitating their respectful pose, Asghar and Zahra contemplated it silently.

'It's absolutely stunning, isn't it?' said Zahra, after a couple of minutes. 'The way the flowers seem to shiver with nervous energy.'

'It's pretty nice,' he replied, relieved that he could now talk. 'You can really tell they're sunflowers.'

'I don't think it's meant to be realistic, as such. Look closer.' She pointed to the encrusted swirls of paint that formed the petals. 'It's like a 3-D painting.'

'Wow,' said Asghar. 'Impressive.'

'That's what doesn't come out in reproductions,' she said. 'It's called *impasto* – Van Gogh basically invented the technique, though you can see it in Rembrandt as well.'

She had scanned the gallery's website on the way over.

'You know a lot about art,' he said.

'I've read a little. But the most important thing is what the artist says to you, personally.'

'I'm glad you're here,' he said sincerely, 'otherwise, I wouldn't know where to look.'

They wandered round the gallery for a bit and then went into the square.

'I love it here,' said Asghar, breaking into a trot. 'Let's see the lions.'

He started to climb one of the black lion statues but kept slipping down: a firm push from Zahra got him up and over. He sat upright with his arms aloft. She couldn't help laughing.

202

'Come up here,' he said. He took her hand, but in trying to pull her up almost fell down himself. Eventually she was securely aboard.

'Did you ever do this when you were a kid?' he asked.

'Never!'

'We came here last Ramzan for a Palestine demo. But we were so late all the main speakers had already come and gone. When it was over we messed around here. Mum and me climbed this lion. My sister was too scared so she stayed down with Dad.'

'You and your mum?' asked Zahra. The thought of Mrs Dhalani scrambling up the statue might, until recently, have made her cringe with embarrassment; but now, sitting comfortably with Asghar, she felt proud that a middle-aged hijabi could so cheekily sit astride the symbol of the British Empire.

'She loved lions back in East Africa,' said Asghar. 'She took us to London Zoo to see them.' From the corner of her eye, Zahra saw two policemen emerging from Charing Cross. She tapped Asghar's side and pointed. 'Let's go!' she cried, and they began scrambling down. Asghar went first and then beckoned Zahra. She tried to descend in stages but it was safer to leap. His outstretched arms cushioned her fall. He took her hand and they ran out of the square away from the policemen, laughing at their own silliness.

'Why don't we get something to eat?' he asked, still holding her hand.

'I'd like that,' she said.

They found a pizza place nearby and sat down. The waiter, a disconcertingly handsome Frenchman, asked whether they wanted to see a wine list. Asghar said they didn't drink alcohol. The waiter removed their wine glasses briskly.

'I always think,' said Zahra, 'that when they take away the wine glasses it's like they're punishing you for not drinking. It's like they're saying: you're only having soft drinks so you can't have nice posh glasses – only ones they give to children.'

'It's money,' said Asghar. 'These guys want tips for pouring the wine.'

'Why do English people want to smell the wine before they taste it?'

'It makes them feel important, I guess,' said Asghar. 'But I don't know about wine – obviously.'

'Trust me: English people don't know anything about it either. I mean, at formal hall they bought the cheapest stuff from the off-licence and just necked it.'

The waiter returned and they ordered two vegetarian pizzas and two Diet Cokes. When the waiter came with her drink, Zahra found it was too sweet.

'I think this is regular coke, not diet,' she told Asghar.

'Waiter!' he called.

'Don't worry, I can have normal.'

'No: if it was wine he would have asked you to taste it beforehand. Waiter, please, this is the wrong drink.' He put the coke to his lips and swilled a little in his mouth before swallowing it. 'It's normal, when we asked for diet,' he said sternly. The Frenchman removed the offending drink and quickly brought its correct replacement.

'Thanks,' said Zahra, taking a sip.

'No problem: my mum always says, if you're paying, then you're the boss.'

'Your mum's a wise woman.'

'If the service isn't good, she always argues with the staff.'

'God, my dad does that as well. It's *so* embarrassing.'

'You shouldn't feel like that. They push it because they think we can't speak English or are too ignorant to say anything.'

'I don't like making a fuss. I suppose I'm quite English like that.'

'English people don't need to make a fuss because they get respect already. We have to stand up for our rights, whether it's about Palestine or—'

'—or getting the right kind of coke.'

'Exactly,' said Asghar with a smile.

The waiter brought round their large bubbling pizzas. He went through the rigmarole of offering to garnish the pizza with pepper and Parmesan. Asghar accepted the pepper but asked if the Parmesan was vegetarian. The waiter said no. Zahra, who loved heaps of Parmesan on her pizzas, had never thought to ask whether cheese could be halal or haraam. Out of respect for Asghar, though, she also only had the pepper.

As they sliced into the pizzas, Zahra admitted to herself that she was having fun; it was nice being out with a boy who just understood the way things were. She wondered what he thought of her – what he would think if he knew how much of a 'Cambridge girl' she had been. But that was no one's business but hers. Outside the sun declined and Asghar became a dark shadow against the falling dusk. The waiter came round to light a candle.

'That's better,' he said. 'I don't like not seeing your beautiful face.' Zahra felt the flickering warmth of the candle and blushed. 'But also because I don't want to be blabbing on without knowing if you like what I'm saying. Do you know what I mean?'

'I liked what you said just now,' she said.

'It's true: I've never seen a girl as beautiful as you.'

'And I've never met a boy like you.' He wiped his hands on his napkin and stretched them across the table. He turned them palm-up, as though in prayer.

'I really respect you,' he said. 'I know you must feel wrong about me talking so openly about . . .' He pointed to her and then himself. 'But I wouldn't be saying this unless I had honourable intentions.' He stuttered over his words. Zahra was frozen into silence. 'You and I suit each other. We are complementary.' Still she said nothing. 'We know each other from way back.' She didn't know what to say. 'I'm in love with you.'

'This seems a bit quick . . .' she stumbled.

'I promise I'll let you do your career, I'll share the housework, do everything like a proper modern husband. We don't even have to live with my parents. I'll do anything for you.'

Her silence had pressured him into pleading.

'There's no ring because I didn't want to put you on the spot. We can choose it together – but it will be a present from me.'

'Can I think about it?' Her cheeks were burning.

'Think about it?'

'Not long. I mean, I won't keep you waiting forever.'

'I'll do it properly if that's better. My mum can call your mum?'

'No!' she said. 'Let me speak to her. I should speak to my family.'

'I've been in love with you since I was ten years old,' he said.

'You're such a sweet boy,' said Zahra, taking his hands and giving them a short squeeze.

After leaving the restaurant, they took the underground until Baker Street where they parted for different branches of the Metropolitan line. Zahra knew she had to speak to her parents quickly before Asghar's family made things awkward with an official proposal. The boy adored her; he was kind; he would probably let her do exactly as she wished. Even as she enumerated these positives, she was wary of the ease with which they tripped off her tongue. If she told Andrea she was getting engaged to a mosque boy she hardly knew so soon after breaking up with Krish, she knew Andrea would cry 'rebound'. But another part of her – a stubborner part – wanted to escape the perpetual judgment of outsiders.

She found Mrs Amir waiting for her at the kitchen table.

'So, what time is this? Swanning off with I-don't-know-who?'

'Mummy, Asghar Dhalani asked me to marry him.'

'What?' she exclaimed loudly. Zahra told the brief story of how Asghar had got back in touch.

'Why didn't you tell me?' asked her mother. 'Meeting behind our backs is not the way to go about these things!'

'I was meeting him as a friend. I didn't know he was going to propose.'

'Ha!' Mrs Amir exclaimed. 'Don't you understand the way these Dhalanis work?'

'I don't think he's even discussed it with his parents.'

'No doubt they'll be rubbing their hands in ghee right now. To have you in this position.'

'What position?' Her mother didn't reply.

'What will Daddy think?' asked Zahra. 'I know he doesn't like them.'

Mrs Amir pressed her knuckles to her temples – something she did when trying to think carefully.

'He's a nice boy. No rumours?'

'He's innocent.'

'The mother will be a nightmare – always interfering. The father is a buffoon.'

'He said we don't have to live with them.'

'Does he have a job lined up? How will he support you?'

'He must have some money. His dad's business is doing well.'

'Oh yes, painting and decorating. They'll want to design the whole wedding.'

'We'll work it out,' she said. Her mother's antagonism had pushed Zahra into arguing for the marriage when she was still unsure what she thought. But as soon as she had told her mother about the proposal, the marriage was sealed. Mrs Amir's questions were purely rhetorical – a way of asserting that her consent would not come easily. In reality, she would accept any reasonably decent boy from the community; her daughter's reputation as a 'Cambridge girl' would likely put off most community boys, who were not as educated as she was. Mrs Amir's voice softened, and she put her palms on Zahra's face.

'Tell me: do you like him?'

'I think so.'

'Could you love him?'

'I could.'

'He's not too immature?'

'He's a bit younger.'

'That's not what I meant.'

'It's my decision, and if I want to marry him I will.'

'It's totally your decision.'

'Yes. My answer is yes.'

Tears welled in Mrs Amir's eyes: 'You have my blessing and, I pray, Allah's,' she said. Mother and daughter hugged.

'Thank you,' said Zahra, kissing her mother's head.

'You've come back,' she said, stroking her daughter's head. Zahra felt a deep calm. So many things could go wrong in life that she might as well go for it. And there was something gloriously romantic about marrying a boy she had never even kissed.

# Chapter Thirteen

A sghar had become skilled at concealing where he went on Tuesdays, having invented a story about some English boys he had made friends with at the careers convention. The personalities of these imaginary boys roughly corresponded with those of his real Muslim buddies: Sheikh Tariq and the two boys, Akbar and Sayyid. Tom, he told Zahra, was a mature student who knew lots about history and politics. He was the sort-of leader of the group. Alex and Samuel were closer to his own age. After meeting and chatting at Tom's house, they would play cricket in the backyard until the sun went down; then they fired up the Xbox. These tales had enough truth to seem convincing. After Tariq's lecture, he did play cricket with Akbar and Sayyid on the floodlit back patio; and Sayyid did once let him play on his PC. Sayyid liked a first-person shooter called *Special Force*. Made by Hezbollah's games division in Lebanon, you played an insurgent fighter trying to take out as many Israeli soldiers as possible. Asghar found the game too fast-moving and usually died within seconds.

On the Sunday that Zahra had visited her parents, Asghar went for a walk with his crew in the Buckinghamshire countryside. (*Chillin' in the Chilterns* as the WhatsApp group was called.) Tariq encouraged them to climb up a steep hill. At the top, overlooking a picturesque village, he led them in prayer, while fluorescent-clad walkers stomped past pretending not to notice them. At first, Asghar felt self-conscious about praying in the open; but Tariq told him he should be proud, not ashamed, to be Muslim. Of course he dared not pray in the Shia style with his new Sunni buddies and, though it felt strange to have his arms folded on his chest, he decided not to make too much of a fuss.

One of the team-building exercises Tariq had planned was for the group to wade together across a fast-flowing river: Tariq led, followed by Asghar and Akbar, the weakest two in the group, with the sturdy presence of Sayyid at the back. They all had to hold each other's hands, no matter how difficult it was to keep their balance. If one of them fell, said Tariq, then they would all fall; but if they stuck together each one would support the other. Asghar, who never got his bronze Duke of Edinburgh award because he could only cope with one day of the hike, was nervous about setting foot on the slippery rocks. He wobbled nervously after each step and once, right in the middle, just stopped completely – unable to see a path for himself through the rushing water. Tariq and the others were a model of patience, allowing him to stand as long as he wanted until, finally, he took a further step in the space between two rocks. He never let go of Tariq and Akbar, and they never let go of him. They celebrated on the other side by roasting some burgers Sayyid's mum had prepared for them.

When he got back late that afternoon, Zahra was still out at her parents' house. She always seemed to be out these days. And even when she was at home she rarely sat in the same room as him: she was either mooching in the bedroom reading a detective novel or wrapped up warmly in their garden on her phone. He had a long shower and heated some tinned tomato soup on the stove. Tearing into a crusty supermarket roll, he heard Zahra's key slotting in the front door lock. She bustled in smiling and kissed him on the cheek.

'Do you want a milkshake? I stopped at the corner shop to get the stuff.'

'What have I done to deserve all this?' asked Asghar.

'A wife can't do something nice for her husband?' she replied, squeezing his neck affectionately. Her fingers felt cool on his skin.

'Shall I help you cut the fruit?' he asked.

'No, no, you finish your soup. I'll do it.' He watched her peel and cut the bananas and strawberries, pour in the honey, milk and ice, and then slosh the mixture into the food processor. After a twenty-second blast she had a thick pink milkshake, which frothed pleasingly as she filled two large glasses.

'When you've finished, come into the living room. You can tell me all about your walk with the lads.'

'It's okay, I'll come now.' His appetite for the savoury soup had gone. He took his milkshake and joined Zahra on the sofa.

'How do you like it, my dear?' she asked.

'It's delicious,' he said, swallowing slightly too large a mouthful. They hadn't spoken like this in ages; it felt good. They sat in silence for a while, enjoying their drinks. She

212

stretched her legs on his lap. He began massaging her calves, working intensively on her legs, enjoying the pleasure she got from his touch.

'Thank you,' she whispered. She took his hand and started kissing it with small pecks. He caressed her face and brought her up to his eye-level. She looked at him with gentle openness. He kissed her instinctively, tasting the fruit on her tongue; her hands stroked his back, while his hands found her sides. His heart beat painfully. He kissed her more forcefully.

'Slow down, sweetheart,' she said softly, 'slow down.' She stood up and closed the blinds. Standing in front of the glowing edges of the window, Zahra became a dark silhouette. She kicked off her ballet pumps and walked barefoot towards him.

When it was over, they hugged with joyful relief. Every so often, he squeezed her shoulders or she scratched his back, enjoying their newfound intimacy. Eventually she disentangled herself and smiled naughtily, kissing him on the forehead.

'I love you,' he said, and Zahra, burrowing her head into his shoulder, carelessly heaving her body back on him, whispered that she loved him too. Desire returned in an unexpected rush. Second time round it was quicker, and for him slightly painful. But Zahra's flushed face looked more beautifully vulnerable than ever.

They lay talking about this and that, tracing the shape of each other's moles – Zahra had a pair circling her left breast – and kissing better those childhood scars that had never healed. When she was a baby hot mosque tea had spilled on her and a shade of burned skin remained on her leg; it now provoked in Asghar a fierce, protective love. She slept in his arms, her face calmer than he had ever seen it. He held her tight – but not too tight – and stayed awake while she rested.

213

No matter what they had gone through so far, he felt, things would probably work out.

Zahra stirred eventually, and slipped off for a shower. He began to tidy the living room, gathering their scattered clothes and stuffing them in the washing machine before unzipping the sofa covers and soaking them in the sink. Usually he found cleaning tedious, but there was a particular satisfaction in putting things back in order after so hedonistically messing them up. He began tackling the piles of post on the dining table that had lain untouched for weeks. Once he had extracted all the important-looking letters and put them in another pile, he gathered the leftover pizza adverts and leafed through them as he made his way upstairs. He could hear Zahra singing a Beyoncé song.

'Pizza?' he shouted through the door.

'What?' The water stopped and he repeated himself.

'There's that new place on the High Road. I got sent a voucher.' The sound of rushing water returned.

Back downstairs, as Asghar returned the pizza adverts to their drawer, his eye was caught by the black and green pamphlet Tariq had given him on his first visit to Umar's house – *Western Sexual Revolution: a New Slavery*. He must have tidied it away without realising. Listening for the shower's steady thrum, Asghar flicked through the pamphlet.

It began by denouncing the sexual freedoms that it said had taken root in the 1960s. When Muslims moved to Britain, it said, they had no idea that the country was about to abandon a thousand years of Christian morality in favour of a liberal-capitalist free for all. Unlike their pious ancestors, modern Westerners – especially Western women – preferred to wallow in their own desires. Sex was now as common as having a cup

214

of tea. Illustrating this argument was a blurred photograph of an Asian girl dancing at a nightclub. The story below was entitled: *A Muslim Girl's Disgrace.* Asghar's heart beat faster. This girl, he read, had been brought up in a believing but liberal family. When she stopped wearing hijab, aged fourteen, her parents had done nothing to stop her. This was where the rot started. Soon she was wandering to parties where alcohol and drugs were freely consumed. She was allowed to study away from home, far from the security of her family and her mosque. She had learned to treat sexual relations casually. Her parents should not have been surprised, the pamphlet continued, when she returned home one day and informed them she was pregnant. The father of the child had abandoned her, she explained, pleading for her father's support. She had allowed herself to be objectified and had been treated like an object in return – discarded like spoiled food, or a broken toy. Despite the pain their daughter had caused them, her parents took her back. But she died the next year of some unspecified cause. 'She broke our hearts,' the father was quoted as saying. But he had missed the point, retorted the pamphlet: '*She should not have been given the chance.*'

It was a pretty stupid story, Asghar thought. Of course it was sad, especially for the parents, but the way it was told seemed unfair. It implied all Muslim girls were out clubbing and drinking when the truth, he knew, was more ordinary. Okay, so they might not all be that religious or even wear hijab, but they had standards. Tariq should be careful about spreading alarmist writings; he would mention it at the next meeting. He was about to throw the booklet in the recycling when he saw it had Allah's name written in Arabic at the top. That meant he couldn't just chuck it away – wasn't there a special way to dispose of paper marked with holy writing? Dropping it in a river, perhaps, or burying it in the ground? Dad would know. For the time being, he left it on top of the pile of pizza leaflets.

As he carried on cleaning up, though, he kept thinking about that poor girl. Did it matter what she had done as long as she had changed? Forgiveness was important, but the past mattered. After all, what was someone apart from an accumulation of their experiences and actions? And even if you changed your ways or regretted what you had done, it would be impossible to return to the space you once occupied. You would always be comparing what was happening now to what had happened before; comparing your current partner with your previous one. And Zahra? He had long imagined her possible entanglements: a crush on an unobtainable figure – perhaps a teacher, as she had told him, or older boy – a love-note written but never sent. That would be forgivable. She had understood his chaste dalliance with Sarah. But what if, for her, things had gone further? What if a Cambridge boy had asked her out? What if she had gone to one of those fancy balls dressed in the pink dress that hung in its dry-cleaning wrapper in her cupboard? What if they had danced, and he had run his fingers down her naked back? What if they had kissed?

He told himself to stop these crazy thoughts.

Still, he wondered: assuming he had existed, had she gone as far with this boy as she had done with Asghar? Perhaps they weren't two troubled virgins taking each other's innocence; perhaps he was venturing where another man had already been? He washed his face from the sink's cold tap. The water dripped down his face and splashed on his shirt. It was important to keep calm. He needed to view the situation like an accountant looking at a set of bad books – calmly working out his wife's moral debt. First, he needed to know the facts. She would be too ashamed to tell him the details; he needed proper proof. Asking outright was impossible. Another way was necessary.

His eye caught Zahra's pulsing laptop on the kitchen work surface. Her password was the same one she always used: sunflowers123. He saw she had quite a few tabs open, including Facebook. Feeling a touch guilty, he clicked on her page. She had 568 friends. He ran through the list, ignoring the girls and searching for boys. There was Mohsen, her brother, whose profile picture showed him wearing sunglasses and a loud shirt at the top of Arthur's Seat. He'd gained weight since he'd last seen him. There were community boys as well: married cousins or husbands of cousins who from a quick trawl of their status updates – links to musical nasheeds praising the Prophet, pictures of their honeymoon in the Maldives – were familiar community types. He found three English boys from Cambridge; but her interactions with them were limited to posting birthday wishes. Asghar abruptly became aware that the sound of running water had stopped from upstairs. Zahra's footsteps pattered across the creaking floorboards between the bathroom and the bedroom. He knew her routine well. She would spend ages drying her body and applying cream; she would then switch on her purple hairdryer and blow-dry her hair. He felt a warm burst of affection for her. He had been silly to get carried away.

He couldn't help thinking about how she had written about him to her friends when they were first getting together – what excitements had she felt, how much had she liked him? It couldn't do any harm just to flick through her private messages and search for his own name. Before he knew it, he had clicked and scrolled further down. And there he found Krish's name – dozens of messages. He read through every one with an intense concentration he never thought he could muster.

Krish wasn't what he had imagined; he was a Hindu with a big nose and gelled hair, and on his page he listed his interests as DJing and Manchester City. Asghar was almost relieved that Zahra had gone for a guy who could almost have been from home turf; but also felt obscurely wounded that she had thrown herself at someone who wasn't all that different from him. Reading their messages from the start, he tried to recreate the progress of their relationship. Krish began by sending her a teasing message punctuated by stupid smiley faces and winks. Zahra replied less effusively, probably holding back to make him come after her more urgently; girls played this game. Soon she started signing her messages with cross-kisses – at first one, then a couple, then, as their intimacy deepened, a generous shower.

The messages were jokey, often sent late at night, as though they continued a conversation left off in real life. Krish cracked jokes about people they knew – including Andrea, whose dress sense he mocked. To this, Zahra had replied with an amused 'Ha!' Asghar had gone out of his way not to say anything bad about Andrea. Respecting Zahra, it seemed, was not the best way to earn her respect. There were many short, practical exchanges about where to meet for dinner or a film. His suspicions about the romantic comedy she had told him she had already watched were confirmed: there was a long message in which she took apart its bawdy sentimentality. No wonder her opinion was so definite: she had already rehearsed it with this other boy. She called him darling and sweetheart, just like

218

she did with him. Asghar knew now that he was a belated presence in her life. Their marriage was replaying in parody what she had already experienced – more deeply and truly – with another man. And if there had not been some emotion left to hide, wouldn't Zahra have told him all about it?

He scrolled to the end of the messages, hoping to see words of rejection or regret from Zahra. But the last message was from Krish, making plans for a daytrip to Grantchester – the rest was silence. Not so long afterwards he, Asghar, and Zahra had begun exchanging messages for the first time. He reread through them as well. He had been so excited to receive them. But now her words read very differently. Compared with the funny, open exchanges with Krish, what he had once taken as natural coyness seemed more like cold, burdened duty. She had been writing from the head, not the heart.

# Chapter Fourteen

Dressing in the bedroom, Zahra felt quietly delighted at how easily she had seduced her husband. True, it had been painful. They had been forced to stop half-way through – Asghar had been cool about that. But the second time had been much nicer. She thought of her parents' failing marriage. How often had her mother – still a reasonably attractive woman – coaxed her husband to bed? Was that the root of the problem? Men needed a bit of encouragement. She looked in the mirror and switched on the hairdryer. It would have been better if Asghar had made the first move. But how long could a girl wait? And how powerfully desired she felt as Asghar's wide eyes roamed over her body. Afterwards, she had felt a wave of tender, almost maternal, love. He looked like the satisfied boy in the childhood photographs he kept on his shelf – munching a pie on a Turkish beach. Walking downstairs, she wondered how long it would be before they could do it again.

She found Asghar on the sofa squeezing a cushion between his hands. The corners looked like they were about to burst.

'What you doing?' she asked.

'I know about him,' he said.

'What are you talking about?' she asked, though she knew.

'You should have told me.'

She saw her laptop open on the kitchen table.

'You searched my Facebook, didn't you? I *cannot* believe you did that . . .'

'You should've *told* me.'

She paused. When she finally spoke each word was tensely controlled. 'What happened before we met, is what happened before we met.'

'It wasn't before we met, actually.'

'I hardly remember that,' she lashed back.

'I'm not saying what you did was – we all make mistakes.' She had never heard Asghar speak this way before. 'I'm not judging you,' he continued. 'Personally, I didn't make that mistake. With girls, I mean. I've been honest about that. I told you everything.'

'So you admit digging round on my laptop?'

'What matters most is you didn't tell the truth.'

'I can't believe you broke into my laptop,' said Zahra, keen to concentrate on how she had been offended against. 'That's worse than anything I've done.'

'Don't turn this on me,' said Asghar. 'You've been caught.'

She pulled up a chair from the kitchen and sat down.

'Tell me something,' she said. 'And I'm genuinely curious about this.'

'Okay,' he said, sinking back into the sofa slightly.

'Before we got married, did you do anything you're ashamed of?'

'I told you, I never even met Sarah . . .'

'Forget girls. I'm talking generally. Did you tell a lie? Or gossip behind someone's back? Or refuse money to a homeless person?'

'Yeah, okay, I must have done those things,' he said. 'Everyone has.'

'And before we got engaged, did I ask you about that? Did I demand a list of every bad act or malicious word?'

'That would have been silly,' he said, 'but . . .'

'But you expect *me* to dredge up every last thing? Every fault, every flaw?'

'It's different.'

'Why? No, really, tell me why?'

'Going out with some guy and not telling me about it is different! Think about our children. How would they feel knowing their mother had behaved like that?'

'You don't tell children everything. You protect them.'

'So you were trying to protect me, like I'm a little boy?'

'Don't you think your dad had a girlfriend before he married your mum?'

'Why are you bringing my dad into this?'

'You know what they got up to when they first came over.'

'So what would you say if our daughter said she was dating some boy? What would you do? Just tell them to have fun and not get pregnant? Say sex is like drinking a cup of tea?'

'*Maybe* I'd be able to understand her better, rather than condemning her without a second thought. That's the problem with our people' – she was getting into her stride now – 'all they care about are rituals and taboos – not morality. Pray five times a day, fast in Ramzan, eat halal, go to mosque and you're done. Is that religion? Never being tested on what you're supposed to believe?'

'It's best to avoid temptation,' he said.

'How can you know something is right, until you feel the pain of what's wrong?' Zahra stood up and circled the room. 'You've never dated anyone?' she asked.

'No, I haven't.'

'Why not?'

'It's not something we do.'

'What about that girl, Sarah?'

'I *told* you nothing happened. I never even met her. I told you the whole story. But you didn't tell me yours. You *lied* to me!' he finished, triumphantly.

'I would have told you one day. When I was ready.'

Asghar clutched his head in his hands. 'Imagine Sarah had replied,' Zahra continued, desperately. 'And imagine she wanted to spend time with you? To have a laugh, to cuddle – what would you have done?'

'I don't know.'

'You must have wanted something to happen.'

'Maybe Allah saved me.'

'Well, He didn't save me.'

She pushed some stray hairs behind her ears and wiped the wetness from her eyes.

'The boy I was seeing, Krish, he was nice. We hung out as friends. For ages we didn't even hold hands, I swear. Then one day he pushed too far. I broke up with him. We haven't spoken since.' She looked at him with appealing eyes. 'Then you came along and I felt innocent again.'

223

'Really?' His head was still in his hands, but there was a quaver in his voice.

'I didn't tell you about him,' she said, 'because I was ashamed. I thought if I ignored it, you would never know. No harm done.'

'You were not ashamed for one bloody minute!' he burst out. 'You loved having your little secret – laughing behind my back.'

'Stop shouting!'

'I'm not shouting!'

'I thought we were sorting this out,' she said, her voice cracking.

'I know what you were thinking all the time,' he said, his voice hoarse with anguish. 'I know what you were saying to Andrea: Asghar's such a pathetic boy, he's never kissed anyone. He doesn't know his wife's already been with some Hindu . . .'

'Stop it, stop it, stop it!' she screamed, covering her ears, afraid he'd say something he could never take back.

'You don't know what I had to put up with. Rumours about what you got up to at university. "But Zahra's good," I said, "You don't know her," I said.'

She thrashed for something to throw back. 'You think you're a real man now, don't you? But it's taken you this long to sleep with your own wife.'

'And whose fault is *that*?'

She was crying and pulling her hair. Her eyes were puffy and her hands trembled. His words wounded her more deeply than she had thought possible. She turned and fled into the kitchen, where she rested her palms against the edge of the sink. After a minute, she opened both taps until the water rushed out in a steaming surge, and she began to wash her face. On top of the piles of letters she saw something she recognised from the trestle-table fanatics on the High Road. She picked the pamphlet up by the corner and flung it at Asghar, as though it were contaminated.

'What the hell is this?'

'Tariq gave it to me,' he said, 'so what?'

'When did Tariq give it to you?' she demanded. From his guilty face she realised what had happened. 'So Tom is actually Tariq,' she said, with a low laugh through the tears. 'You've been hanging round with those crazies from the stall. No wonder you've gone all fundo on me.'

'I'm sorry,' Asghar said tentatively, from the doorway. 'I didn't mean to lie to you.' His anger seemed spent. But she just sat down at the kitchen table and wept. Her mind was a mess. Her throat was sore. Still the tears kept coming – she, Zahra, who never cried even at children's films.

'Don't worry,' he said softly, 'I forgive you.'

'*You* forgive *me*?' She banged the table and went upstairs.

For the rest of the evening they prowled round each other. Asghar stayed downstairs while Zahra went to the bedroom and switched on the television. She tried watching a sitcom but the jollity of the audience laughter could not drown out her sorrow. Her mind reeled with confusion. She blamed Asghar for dragging into the light what should have stayed in the dark. So what if she had kept Krish a secret? She was the one who had broken things off when he went too far. She had been sent a test and she had – eventually – passed it. But another fugitive thought crept up on her. What if it wasn't principle she had acted on in rejecting Krish. What if it was a pathetic failure to grow up; the remnant of childish fears?

She began her nightly routine. After brushing her teeth, she pulled her hair up with an Alice band and moisturised her face, arms and legs before changing into her night bra. She had followed the same routine since she was fourteen. She tried to read some Dorothy Sayers but not even Lord Peter Wimsey could cheer her up. She switched off the light and listened for Asghar's footsteps. When he finally creaked open the door, she was still awake. She heard him change into his pyjamas and slip quietly into bed. She wondered whether he would lean over to kiss her, or even place an affectionate hand on her back. But he didn't.

Over the next few days, they spoke with the wary politeness of strangers. Asghar stayed late at the college library; Zahra spent more time at the office, where there was always more work to be done. When she got home and found Asghar still out she felt relieved. The sound of his key in the lock prompted her to leave the sitting room – where she was usually eating a bowl of pasta in front of the television – and go to the bedroom, where she carried on watching her programme until her eyes closed. Later, Asghar would creep in guiltily.

She was too embarrassed to confide in her mother, who was dealing with her own marital problems. She couldn't breathe a word to anyone from the community – not the cousins her age who might have gone through something similar – for fear of an exaggerated version of events getting back to her parents. And Zahra could not bear to hear Andrea's I-told-you-so speech.

The only person left was Mohsen. Until recently, she had regarded her younger brother as the kid who stole her lipstick and drew on the walls, or knocked on her door and ran away when she had friends round. But since he had gone to Edinburgh, he had grown into confident adulthood. He didn't seem plagued by doubts when it came to the opposite sex. He mentioned girls to his parents all the time and they teased him about his popularity. At the same time, he made sure to keep in touch with the old mosque. He organised career fairs and public-speaking competitions, recited the Quran during Ramzan.

She texted him, asking whether he was around for a chat. Straight away he rang back.

'Salaams, my dearest,' he said, in a lush voice that made Zahra smile. He had become quite the dandy at Edinburgh – all pink shirts and chunky cufflinks.

'Can you talk?' she asked. A confusion of voices and music drowned out his reply. 'What?' she repeated twice.

'Wait a tick,' he said, 'just going outside.' The noises faded. 'I'm all yours, sis.'

She told him everything in a swift babble – Krish, Asghar, the rushed engagement and honeymoon disaster, ending with the big argument and the present impasse. She didn't mention Tariq and his group, though. She knew that would worry Mohsen too much.

'Mo,' she said, 'I don't know what to do. I can't imagine staying, and I can't imagine leaving.'

'I always thought he was a bit of a dweeb – but you insisted it was a love match.'

'It was a love match. Well, it wasn't arranged.'

'But you didn't love him?'

'They say love comes after marriage,' she said, laughing weakly.

'Have you talked to Mum?'

'God no! I can't burden her with all this.'

'She wasn't that keen on him either.'

'I know, and so—'

227

'—she won't lose the chance to say that.'

'Exactly.'

'But silence isn't a long-term solution.'

'Do you think I should tell her?'

'She might be helpful. But I think you've already made up your mind.'

She heard Asghar coming in the front door. 'He's home,' she said. 'I don't know if I can talk much longer.'

'Call me back if you need to. It's hard, I know, but if it's not working then you have to make a decision.'

She was silent. A welter of female voices surrounded her brother.

'Got to go,' he said, 'but call me anytime, love you, bye.' A double beep signalled he was gone.

She felt terribly alone. On her top shelf was the Quran she had brought from home, looking equally unloved. She pulled it down and flicked through its thin delicate pages. Stopping at random she read some lines aloud in Arabic. There was no English translation so she didn't understand what she was reading. She wondered if she preferred it that way. The mere sound of the words was more of a balm than their literal meaning, which inevitably strayed into sermons on hellfire and damnation. She went downstairs and found Asghar staring at his laptop.

'Are you watching something?' she asked.

'I was going to look for a film,' he said.

'Can I join you?'

'Sure. Why don't we choose one?' He sounded more cheerful.

'Before then maybe we could talk?' Now he looked disappointed. She sat on the sofa opposite.

228

'We've been married how long now?' she asked.

'Our anniversary's coming up.'

'We both agree things have been . . . difficult?'

'If you say so,' he answered.

'That living together hasn't been as we'd hoped?'

'Tell me what you want to say.'

She breathed deeply. 'Maybe we rushed things.'

His eyes brimmed with tears.

'Maybe we didn't get to know each other properly before getting married,' she added.

'Are you saying we should divorce?' He sounded like an injured child.

'No, I'm not saying that – don't put words in my mouth.'

'That's what you're thinking.'

'Maybe we need a break from each other – to rethink.'

'We hardly see each other now.'

Zahra massaged a knot in her neck. 'I'm trying to keep calm and do what's best for us both,' she said, more forcefully. 'We can't carry on like nothing's wrong.'

'I'm sorry,' he said; a small tear was caught in his meshed eyelashes.

'You basically called me a slut.'

'I never said that word! I was upset. I would have forgiven . . . no, that's not what I mean. I would have understood. If you'd told me.'

'I should have told you, Asghar,' she said. 'I was wrong. But I've been thinking and the reason I didn't tell you was because I felt I couldn't trust your reaction. What does that say about our relationship?'

'You didn't even give me a chance. You just assumed I'd judge you.'

'Was I wrong? Now I find out you're messed up with Tariq and God knows what.'

'It's just a discussion group. We just talk and stuff. Don't make it into something bigger than it is.' He paused. 'This is so important you'd break up the marriage?'

'Why do you think people break up? It's because of stuff like this.'

Asghar leaned forward so he was on the edge of the sofa. 'I'm begging you,' he said. 'I'm begging you not to leave. I promise things will change. I don't care what happened ages ago; I was angry. I'm sorry, I'm sorry.' He looked in anguish at her. 'I've loved you since we first met at the old mosque – I know you're not that girl any more,' he added, 'but when we met the second time, I fell in love with you all over again.'

'I don't know if I can say the same,' she said slowly.

'I don't care,' he said. 'Just let me love you.' Zahra looked at his pleading eyes and put her hands on his cheeks. She lightly kissed his forehead.

'You deserve more.'

She left Asghar and went upstairs. From the landing, she saw him begin to rock back and forth, as though he were praying in a Sufi circle. There were prayers for every occasion, she thought, one for protecting your home and one for finding lost keys. But there was none to make someone love you. She took out her phone and called her mother.

# Chapter Fifteen

M rs Dhalani cracked another egg into a bowl. 'You know I knew that girl was no good. At the wedding breakfast she was so aloof – hardly said a word! But I kept my mouth sealed – why should I be blamed for spoiling everything? I told your father, if Asghar wants a love match, let him make a love match. I'm an open-minded lady – ask anyone – but this girl was a bad egg from the start. Asghar, bring the salt and pepper, please? Her manners were too . . . proper. She never spoke like *we* spoke, never laughed at *our* jokes. And whose fault is that? Asghar, beat up these eggs – I need strong arms. I'll tell you whose fault. The mother. The father we know about. But her mother let her go gallivanting to Oxbridge. For three years she disappeared: no weddings, funerals, Ramzan, Muharram – nothing, even during summer holidays. You were such a different boy – never talking back, at mosque every Friday. Add milk – more – a bit more – not that much! Good riddance!'

She poured the omelette mixture into the frying pan. Asghar looked on as it crackled.

'Don't look so sad,' his mother pleaded.

'I'm not looking sad,' he said. 'I'm just looking at the omelette.'

'Everyone knows it's all her fault – Zohra, Zahra, whatever her name is. She was being unreasonable, wasn't she?'

Asghar said nothing. Since he had returned to his parents' house a month earlier, his mother had been pressing him for damning evidence against Zahra. But he had held back. She was, after all, still his wife.

'She made you unhappy, didn't she?' insisted Mrs Dhalani. 'She treated you badly?'

'It's private,' he said, taking over the cooking from his mother. He flipped the omelette clumsily, splashing hot oil on his shirt.

'Careful what you're doing!' his mother cried, tearing off some kitchen tissue paper.

'I don't want you discussing us at the mosque.'

'We have to put our case forward,' she said, wiping the oil stains on his shirt. 'You must understand.'

'I do understand.' In the eyes of the community separation by mutual consent was a legal fiction. The breakdown of a marriage so traumatised its moral imagination that it demanded someone to blame, preferably with added juicy gossip. Within hours of the news getting out, competing mothers would be on the phone to the mosque's biggest gossip-mongers, justifying their child's behaviour: the boy was too Islamic, not Islamic enough; the girl was career-minded, her parents interfered. Privately these mothers knew that the complex flow of human relations could not be reduced to such clean lines – that it takes two to make a marriage and two to break one; but they also knew that the chances of finding another spouse from within the community (especially for a girl) depended on your story becoming the established narrative. Mrs Dhalani knew Zahra's mother must be saying terrible things about her son, and she wanted to chuck some gossip grenades of her own. With just one hint from Asghar about Zahra's irregular past Mrs Dhalani could have blasted Mrs Amir off the moral high ground. But the silly boy would not cooperate.

Asghar was picking at his omelette when his father walked in.

'Do you want some food?' he asked, half-rising from his seat. Mr Dhalani had taught him from childhood to stand up when he came into the room, and Asghar had never lost the habit.

'Isn't your mother making anything fresh?' he answered gruffly.

'Wait, I'm just making you another one,' said Mrs Dhalani, rushing to the fridge. 'Asghar – put the kettle on.'

'Quick then: I have a meeting in an hour.' He sounded agitated. There were rumblings at the new mosque of a challenge to him at the upcoming election. At Asghar's wedding, he had boasted of hugging more than a thousand supporters. Now his son's broken marriage was being used to attack him.

'Here you go,' said Asghar, placing a brimming mug of tea in front of his father.

'Sweetener,' he said without looking up. Asghar fetched the dispenser from the cupboard. Mr Dhalani had gained weight with the stress: the buttons on his striped shirt bulged, and flesh peeped out from under his silver rings.

'When is your deadline?' he asked, devouring his omelette with streaks of ketchup and an avalanche of salt.

'I've still got time,' replied Asghar.

'Studying hard?'

'I was just having a break, but I'm going back upstairs now.'

'Don't let us down,' he growled. Asghar had made his father look foolish by messing things up with Zahra. He could not make another mistake with his coursework.

'Take some biscuits with your tea,' said Mrs Dhalani, piling a plate with custard creams. 'He's getting fat,' said her husband, as Asghar left the kitchen.

Upstairs, Asghar sat at the wooden desk his parents had bought him as a reward for getting into Enfield House. He ate his biscuits and drank his tea. Zahra had promised to keep in touch via text. She said that way she could check he was feeling okay – and vice versa. This also left open the path to reconciliation. But after a few weeks her responses had slowed and finally stopped altogether. He tried tracking her through Facebook but she had deleted her account. He filled the silence by imagining the worst: her partying with Cambridge friends; drinks after work with sharp-suited colleagues; hooking up with that Hindu boy. To quell his torment, he immersed himself in childhood reading. He took out an old pile of storybooks about the prophets before the Prophet. The trials of Adam and Ibrahim, Yusuf and Salih became his own. In darker moments, he relished the fate of Nuh, who abandoned his wife to the cleansing flood.

His sister Fatima looked round the open door. She had come straight from madressa and was still wearing her black cloak and hijab. Matched with her oval glasses, she looked more like a middle-aged auntie than a teenager.

'You okay?' she asked.

'Fine,' he replied.

'Don't sound fine.'

'Fine then, I'm not fine.'

'Can I come in?'

'Suit yourself.'

She sat on the bed while he pretended to work. 'It smells in here,' she said.

'If you're going to be like that, then get out.'

'All right, I was only exaggerating.'

They sat in silence: Asghar copying from a textbook, Fatima leafing through his storybooks. 'Will you get married again?' she asked.

'I'm already married,' he said. 'We're going through a period of adjustment.'

'You could take another wife,' she giggled.

'Shut up, Fatima. You don't know anything. And take off that hijab – you're inside now.'

'I like wearing it,' she said, fiddling primly with her pin.

'Suit yourself.' He went back to pretending to work.

After a minute of silence, she said slyly: 'I've got something you might be interested in.'

'First time for everything.'

'I've found the perfect girl for you. One of my friends from madressa – I won't say her name, she's a respectable girl, but she's definitely interested in you.'

'I'm not taking a second wife. That's not how things work these days.'

'No, you idiot, after you divorce Miss High and Mighty.'

'How does she know me?' said Asghar, his annoyance tempered with curiosity.

'I've told her all about you. I said you were properly devout – studying hard for a job, saying your prayers on time, never missing a fast. That's the kind of guy she wants.'

'What does she look like?'

'Why is that always the first question boys ask?' cried Fatima.

'What, and they don't ask if he's tall and handsome?'

'Do you know what girls ask first?'

'What?'

'"Is he religious?"' she replied, glorying in the maturity of her gender.

'Tell her I know the whole Quran by heart.'

'You know, like, three surahs.'

'Oh, well: wasted youth. She sounds too young for me anyway.'

'She's not so young. She's from Tanzania and is two years older than me.'

'So she wants a Muslim man with a passport. I get it.'

'No, she's really lovely. No airs and she'd cook, clean, everything. And she loves English accents.'

'Mum sent you here, right?' He recognised her criteria for an ideal bride.

'Mum knows,' she admitted, 'but think about it properly. You made your own choice and look where you are.' Fatima opened the window and a chill wind fanned through the room. 'Oh, and by the way she is slim, and beautiful.'

She skipped from the room with her hijab trailing behind her.

When Asghar had met community girls from East Africa, he had found them quite appealing. He liked their aspirational American accents picked up at international schools. They hoped to migrate not to escape poverty (relatively speaking they were richer at home than they would be in England), but rather to follow the expected trajectory westwards. These girls had no nation, only a shared tribe spread across India, Africa and the West, and it was only logical for them to be attracted to high-ranking members, such as himself. Being British gave Asghar an advantage: he would have status, be deferred to. Maybe he should ask his mum to arrange a meeting?

No. He forced himself to stop. It was exactly this sort of idle fantasising that had led him to stumble blindly into Zahra's arms. He needed to curb his imagination.

He heard his mother calling him from the ground floor. He loped down the stairs and entered the kitchen, where he found his parents arguing about him.

'It's the girl's fault,' said his mother. 'Get rid of her and start again. He's still young.'

'The Quran says we must allow time for reconciliation,' pronounced his father in his best religiously authoritative tone.

'They should speak to Maulana Haider, then.'

'I'm not airing our dirty linen in front of him! The boy is the problem,' he said impatiently. 'Look at him – he can't be a man to any woman.'

'Listen to what you're saying in front of your son?' cried Mrs Dhalani.

'Oh no, you carry on,' muttered Asghar.

'I'm ringing Dr Amir to sort this out . . . wait,' he said, reconsidering, 'you should speak to the wife – one mother to another.'

'Me! What will I say!'

'Tell her to speak to her daughter. Tell her we can't have a divorce hanging over us – especially not with the election coming. Say there is dirty water to be drained but don't throw out the whole bathtub.'

'I don't know . . .'

'You're always mollycoddling him!' he exclaimed. 'It's done him no good. Pick up the phone and dial the number.'

She washed her floury hands and dried them with a kitchen towel. She cracked her knuckles, as though trying to expel stressful thoughts.

'Put it on speaker phone,' said Mr Dhalani, as she dialled.

'Hello?' said Zahra on the other end, 'who's calling?'

'Salaam aleikum,' said Mrs Dhalani. She seemed affronted that Zahra had answered so confidently. She switched to Gujarati.

'Is your mother there?' she asked. 'I need to speak with her.'

'Of course, auntie,' said Zahra with level politeness. 'Just wait a moment.' Asghar thought her voice sounded different; but maybe that was because it had been a while since he had heard it.

'Hello?' said Mrs Amir cautiously. She always answered the phone in English, even if she knew who the person on the line was. She didn't want to be caught revealing her foreignness to strangers.

Mrs Dhalani began by enquiring about Mrs Amir's cousin, whose poor health had been announced at the new mosque recently.

Mrs Amir said she had heard from Toronto that she was doing much better.

Illness strikes at any time, said Mrs Dhalani philosophically, adding that we should all consider each day as our last.

Mrs Amir concurred. Her own mother's death anniversary was approaching – always a painful time. By now Mr Dhalani was rolling his hands to indicate she should speed up the conversation.

'I'm phoning about the children . . .'

Mrs Amir agreed with Mrs Dhalani that casting full blame on either side was not fair and that, yes, perhaps a meeting between the two families might be helpful.

'Just the parents,' she responded.

'Oh,' said Mrs Amir. 'You mean meet without the children?' She paused. 'I think it might be better if Zahra and Asghar were also there. They are the ones who are married . . .'

Mr Dhalani made a frantic throat-slitting sign. But when Mrs Dhalani turned her eyes towards Asghar, he gave a small nod.

'That would be fine. Yes. All together.'


The reconciliation was set for Sunday afternoon. Driving to the Amirs', Mr Dhalani wondered aloud whether they should, traditionally speaking, have accepted Mrs Amir's invitation. If this had been a marriage proposal, of course, they would have been correct in visiting the girl's house; but once the couple were married, the boy's family took priority in hosting.

'What are the rules when there is a separation?' his wife asked. Mr Dhalani didn't reply.

'Everything will be all right,' said Mrs Dhalani, turning to Asghar, who was staring quietly out the window. She started coughing. 'I'm okay, I'm okay,' she said, smiling. 'Just feeling a bit dizzy.'

Her husband pulled the car into the Amirs' driveway and waited until she had recovered. Asghar got out of the car and led the family to the front door. He hammered on the door using the gargoyle knocker.

'Why have this devil face, I don't know,' said Mrs Dhalani. 'Allah protect us.'

Mohsen opened the door and greeted them warmly. They exchanged salaams.

'Where shall we put our shoes?' asked Mrs Dhalani. Mohsen pointed to a rack in the corner. The Dhalanis spent a minute precariously leaning on the walls and untying their shoes. Mohsen invited them into the lounge and asked if they wanted chai. All three refused.

'Please have some! I have leaves I bought from India,' said Mohsen.

'Where were you in India?' asked Mrs Dhalani.

'Kerala – I volunteered during my gap year.'

'South India,' said Mr Dhalani doubtfully. 'Why did you go there?'

'It's where the gap-year company sent us.'

'You didn't go with your family? Visit Gujarat, the old town Bhavnagar?'

'No.'

'Shame. It's important to know where you come from.'

'Have you been to Gujarat, Dad?' asked Asghar, who knew the answer.

'Not personally, no, but my father went with his brother in the 1950s. They visited their ancestral village.'

'How did they find the place?' asked Mohsen.

Mr Dhalani paused. 'It was very hot, they said.'

'I will have some chai,' interrupted Mrs Dhalani.

'Yes, I'll try a cup as well,' said Asghar.

'Uncle?'

240

'PG Tips for me.'

Mohsen opened the frosted door that led to the kitchen and disappeared inside. Asghar saw that his parents were nervous: his mother's hands were shaking. In contrast, he felt a fatalistic calm. Whatever else happened, at least the situation would be clarified. Just then, Zahra and her mother entered the living room. Zahra looked good in a long red skirt and crisp white blouse. Mrs Amir looked stressed; her bloodshot eyes were wrinkled at the edges.

'My husband is at the hospital,' said Mrs Amir. 'He's coming home soon, but he said to start without him.'

The adults exchanged pleasantries while Mohsen served chai. Asghar stole a glance at Zahra, who was sitting on a chair next to the sofa where her brother and mother sat. She glanced at him and looked away. In another world they might have been prospective marriage partners, shyly checking the other out.

Mr Dhalani sipped his PG Tips and smacked his lips with satisfaction. Then he put on his serious face. 'Your daughter and my son are having marriage problems. About this we must be honest. We cannot blame solely the boy or the girl. Fault is on both sides.' Mrs Amir responded by blowing on her tea. 'In our day, sister, these problems were ironed out by the parents. But we are moving with the times.' He pointed airily to Asghar and Zahra. 'They are being included now.'

'In our day,' said Mrs Amir, 'things were very different.'

'Yes,' agreed Mrs Dhalani.

'Good – we're getting somewhere. Now,' Mr Dhalani continued, 'I'm going to address my son so everyone can hear me.' He beckoned to Asghar. 'Sit forward.' Asghar shuffled an inch up the sofa. 'Come closer! Let me speak to you properly.

Now Asghar,' he said, settling into the presidential tone he used at the new mosque, 'it was your choice to marry Zahra – and yours alone. We did not pressure you in any direction. When you said you wanted to get married, we gave you our one hundred per cent blessing. But we also warned you that marriage is hard in the early days. Even your mother and I had difficulties. We learned to compromise and now look at us. That's right, my dear?'

'Absolutely,' said Mrs Dhalani. Asghar couldn't remember the last time his father had called his mother 'dear'.

Mr Dhalani now addressed Zahra.

'Zahra,' he said, 'as your father-in-law, it's my duty to speak. Don't jump at the first sign of trouble. A wife should understand her husband's problems – whatever he faces, you face together.'

Asghar saw Mrs Amir twist her scarf into a knot.

'You must remember the duties you owe your husband . . .' continued Mr Dhalani.

'What about the duties he owes me?' said Zahra.

'I don't know what your daughter is trying to say,' said Mr Dhalani, speaking to Zahra through her mother, 'but she should let her father-in-law finish speaking.'

'Did you have more to say?' asked Mrs Amir, who seemed unworried by her daughter's interruption. 'Perhaps it's time to give the children a chance to speak?'

'Fine,' he said, slapping his knees. 'It's your decision completely.' He sat back sulkily.

Mrs Amir gestured at her daughter. Asghar looked at Zahra, trying to sense what she would say. She was about to speak when the door rattled and Dr Amir entered, his suit crumpled and his thinning hair uncombed. He apologised for being late and sat down next to Zahra. Asghar noticed that he didn't address or even look at his wife. Dr Amir and Mr Dhalani greeted each other with pointed politeness. During the wedding the old rivals had barely spoken to one another, leaving the women to negotiate the arrangements.

'My daughter is unhappy at the way she has been treated,' said Dr Amir. 'She has not been given the respect due to her.'

'What about my son?' snapped Mr Dhalani, his conciliatory tone forgotten in a flash. 'Your daughter didn't make Asghar feel comfortable. She was out working all day, forgetting the duties of a wife.'

'Dad,' said Asghar, 'I'm not sure—'

'No, no – your father is speaking now. We are a respectable family. We have worked for the community like servants for many years, and our son deserves to be treated as the man of the house.'

'Well, like you brother, our family has *also* been serving the community—'

'The *old* mosque,' said Mrs Dhalani.

'Yes, the old mosque,' said Mrs Amir, 'so what if it's the old mosque? It's the place where the community began!'

'You haven't noticed, but we've moved on to the *new* mosque.'

Asghar listened to the argument go back and forth. His parents and his in-laws had strayed from discussing him and Zahra into replaying this ancient grudge. At that moment, hearing their pointless bickering, he felt disgusted. What was this community anyway? There was no unity, only rivalries. They wanted you to marry inside only because it was a way of carrying on an argument they had been having for generations. He looked at Zahra. She looked tired. Her eyes were ringed with shadows. He noticed she had done something new with her hair; it seemed shorter, more restrained. When he had first met her properly, she had seemed impossibly glamorous, floating above the ties of community and religion, living life on her own terms. That was why he had been drawn to her in the first place. But now he was seeing the backstage suburban reality. He felt terribly sad at the part he had played in her diminishment.

The parents stopped arguing for a moment. Asghar cleansed his dry mouth with tea.

'I think I should be allowed to speak?' The two older men reluctantly deferred to him. 'I don't want to rake over everything,' he said, looking at Zahra directly. 'It won't do any good. Those things should remain between us. I'll say only one thing. We've known each other since we were children. We were at the old mosque together, remember? When we met up years later, I thought we could pick up . . . But after marriage it didn't work,' he said, keeping his gaze level. 'I'm sorry. I'm very sorry for what's happened. But that's it.'

'You can't throw everything away like that,' cried his mother.

'You can't force two people to love each other,' he replied.

Zahra rushed from the room, followed by her mother. The others sat in awkward silence for a moment.

'We'd better take our leave,' said Mr Dhalani.

Dr Amir stood up straight away, not bothering with the conventional effort to make them stay. Mohsen showed them out.

On the way home, Asghar's mother asked why he had been so final. 'You should have discussed it with us beforehand.'

'It's my decision,' he said calmly.

'We're better off without that family,' said his father. 'It's good for Asghar to stand up to them. We'll divorce and move on. There are plenty of other girls, good community girls, not like this pretend Englishwoman. Fatima knows a nice girl at madressa. We'll arrange a meeting.'

That night Asghar composed an email to Zahra. The subject line was 'The Future':

*Dear Zahra,*
*Today was awkward, I know. It probably wasn't the best way for things to turn out, but perhaps it's good to bring things to a head. In the last few weeks I've tried to be as honest as possible about my feelings. I love and care for you . . .*

He retyped that last sentence:

*. . . I loved and still care deeply for you.*

And once more:

*. . . I loved you and care for you. But do I love you now? I'm not sure it's possible. Too much has happened to recover what we might have had. Maybe if we'd started from a blank slate. So it's probably best if we decide for ourselves (under no family pressure) to leave everything – a clean break. Then we can get on with our lives and find more suitable partners.*

He blinked at the screen and deleted those last words.

*Then we can get on with our lives. Lastly, I want to apologise for anything bad I've said or done. Nothing was done with bad intentions, I promise. Of course, I forgive you for anything you might have said or done, without realising. You don't have to reply to this now or ever. But if our paths do cross again or you want to write to me at any point, please know you have a friend who cared for you and still does.*

He pressed send.

246

## Chapter Sixteen

Zahra was sleeplessly checking her phone in bed when Asghar's email arrived. She scanned down for its essential message, and when she realised his meaning she felt a pang of rejection. Immediately, though, she chided herself: it was *she* who had left *him*, not the other way round. Rereading the email, she noted its careful tenses: *I loved you and care for you* . . . His words had an unmistakable tone of finality. Putting her phone on her bedside table, she propped herself up on her pillows. Since leaving the Kilburn house, her mood had swung between elation and embarrassment, relief and longing. To convince herself she was doing the right thing, she had taken an old school notebook, scored it down the middle with a pencil and tallied up the reasons for and against staying with her husband. Switching on the lamp, she found the notebook in her drawer. On the pro-Asghar side she had scribbled: *sweet, reliable, friendly, can be kind, adores me, Muslim*. On the anti-Asghar side she had written: *judgmental, boring, few outside interests, bit of a fundo.* She picked up a pen and went over the anti-Asghar side in permanent ink, thickening the letters and underscoring the words. This calmed her down. But when she put the notebook away and tried to sleep, a familiar discomfort tightened her chest.

The next morning, she texted Krish asking whether he wanted to meet up. To her surprise, within a minute he sent back an enthusiastic yes. He said he would be down in London that weekend for work anyway, adding that he had wanted to get in touch for a while. Nervously, she rehearsed what she would say, and what she would not. She would pour every ounce of her charm into her self-presentation. She didn't yet know exactly what she wanted – apart from more options.


They met at a pop-up Indian cafe on the South Bank. The weather was blustery and the cafe packed with young couples and prams. Zahra and Krish were forced to sit outside on the damp benches shielded only by parasols in green, white and saffron. Krish was sporting a well-groomed beard and a grey, hand-knitted scarf wrapped round his neck. She told him he looked good.

'Cheers! Love your red coat,' he said. 'Is it new?'

'Quite new,' she said vaguely. She had asked Asghar to buy it for her birthday.

Drinking cardamom chai and munching vegetarian mini-samosas, they discussed what their mutual friends were doing after university – who was dating whom, who had gone abroad to teach English, who had their dream job, who was still drifting. Zahra had forgotten how much she enjoyed spending time with him, laughing at the same silly jokes about Adam and his fondness for old-time jazz.

'What are you up to then?' she asked coyly.

'Helping the people of Manchester get some soul in their lives.'

'What, in temple?'

'I'm putting on club nights playing classic soul music. Marvin Gaye, Otis Redding, that kind of thing. We've done three so far, and they've gone well. Not packed, but getting there.'

'Is that what you're doing, like, full time?'

'It's a full-time job! You've got to sort out the licences, book the venues, do all the online promotion, find the DJs. That's why I'm here this weekend. I'm going to a club night in Tooting, meeting a promoter who has this ace new DJ. He used to rep the Scarlett Pimps before they broke up.'

'What happened to law?'

'Still an option – but you've got to follow your dreams, right?'

'Right,' she said. 'The bank's going well by the way, thanks for asking.'

'Glad to hear it.'

Krish was always careful with his appearance: hair precise, sideburns shaped, face moisturised. Now, though, she spotted dark eyeliner round his eyes – an odd feminine touch.

'That's a nice scarf,' she said.

'It was a present,' he said quickly. 'It's hand-knitted. The wool's from this special sheep from Scotland . . .' As she listened to him explain the scarf's rare origins, she became certain that this was a present from the new girlfriend – and even more certain that she wasn't Asian. Knitting for English girls meant embracing the homely crafts their mothers had shunned. For Zahra, knitting was still too close to the image of the traditional Indian housewife.

'So who made you that scarf?' she asked casually. Krish stopped chewing his mini-samosa. He sipped some chai and tapped the table, as though setting himself straight.

'I'm glad you asked to meet up,' said Krish, 'because I wanted to talk to you about something.' She opened her eyes wide. 'I have some news,' he continued. She felt like she was about to throw up. 'I'm getting married.'

'Oh congratulations . . .' Zahra felt her cheeks stretch as though someone were pulling her skin. 'Wow, I'm so pleased.'

'Cathy and I were in India,' Krish continued, 'and I asked her outside the Taj Mahal – right on the Princess Di bench. It sounds corny but it *was* really romantic. When she said yes, all the tourists applauded. You remember Cathy? I mentioned her, didn't I?' How could she forget his ex-girlfriend – no longer ex, of course. 'We saw each other when we were doing A levels, for a bit, but we were both too immature. After graduation, we gave it another chance.'

'So you went back to her,' she said flatly.

'I suppose we had both grown up.'

'Had you now?'

'I don't want you to be upset,' said Krish, a little impatiently. 'But you got married without even telling me,' he reminded her.

'Your family's okay you're marrying a white girl?'

'Better than marrying a Muslim.'

'Oh, thanks.'

'Don't push it,' Krish said sharply. 'I spent ages behaving like a perfect gentleman. Just when things got serious you rejected me. Remember what you said when we broke up? "I felt like I was violated." For God's sake, it was only a kiss!'

'It wasn't *only* a kiss.'

'You wanted to,' he lowered his voice, 'do all that stuff as well. Then you go and make me feel like some kind of rapist.'

'Well, I'm sorry if *I* treated you so badly.'

'Yes, you did.' He did not avert his gaze.

'My parents are getting divorced,' she said suddenly. 'Twenty-seven years together, just like that, gone.'

'I'm sorry.' Krish seemed unsure how to react to her abrupt news.

'Don't be. It's for the best, I'm sure. They've barely had a proper conversation in years. Turns out Dad was waiting for me to get married before he split from Mum.'

'Is there someone else?'

'Of course not.'

'When someone wants out of a relationship fast, they've usually found someone else.'

'It wasn't anything like that with me and you.'

'I know, you told me you met your husband later. I'm speaking generally.'

Heavy raindrops began to patter on the parasol. Zahra sipped her cold chai and stared at the turbulent Thames.

'It's funny how things turn out,' she said, 'because you've just told me you're getting married, and I came to tell you I'm getting divorced.' He looked shocked.

'Oh, babe . . .'

'Yes, just like my mum and dad. Probably. We're just separated now but there's not much hope. I know I rushed into it. I've only myself to blame for all this. I've made all the wrong choices . . .'

Krish gave her a handkerchief monogrammed with his initials. She blew her nose forcefully.

'Sorry, was that a present from Cathy?' she asked, laughing through her tears.

'It's okay,' he said, 'you keep it. She got me a dozen.' Zahra tucked the handkerchief up her sleeve.

'Relationships are complicated,' he said. 'After we met at Lighthouse, I couldn't stop thinking about you, wanting to talk with you, wanting to be with you. I was infatuated. And I think you knew that.'

'I really enjoyed spending time with you,' said Zahra.

'Thanks,' said Krish, with a hint of sarcasm.

'No, I felt more than that, Krish . . .'

'No need to go back over everything: I was the foolish one. I thought that just because a girl spends every other night hanging out with me, going to the movies together, taking long walks together, I thought it wasn't ridiculous to think romance was on the cards. But I know what you were up to.'

'I wasn't "up to" anything.'

'I couldn't work out why you wanted to hang out with me. Your parents wouldn't have approved of me being Hindu. At first, I thought you were rebelling, and I was cool with that. Later, I thought you weren't rebelling at all. It's *because* I'm not Muslim you got involved with me. I was safe because I was untouchable. There was no chance of anything serious, so you could have your little dalliance in the full knowledge you'd eventually cut it off saying, "Oh, I'm Muslim, you're Hindu, it would never work."'

'Krish, you know it wasn't like that—'

'I've noticed that about Muslims. You guys never leave your religion behind. Once you've been taught your Quran and your Prophet, you never stop being Muslim. Even those guys who drink and do drugs and sleep around, they'll always be fasting in Ramzan – I guarantee it. And even those "ex-Muslims" can't stop banging on about hating Islam. It's like a childhood romance they can't get over. Hindus are more chilled. We kind of make it up as we go along.'

'When did you ever hear me talk about religion?'

'You lot can't progress because you've got this huge weight of guilt: that if you stray from the straight path you'll go to hell. Now all religions have their extremists. Those Shiv Sena guys are crazy, I know that—'

'You seem to have been listening to them pretty closely.'

'—but most Hindus here don't care about that bullshit. They leave it in the mother country.'

'That's totally unfair.'

'You weren't exactly fair to me,' he said, his voice hardening. 'And now you want to reactivate me, recharge me like an old phone that's been dead for months.'

'I thought we could be friends.'

'Friends like we were in Cambridge? Just friends who went on walks in Grantchester, and spent the afternoon lying in the sun – just friends like when we parked in college?'

Zahra banged her chai cup down on her plate. 'I *cannot* believe what a fucking idiot you're being,' she said. She grabbed her handbag and stood up.

'Walk away then, walk away,' said Krish. 'Be angry because I'm happy!'

It was the first time she had heard him so upset: his voice, she thought as she strode away, seemed to have taken on a slight Indian tone. She carried on until she reached the yellow stairs leading to the riverbank. But they were closed off for repairs and there was no way out except back past Krish. She looked across the grimy Thames and wept. Exhausted, she turned round and walked back towards the cafe, half hoping and half dreading he would still be there. She saw him speaking on his phone, cupping the handset intimately to his mouth. She hovered behind a pillar until he left.

She took the Tube in a daze. When she got home her father was out – he was rarely in these days – and her mother was upstairs, climbing up the attic stepladder. She stepped over some disintegrating cardboard boxes and a couple of bulging bin bags teetering against the wall.

'Oh good, you're back,' said Mrs Amir, her voice echoing from the attic. 'You can help me unload all this stuff. How was Andrea?'

'She was a bit weird,' said Zahra, composing herself. 'I'm not sure if I still want to be friends with her.'

'Why not? She's been such a good friend to you all this time: you Skype all the time. And remember the wedding? Andrea looked so beautiful, and Carl is such a good-looking boy!'

'Mum, don't call Carl good looking. It's weird.'

Mrs Amir eased herself off the stepladder, making sure her green Moroccan gown didn't get caught on the loose screws. 'I can say he's good looking if I want. Soon I'll be a single lady.' She winked before bending down to pick up a box. 'Come, take this.'

Zahra took the box and started coughing; the dust made her fingers tingle. Avoiding the spider corpses, she found piles of old letters and photographs.

'What's all this?' she asked.

'It's your parents' marriage, in boxes,' replied Mrs Amir. 'Letters, photographs, plane receipts – I kept everything.'

'Can I look?'

'I'm throwing them all away,' she said. 'There's no point now the marriage has turned to dust.'

'I didn't know you wrote love letters.'

'There's plenty you don't know.'

After a show of resolution, her mother was coaxed into telling the story. She was twenty years old and living with her parents in Nairobi when the recently qualified Dr Amir had visited the family home. He was the first man to ever visit her, and she had fallen in love with him right away. He charmed her with tales of studying medicine in London – white fog, eccentric landladies, Windsor Castle. A day later, her match-making aunt conveyed a proposal from his family. She eagerly accepted. For a year they exchanged letters between Nairobi and London.

Zahra withdrew a thin blue envelope from the box and saw her mother's name in her father's indecipherable hand-writing. The envelope was roughly ripped, a sign perhaps of her mother's impatience.

'Come on, let me look at one at least.'

'Love letters are all the same: "You're the most wonderful girl, the most beautiful." Probably your father wrote something like that. Then you get married and you don't need letters because you have each other. Then twenty-seven years later, he comes home to say he's divorcing you and the letters are worthless paper. Like clothes that don't fit any more. Fit for junk.'

'What about the letters you sent him?'

'Your father threw them away. He was never sentimental like me.'

'Me and Asghar only have a few emails,' she said.

255

Her mother looked at her softly. 'Are you sure it's over?' she asked.

'You heard what Asghar said on Sunday.'

'I saw the way he looked at you. That boy is still in love; give it another chance, you could make it work.'

'I think it's too late,' said Zahra mournfully.

'If it's too late, it's too late. I can give you my lawyer's email,' she said briskly, returning to a sorting-things-out mood.

'Will you and Dad sell the house?'

'Don't worry, I'll find a place where you can stay as well.'

'And Mohsen?'

'I'm sure he'll go with your dad. Or move in with friends.'

Mrs Amir dived into a box and brought out an old photograph of her husband as a student in London. He was posing outside a posh-looking building – a hospital perhaps? – wearing a brown suit and a fat green tie; he had long hair and wore dark glasses.

'Wow, he looks so seventies!'

'It was the seventies,' said Mrs Amir. 'He was very fashionable.'

'Did you take that photo?'

'This was before my time. Look, I'll show you something else.' She shuffled through the faded Polaroids until she found a picture of a Mediterranean-looking lady wearing a white skirt and white jumper. She was shielding her eyes from the sun and smiling.

'That was your father's girlfriend, Jacinta. She was a nurse at the hospital.'

'Girlfriend?' said Zahra, surprised to hear that word in her mother's mouth. When he was feeling jovial, Dr Amir had alluded to his youthful adventures – the nurses were far prettier in their old uniforms, he claimed to Zahra's discomfort – but never went into details.

'Was it serious?'

'They lived in a flat in Hounslow,' said Mrs Amir. 'He told me about her when I found these photographs in a shoe box under the bed. He promised to throw them away.'

'You must have been upset.'

'The past is the past. An experienced man is better in some ways. Your father said he got out all his bad habits with Jacinta. It wasn't true: he still had the same bad habits. But it made me feel good when he said that. So I forgave him.'

'Mum,' she said, 'didn't you feel bad that he was your first love, but it wasn't the same with him?'

'It's different for men and women. Or maybe we're told it's different and we believe it.'

Her mother started dumping the bundles of papers in a black bin bag. Zahra helped, often stopping her to ask about this or that piece of paper. She came across a legal file marked Egypt Air. The holiday her father had planned had been cancelled because of a terrorist attack. It was family lore that instead of seeing the pyramids at Giza, Mrs Amir was taken to a pebbly beach in Brighton. There she mistook the Pavilion for a mosque and asked her husband if they could pray there. He teased her for the rest of the holiday and, when the children came along, he passed the joke on. Zahra had laughed along with her dad and brother, but the humour now seemed less good-natured than she had once thought.

'Rubbish,' said Mrs Amir, dropping the file into the bin bag. 'And this . . .' She picked up the old photographs of her husband and Jacinta and chucked them away.

Zahra objected. Her mother was within her rights to destroy

everything that belonged to her married life; but those pictures belonged to a different world, her father's world.

'He never looks at them. He's probably forgotten they even exist,' she said.

They spent an hour throwing more stuff away before carrying the bin bags to the backyard, ready for collection. After four trips up and down the stairs they decided to reward themselves with a cup of tea in the kitchen.

'I'm thinking of dyeing my hair,' said Mrs Amir, washing her hands in the sink. 'Reddish I think would look good.' She pushed her waves of grey round her ear.

'You'd look ten years younger.'

'I might take off my hijab as well.'

'What? Really?'

'I'm not changing my hair just for those women at the mosque. You know what they'll say? If only she hadn't neglected herself, her husband wouldn't have divorced her.'

'But you've worn hijab forever.'

'In Nairobi I never wore it. When I got married I never wore it. It was in the 1980s when Imam Khomeini told us to become better Muslims that everyone started wearing it, and so did I. Now things are different. I might go out a few times without it. See how I feel. It will be easier getting a job. There are a lot of prejudiced people these days.'

'Why should you change yourself just because of what other people think?'

'You don't wear it – you don't understand how people look at you. Like you can't even speak English or something.'

It was true: Zahra never wore a scarf except at the mosque. She had, however, always found it reassuring that her mother wore one. In conversations with non-Muslims, she invoked her mother as an example of the archetypal Muslim woman who wears hijab for religious, not political, reasons. Her mother's desire to discard the hijab made her feel uncomfortable. It felt strange that her mother was throwing away her married identity – first the letters, now the hijab. Did she realise how difficult it would be to shed a skin you had worn for a quarter of a century? The past was not something to be discarded – it had to be acknowledged and absorbed and transformed.

'If your father can do what he wants, then so can I. The Quran doesn't say you have to cover your hair.'

'That's what I say when people ask why I don't wear hijab.'

'Maybe I've copied you.' She drained her tea with a twinkle in her eye.

When her mother went back upstairs, Zahra slipped out of the side door and found the bin bags. They were slippery with rain, and it was hard to unpick her mother's tight knots; frustrated, she ripped a hole in one bag and took out a bundle of her father's letters. She would keep her promise not to open them; instead she would put them somewhere safe in case her mother ever wanted to look at them. The record of her parents' courtship was too important to destroy for the sake of petty vengeance. Besides, it was her own history as much as her parents'. Before leaving the bag, she also saved the photograph of her father on a sunny suburban street. And the one of the nurse Jacinta, the girl who was her father's first love. These she would keep for herself.

# Chapter Seventeen

Since visiting Zahra, Asghar had barely left his room. When his worried mother came to him with hot soup and buttered toast – the same comfort food she gave him during childhood illnesses – he kept telling her not to worry. All he needed was some time to think, to reflect. She would shut the door and listen out for a minute with her ear cocked. All she heard was shuffling and the occasional bout of heavy breathing as he dropped off, catching up on the sleep he had missed during his restless nights.

He stayed up late and watched films on his laptop. One of his favourites was *Titanic*, which he had first seen with his mother one Valentine's Day a few years earlier. She had bought the DVD from a stall in Southall, hoping to watch it with her husband. But Mr Dhalani had an emergency decorating job to complete for Mrs Sachoo, whose in-laws were visiting from Canada. ('And it will only make me seasick,' he added.) Fatima only watched religious films like

*The Message* or *The Alchemist of Happiness*. So Mrs Dhalani invited Asghar to join her in the living room. He was immediately drawn in by the romance across the social divide, inwardly jeering at the posh people keeping the beautiful and soulful heroine apart from her poor but noble lover. All was going wonderfully until the hero painted his lover in the nude. That was excruciating. Why did English films have to shove sex in your face the whole time? Re-watching the scene alone in his bedroom, he would skip the nudity and go straight to what really excited him – the emotional climax of the sinking ship.

He stopped attending Tuesday meetings at Umar's house. After missing two weeks in a row, Sheikh Tariq called him personally. Asghar told him the news about Zahra, though he didn't go into details.

'So you're now a free man,' said Tariq jovially.

'It's only a trial separation. I don't know about the future.'

'Why wait? You can divorce her straight away. Simply recite three times: "I divorce you, I divorce you, I divorce you."'

'Is that allowed? The maulana at our mosque says you have to meet all these conditions . . .'

'Of course it works! Tell him to read the Quran,' said Tariq impatiently. 'It's all there in clear sentences. No clever interpretation needed. But remember one thing: you have to say it face to face. Once in Granada a man came to me. He was too nervous to divorce his wife face to face in case she made him change his mind. She was a very persuasive lady. So he left her a voicemail: "Hello, this is your husband. I divorce you, I divorce you, I divorce you." Can you believe it? Of course, I told him it wasn't sharia compliant.'

'It wasn't?'

'How would he know if she heard the message?' he asked. 'Or turned it off after the first "I divorce you"?'

'Well, we're not thinking about divorce – not yet.'

'Zahra was never the right woman for you,' said Tariq. 'I disliked her straight away when I met her. Girls should keep custody of the eyes. They should never address a man directly, only through her husband. But she looked at me with a direct gaze. Like she was judging me.'

'She looked down on me all the time,' said Asghar. 'I could tell when she thought I'd said something stupid. She would have this little smile.'

'This is what the West does to women. Only Islam can teach them to behave as women, not imitate men.' Asghar felt a guilty pleasure in having his resentments so confidently theorised.

Tariq told him he should seriously consider coming back to Umar's. But in the meantime, to keep him in the loop, he would be adding him to an exclusive WhatsApp group. On *Strangers of Europe* Umar, Sayyid, Akbar and a few selected others exchanged updates, wisdom quotations, charity appeals and political opinions.

'We won't abandon you,' said Tariq, before saying goodbye. At least someone was on his side, thought Asghar. Meeting Tariq was the only good thing to have come from that disastrous honeymoon in Spain. He recalled Ian's painting, *The Muslim Bride*. When Zahra had left the house in Kilburn, he had dragged it out from under the bed and chucked it in the skip outside the house a few doors down. It clattered on the sharp debris and slid down to rest on a broken mirror. He had felt a rush of intense relief for a few moments; followed by desolating emptiness.

His mother rapped on his door twice and entered.

'Behta, do you want something else to eat?' she asked. Asghar put the phone away, hoping she hadn't heard him speaking. She would rather he sought advice from Maulana Haider than some random Spanish sheikh.

'Not hungry,' he replied.

'I'll bring tea and biscuits.'

'It'll only be wasted.'

'I'm going to the gym. Why don't you come with me?' she asked, almost shyly.

'I've got university work to catch up on.'

Her tone sharpened: 'You can't lay about all day.'

He glanced at his computer screen: his inbox was empty. Zahra hadn't replied to his email yet. He knew he had said that she didn't have to – but it would have been nice to get even a short message. He closed his laptop: 'Let me get dressed.'

'Five minutes!' she cried, and flew downstairs. He pulled out his oversized blue jumper and black jeans. On his way down he passed the old spider plant housed in a faux-Victorian pot his mother had kept alive for years. The leaves were yellowing; it seriously needed a prune. In the kitchen, he found her washing some tea-stained mugs. She drained the greasy water from the cooking pot but it was still stained with burnt onion and needed another scrub. She refilled the pot with soapy warm water and left it to soak. She quickly scribbled a note to her husband. *I'm off to the gym, and after I'll bring takeaway food*, she wrote, reading her words aloud as the pen scratched the page. *Chicken and chips – I won't forget wings!* Those were her husband's favourite. She removed a safety pin trapped between her teeth and fastened her hijab.

'Come, my best boy,' she said, smoothing his hair. 'Let's go.'

They got into the family Mercedes, still dented from the week before the wedding. She pressed the accelerator and lunged the car backwards – then applied the brakes sharply.

'Just waking you up,' she said, twisting her head towards the rear window. Once they were safely on the road, Asghar switched on the radio.

'You don't want to talk to your mother?'

'Why do we always have to talk?' said Asghar.

'Okay, fine,' she replied, 'but I don't want men shouting their heads off about football. Put on Sunrise.' He twiddled the medium-wave knob until he found the Asian radio station. The deep-voiced host was speaking Hindi. The programme's name was *Golden Oldies*. The title, Asghar thought, seemed to refer to both the songs and the listeners.

Down the line was Geeta from Wood Green reminiscing about growing up in Bombay. Her late husband had taken her to the Raj Kapoor and Nargis classic, *Shree 420*. She had been a schoolteacher and always loved the classroom song. Could they play it?

It would be a pleasure, the host replied, clearly an expert at charming Indian women of a certain age. Asghar expected the song to be mournful and romantic, like other old Bollywood songs he had heard; but to his surprise it was chirpy and cheerful.

'We used to sing this in school assembly!' cried Mrs Dhalani, humming along and filling in the lyrics with a sing-song voice.

'What's it about?'

'They're puzzles,' she said. 'In the film, Nargis is teaching the children names of fruits and vegetables. Raj is a ragamuffin – like Charlie Chaplin – eavesdropping on her.'

'Let me guess: Raj loves Nargis.'

264

'Of course!'

'Why are all Bollywood movies about love?' he sighed. 'Aren't there more important subjects in India – poverty, corruption, Hindu–Muslim riots?'

'You can't talk about life without love. Look! Raj is joining in now.'

They listened to the singing voices playfully entwine. After the song ended the adverts came on. The first was for a match-making website. 'All religions, sects, castes catered for,' the service boasted. For millions of Indians, the real marriage trade was unromantic – a matter of practical bartering and brokering. That must be why Indians loved sentimental movies, he thought. They satisfied their romantic yearnings through the fantasy world of the cinema. Perhaps that was the safest option.

'I'd like to watch those old movies,' he said.

'You wouldn't like them,' said his mother. 'The singing and dancing is so old-fashioned. The modern ones have the hip moves.' She wiggled her hips in her seat and giggled.

As the car veered to the side of the road, Asghar begged her to concentrate. 'I'm serious, we can watch them together. Like we used to. I can find them online.'

'What's this find them online nonsense?' she said. 'I can get the DVDs for two pounds in Southall. We can stop by after the gym.'

The traffic was bad and they arrived at the gym almost exactly as Mrs Dhalani's class was due to start. They rushed up the stairs and she waved her pass at the electronic barrier.

'My Bolly-robics instructor is very tough in the warm-ups,' said Mrs Dhalani, taking the lime green bag that Asghar had carried up for her. 'If you're late she makes you run round the gym twice.'

'Bolly-robics?'

'You exercise to Bollywood music. It's good fun. Why don't you join us? I can get you a day pass.'

But Asghar said he didn't feel like working out.

'Exercise will help you sleep,' she added.

'Don't worry about me,' he said, wondering how she knew he had trouble sleeping. She surprised him sometimes with how well she read his emotional states. He said he would wait in the cafe until her class finished. She kissed him lightly on the forehead and pushed through the double doors towards the ladies' changing room.

The empty cafe smelled of chlorine. At the counter he noticed a glass cabinet filled with pastries, lit by small spotlights. He ordered a croissant and a coffee from the pretty fair-haired girl at the counter. According to her badge her name was Magdalena and the red-and-white flag underneath told him she was Polish. Good for her, he thought. She poured coffee from a filter jug into a Styrofoam cup, and used her gloved hands to retrieve a croissant and place it on a plastic plate. She smiled at him broadly.

'Thank you, Magdalena,' said Asghar, putting on his best English accent. 'This looks delicious.'

'You're most welcome,' she said, inclining her head. She really was very attractive. Just as he was turning away, she started speaking to him. 'I must learn to speak with this accent.'

'Why, thank you. I've been practising it all my life.'

'You are born here?'

'British born and bred.' He sensed she was impressed. 'There are many Indian people who were born in this country,' he said. 'London is very multi-cultural.'

'I know. I have studied this in Poland.'

266

'Welcome to England,' he said. She gave him a little wave as he walked away.

He found a table facing the counter. Was it his imagination or was Magdalena flirting with him? She had responded well to the English gentleman act. It was strange: proper English people like Mr Powell treated him like an outsider, making him feel as though he would never learn all the unwritten rules he needed to feel accepted. Yet with this Polish girl, he could not have felt more like a native. Maybe he would only ever truly feel English if he lived abroad – in Europe or America – where they would be impressed by his accent.

He was about to bite into his croissant when his phone vibrated. Tariq had added him to *Strangers of Europe*. He tapped out his first message: *Salaams, Asghar here.* Straight away, Tariq messaged back welcoming him to the group; five or six others also salaamed. *Great to chat here*, he typed. He took a bite of croissant – which he quickly spat out. It was doughy and under-baked, almost inedible. He looked up and saw Magdalena cleaning the sink. He considered complaining but didn't want to make her think she was doing a bad job. In any case, the croissants probably came straight from the bakery. It was tough for newcomers to get things right. In solidarity with Magdalena, he took another bite – but it was still horrible. He drowned the taste with sugary coffee.

A message appeared from Umar. *Watch this, brothers – Sheikh Tariq burns a Zionist!* Below he had included a video link to a panel discussion in Tower Hamlets that had been held the night before. It was entitled 'Israel: Democracy or Occupation?' Umar praised Tariq's performance. *You wiped the floor with that journalist.*

Asghar plugged in his earphones and clicked on the link

with excited anticipation. This would cheer him up, for sure. For the first few seconds the picture was blurry and then it cleared up. On the far left of the panel was Tariq, dressed in traditional Arab clothes; sitting next to him was a paunchy middle-aged English guy from a think-tank called Lyceum; moderating in the middle was a smart Muslim lawyer in hijab; and beside her was a dark-haired woman from *The Times* – surely the journalist Tariq was about to slay. Asghar pressed the white tracking line and fast-forwarded past the introductions. He stopped when he saw Tariq gesticulating towards the dark-haired journalist. They were arguing fiercely over the one-state solution. Tariq asked why Israelis were so afraid of democracy; she said she was surprised that Tariq seemed to be such a fan of democracy: didn't he want a caliphate in Europe? Tariq accused her of avoiding the question. The mainly Muslim audience cheered Tariq.

The camera lingered on the female journalist long enough for him to see her nametag: 'Sarah Seeley, *The Times*.' It took him a few seconds to place the name. Sarah Seeley – could she be Danny's sister? He had always assumed that she was, like her brother, fair-haired, but this Sarah had dark curls. He stopped the video and searched for her on Google. She was famous enough to have a short Wikipedia page. Sarah was four years older than Asghar and had gone to school not far from Enfield House. After studying theology at Oxford, she joined *The Times* as a trainee. She had been awarded fellowships in Washington, Barcelona and Tel Aviv. The page didn't say anything about her personal life, whether she was married or not. He returned to the video and watched the rest of the debate. Sarah was arguing that the Palestinians were better off under Israeli control than they would be under an Arab despot.

In Israel there were functioning courts, democracy, freedom of speech and human rights – more than could be said for most Muslim nations. The audience bellowed its outrage; but she was undeterred. 'And if you're going to boycott Israel, which, I admit, has some troubling policies' – Tariq shouted 'shame, shame' – 'then we should boycott India for how it treats Muslims in Kashmir or China for what it does to the Uyghurs. Why single out Israel?'

Asghar had never thought of that before. Tariq began shouting 'warmonger' and 'Zionist', and encouraged his vocal supporters to drown her out with clapping. The camera caught Sarah flinch and Asghar's heart leapt to her defence. He paused the video.

He couldn't help feeling oddly proud of Sarah. Here was a beautiful and intelligent *Times* journalist – and he knew her! He wasn't so troubled that they were on different sides of the argument. Why shouldn't Sarah defend her own people? Muslims defended Pakistan or Iran when they were misrepresented in the media, even though their governments did bad things sometimes. She took pride in her Jewish identity. He could tell from the way she spoke that this was personal, not merely a debating point. He could respect that. He restarted the video. Tariq was leading his supporters in collective clapping whenever Sarah tried to speak. Asghar had never seen him like that – his face contorted with fury. He wanted to tell him that there was another side to Sarah, the side that was curious about Islam, and that she had once been friendly to a young Muslim boy.

Back on *Strangers of Europe* he scrolled down and read more comments. *You told her, Tariq*, said Akbar. *Shekels from Murdoch*, said Sayyid. *Stupid Jewess*, said Umar.

Someone posted a picture of an Israeli flag on a toilet roll, which provoked waves of amusement.

Asghar felt ashamed. Wasn't the Star of David a sacred symbol of a prophet? What if someone put the Saudi flag – with Allah's name – on a toilet roll? He recalled his argument with Zahra in Cordoba's cathedral-mosque. At the time, he hadn't understood what she was saying. How could Christians lay claim to a place Muslims had built? But he was beginning to see her point. All things being equal, maybe somewhere could be a mosque and a cathedral at the same time.

He typed quickly. *Not saying I agree with her, but the journalist lady should be treated with respect. She is from the People of the Book, and the Prophet said we should debate with each other peacefully.*

At first he took the silence for chastened agreement. But when Sayyid replied with a cursory, *What you chatting about?* the messages started flooding in.

*Brother, don't be fooled.*

*She has Muslim blood on her hands.*

*The Jews started it.*

Tariq waited until his lieutenants had exhausted their disapproval before he sent his message. *Our brother is misguided. Those who commit evil don't deserve compassion. Hopefully, in time, we will educate Asghar about the true meaning of Islam.*

Who was he, a convert of a few years, to lecture him about the true meaning of Islam? How dare he wield those words as though he owned them? Asghar twirled his wedding ring, fuming.

He started typing a response but Magdalena interrupted him.

'Excuse me, sir, you are this lady's son? With the scarf?'

He nodded. Her formal tone sounded odd.

'Something happened. Your mother is not feeling well. Come with me.'

'What's wrong?'

'Come with me,' she repeated. Asghar followed her through the double doors and towards the exercise class. Inside he saw the instructor loosening Mrs Dhalani's scarf. His mother was lying on the floor, apparently unconscious. Asghar called her name but there was no response. He knelt down, pulled back her trailing scarf and saw her face. It looked like an overripe pear. Asghar's heart thumped, his palms sweated.

'We were doing the warm-down, and she collapsed,' said the instructor, an Asian woman. 'I don't know what happened. We did the same exercises as normal.' He put her hand over his mother's mouth and felt some warmth. That was reassuring.

'Someone get a doctor!' he called out. No one in the exercise group replied. He pulled out his phone and dialled 999. He asked Magdalena for the gym's exact address.

'I can't . . .' she stumbled, her English collapsing.

'Tell me!' he demanded. Magdalena recovered and told him; he repeated each line of the address to the emergency services operator.

'She's breathing,' said Asghar, responding to the operator's question. He squeezed his mother's hand. She did not squeeze back.

Asghar told Magdalena to wait outside for the ambulance. The instructor said she could try reviving her; but Asghar said she was already breathing, just unconscious, so there didn't seem any point. He reasoned it was best to wait for the professionals. They were alone on the foam gym floor. He stroked

271

his mother's face while looking at his watch. Waiting for her was a familiar feeling. Often when she picked him up from school, she would come ages after she had promised. He would stand alone at the gates, scanning the road for her car, hoping and cursing. Just when he had convinced himself the worst had happened, she turned up with a wave and a wide smile. All his anxiety was dispelled in an instant. It would be the same this time, he hoped.

The paramedics burst in with Magdalena following. They checked Mrs Dhalani, put an oxygen mask over her face and hauled her on to a stretcher. 'Please sir, give us some space,' said the paramedic firmly.

'I'm her son,' he said.

'Follow us,' he instructed. Asghar jogged behind them as they rolled his mother through the corridor. Over his shoulder he saw Magdalena ticking behind him in her black heels. Outside on the pavement, they loaded his mother into the ambulance like an awkward piece of furniture. He climbed into after them and sat on a small orange chair designated for relatives. The siren sounded. He saw Magdalena give him an optimistic wave before crossing herself as the doors slammed shut.

# Chapter Eighteen

Asghar stepped from a sunny morning into the dark washing room. He went through the back door that led to a small room stacked with plastic chairs. In the centre lay a humming metal box shrouded in cold steam: the coffin used to store the body overnight in the new mosque. He rubbed the glass to reveal his mother's sweet crumpled face. She had suffered a serious heart attack at the gym. After being rushed to hospital the doctors had done all they could, but her heart was too badly damaged. The Iraqi heart surgeon asked Mr Dhalani if he wanted to switch off her life-support machine; he refused. Two hours later Allah saved the family from further agony. Mrs Dhalani's pulse slowed down and the machine's bleeping became less frequent, as though she were communicating in fading Morse code. To counter the terrible thirst of the dying, Asghar had wetted some cotton buds and dripped cool water down her throat, whispering that she would soon be drinking heavenly milk. When it was all over, after the rush to get the death certificate and burial certificate before sundown, she was transported to the mosque where the ladies whom she had once helped to wash the dishes now ritually washed her corpse.

Along with his father and sister, Asghar had stayed with the body until midnight. Such was Mr Dhalani's terrible state – weeping uncontrollably, battering the coffin with his fists, wailing at Allah's unfairness – that the lady in charge of the ritual washing, Maryam Auntie, had told him to go home with Fatima. Mr Dhalani drooped his head on his chest. Fatima rummaged in her mother's handbag and found a tissue packet. Her father wiped his eyes and blew his nose.

'Your mother always has tissues,' he said admiringly.

'Why don't you go home?' said Asghar. 'I'll wait here.'

'She's only fifty years old,' said Mr Dhalani, who didn't seem to be listening. 'How can she have a heart attack? She was always dieting, always eating the right things. It's me who has kebabs, chips and everything. I never do exercise. So why is she gone, and not me?'

'It is Allah's will,' said Maryam Auntie with gentle firmness. 'We must have patience.'

Mr Dhalani looked at her angrily; he wasn't in the mood for religious consolation.

'I'm going to stay and read Quran,' said Asghar.

His father stood abruptly. 'Do what you want,' he said. 'Yes, you read Quran. Maybe by a miracle she will come back to life, like Jesus and the clay birds.' He gave a small, half-deranged laugh.

Fatima took her father's hand and led him towards the door.

When everyone had gone, Asghar drew up a plastic chair and opened the Quran. After reading a few pages, he went

274

over to the metal box, wiped the cold condensation from the glass and looked at his mother: her eyes were closed and her skin had drained to a grey-green hue. It was too upsetting to stay for long and he went back to his chair to read Sura 94, reportedly revealed to the Prophet when he was weighed down with strife in Makkah:

Did we not expand your breast and remove your burden – the one that weighed upon your back – and then raise your reputation high? For surely with hardship comes ease. Surely with hardship comes ease. So when you have finished your duties, stand up – and direct your longing to your Lord.

He dozed off with the Quran on his lap. Waking up, he found it was a brilliant spring day: cold and sunny. The funeral would at least be dry. Stretching his legs, he walked round the new mosque's large grounds. He went past a grotto which, according to a tarnished bronze plaque, had once housed a religious hermit, a favourite of the lord who had once lived there. Now it was sealed up and overgrown with brambles. The plinths where the naked female goddesses had once stood were now weathered and weedy. Rainwater had collected in the dried-up fountain under a green carpet of algae. He dipped his finger in the water and watched the algae break and reform.

Back at the washroom Maulana Haider was waiting for him, dressed casually in jeans and a black shirt. Asghar hadn't spoken to him since the wedding.

'Sura al-Fatiha,' said the maulana, running his fingers on the glass-topped sarcophagus.

They recited together. 'The soul does not rest until the body is buried. It is present here.'

The maulana pointed upwards. Asghar tried to sense his mother's spirit hovering benevolently over them; but he felt nothing. His gaze returned to his mother's face: the cheeks he had kissed, the lips that had kissed his.

'Imam al-Ghazali said something wise about leaving this world: "A man is like a prisoner in a gloomy chamber from which a door has been opened on to a spacious garden stretching as far as his eyes can see, containing diverse trees, flowers, birds and fruit." We pray that such Paradise awaits her.'

'I've read nearly half a Quran,' said Asghar, holding up his gold-embossed book. The maulana nodded in approval.

'If it's too much, you can pay someone in Pakistan to read the rest.'

'I'd prefer to do it myself,' replied Asghar. 'I'm reading the English translation.'

He was proud of his achievement. His concentration had never been strong enough to read such a large chunk in one session. Sitting with his mother last night, however, his mind and desires had been united. Instead of scaring him, as they usually did, he found the Quran's moral imperatives invigorating; and the rounding merciful phrases that melted divine justice – his mother's favourites – filled his heart with love for her.

'Have you had breakfast?' asked the maulana.

'I don't feel hungry.'

'Let's find you something.'

'I want to finish my Quran.'

'There is time,' advised the maulana. 'I'll bring you something.'

'No, I'll come with you.' As the grieving party, it was his privilege to be served, but it felt strange sending the maulana to do his bidding.

Together they walked to the main building and down some side steps to the kitchen. The volunteers were preparing the funeral food. Maryam Auntie was pouring rice grains from a hessian sack into an enormous pot filled with boiling water. When she saw them, she stopped and leapt forward to hug Asghar.

'Don't worry, maulana sahib,' she said, reassuring him of the rectitude of her physical gesture. 'Asghar is my son now.'

'Thank you for washing her last night,' Asghar said.

'Kulsum was one of us,' she said simply. Asghar looked round the kitchen. Here she had not been Mummy or Mrs Dhalani but Kulsum, one of the women who toiled for hours to feed the mosque's congregation. He thought of all those meals, all those mouths – all the pleasure she had given to people in Ramzan who had sat hungrily through the sermon and prayers before feasting on her food.

'Is there any breakfast?' asked the maulana. Maryam Auntie opened an industrial-sized fridge and found two leftover kebab rolls in silver foil. She warmed them in the microwave and wrapped them in a carrier bag with a tub of relish.

'We're making lots of rice today,' said Maryam Auntie. 'Many people are coming for the funeral.'

'She was an honourable lady,' said Maulana Haider. 'When I came home for dinner, she always cooked delicious biryani. She joined us for chai and asked the most intelligent questions – in fluent Urdu. Better than your father's.'

'We'll miss her,' said Maryam Auntie, taking Asghar's hand and rubbing it gently.

Asghar left the kitchen with the maulana and trudged back to the washroom. He looked up as the sun moved behind the sky's only cloud, barely containing its superb brightness.

'Come and sit outside,' said the maulana.

'I've already left her too long,' said Asghar, shivering slightly in the door's shadow.

'We'll sit by the entrance: half-in, half-out.'

Asghar set up two chairs at the door, within earshot of the humming metal box.

'I spoke to your mother only two weeks ago,' said the maulana.

'Oh?' said Asghar.

'She phoned me about your current situation.'

'Oh,' said Asghar, suddenly feeling extremely tired.

'She told me you and Mrs Dhalani are living apart?'

'Mrs . . .? Oh, you mean Zahra.'

'That you are having problems?'

'Something like that.'

'She's worried about you. She wants you to be happy.'

Asghar sighed. 'Things aren't that easy,' he said. 'Zahra and I had different expectations of married life.'

'Marriage is not like a bed of roses.'

'She didn't understand me,' said Asghar, thinking for the first time that the maulana's favourite metaphor – he had used it during their wedding sermon – didn't make much sense. Surely marriage *was* like a bed of roses: it needed feeding and watering, care and attention; there were prickly thorns as well as silky petals. But he let it go. 'No matter how much we speak to each other,' he said, 'we never speak *to* each other.'

'Do you listen to her?'

'I gave her everything she wanted.'

278

'Listen. Once an unhappy man came to me for advice. He had lost thousands of pounds gambling on the internet. He had to borrow money to pay off his losses. He didn't tell his wife. He hid the letters from the debt collectors. But the secrecy meant he began to hate his wife for making him feel so guilty. He became petty – the dinner wasn't cooked nicely, her mother called too much. All this he admitted to me.'

The maulana unwrapped his kebab and took a bite. Asghar did the same.

'He wanted to keep his secret, but also get rid of it. He wrote her a letter explaining everything and disappeared. When she found the note – Allah forgive me – she thought the worst. You can imagine the night she had.'

'What happened?'

'The police found him at the Holiday Inn in Birmingham.'

'Alive?'

'Just.'

'His poor wife!'

'When he came back, he expected her to throw plates. But she didn't.'

'She forgave him?'

'He begged for mercy but she refused to say a word. Then, at last, she told him she had saved some money for the school fees. Instead she would use it to pay off his debts. He insisted she pay only half. That's when he came for help.'

'What happened?'

'In strictest confidence, I arranged for the mosque to pay his debts.'

'How are they getting on?'

He shrugged. 'They had another child. I saw him dropping her at the mosque crèche.'

Asghar chewed his kebab thoughtfully.

'Okay,' said Maulana Haider. 'I need to put on my superhero clothes, as my boy calls them.' He touched Asghar's shoulder before disappearing round the corner in the direction of the cottage.

Across the field, Asghar watched the old caretaker opening the iron gates. Gradually the mourners began to arrive. First came the regulars: the retirees who lived close enough to walk and for whom every funeral was a social occasion. Then came the businessmen in suits making deals on their phones as they emerged from their cars. And then his mother's legion of relatives: sisters and cousins, aunts and uncles. Should he be greeting them at the entrance? No, he remembered, that was for weddings, not funerals. He hoped his father was on his way. Mr Dhalani had been wrecked by his wife's death. How many times had he reminded her with playful solemnity where he kept his will – only for her to chide him for being so morbid: they would, she assured him, live as long as the two parrots she had kept as a child in East Africa – fifty years, a hundred years, she exaggerated.

A familiar car nosed nervously through the gates. He recognised the number plate: A786 MIR. The car slowed down and Zahra emerged from the driver's seat. She was wearing a black chador slung over blue jeans and a white scarf that barely covered her head. She opened the door for her father, who stepped out. The caretaker shouted that the car was blocking traffic and so Zahra – after scanning the mosque grounds but apparently not finding the person she was searching for – got back in and drove round to the car park on the women's side. Dr Amir didn't know where he was going. He tried the wrong door and found it was locked.

Asghar jogged over and greeted his father-in-law with a respectful salaam.

'Son,' he said, 'accept my deepest condolences. In this difficult time we must ask for patience.'

He cupped his hands and raised them to the sky. They prayed together.

'Thank you for coming,' said Asghar.

'It is my duty,' insisted Dr Amir.

'I'll show you the way.' He grasped his hand and led him inside the mosque.

When they walked into the prayer hall together the crowd stared – the bereaved always being objects of fascinated attention, and especially so since this was the first time Dr Amir had set foot in the new mosque. They continued staring as Asghar led his father-in-law towards the front. At least Asghar thought they were staring. Stepping over the cross-legged men, he noticed that not everyone *was* looking at him. Some swiped their phones, while others shielded their eyes from the sunshine streaming through the windows.

Taking his place in the front row, Asghar heard salawaat rippling from the back of the prayer hall. He turned to see Maulana Haider among those bearing his mother's black-draped coffin. The congregation stood up and formed two lines on each side, passing the coffin on their shoulders – as though his mother were crowd surfing, Asghar thought weirdly. Should he join them or was his role to stay at the front? His father would know but he was still nowhere to be seen. He decided to join in. Bearing the coffin's weight on his shoulders, he was jostled by uncles and ended up underneath the coffin, carrying its heaviness on his back. Stumbling forward the front edge scraped his neck. He and the others lowered Mrs Dhalani in front of the mihrab and prised open the coffin. Wrapped tightly in her white shroud, she looked as though she were napping on a cold afternoon.

'Should we expose her face?' whispered Maulana Haider. At men's funerals the face was usually open, but did the same rule apply to women? Since the maulana had asked the question, a choice was clearly on offer. He wanted to see his mother's face for the last time. Yet it would have offended both her modesty and her vanity to be exposed to the men in such a state. He told him to keep her face covered.

'Shall we start,' asked the maulana, 'or wait for your father?'

'Let's get going,' Asghar said. His mother was waiting. The men grouped close together. You did not need ritual purity to perform the funeral prayers, making it easy for anyone to join in; it was Allah's last concession before the trials of the grave. Asghar looked along the row at the old men who ran the community. Finally, after years of praying behind them, Mrs Dhalani was front and centre.

Once the prayers were done, the coffin was resealed and carried towards the barred doors that led to the women's section. The caretaker was about to open them when a voice called out. 'Wait! I must see my wife!' Mr Dhalani barged through the parting crowd and threw himself on the coffin. 'She was my only wife,' he cried out, 'my only wife,' sounding a bit like he wanted credit for not taking a second wife.

He had arrived late, and now he was wailing without restraint. Asghar put a firm hand on his shoulder and told him to stand up.


On the women's side, Zahra heard the double doors being

rapidly re-bolted. Maryam Auntie made pacifying gestures to the other women who were expecting to receive the body. She bent down and squinted through the keyhole. Just behind her, Zahra listened in mute distress to a man's voice wailing – was it Asghar or his father? When she had heard the news the night before she had wanted to ring Asghar straight away; but she felt too embarrassed. Did he even want to hear from her? Was she even right to come to the funeral? That day she was due to have an important meeting with a Qatari client. When she told Sally that she really felt she ought to be at the funeral, she was asked by her frustrated boss why everything was happening so quickly. The client might be unhappy about rescheduling. She shouldn't worry, Zahra told her – he'll understand. He's Muslim, like me.

The doors opened and Zahra saw Asghar holding his father in his arms. He handed him over to her father, Dr Amir, who was with the mourners at the front. Along with the other men, Asghar and Maulana Haider picked up the coffin and brought it to the threshold between the men and women's sections.

'Go and take her,' Maryam Auntie instructed Zahra.

Separated or not, she was still married to Asghar, and was the only woman present who was allowed physical contact with him. She stepped forward. Asghar stopped at the doors and steadied himself. He looked up and saw Zahra's outstretched arms.

'Thank you,' he mouthed, carefully putting the coffin in her hands.

'I'm so sorry,' she said. Maryam Auntie and the other women joined in quickly and within moments the coffin was safely grounded, and the doors bolted once more.

Maryam Auntie opened the coffin and uncovered Mrs Dhalani's face. The pursed, slightly frostbitten lips of her mother-in-law reminded Zahra of Asghar when he was sleeping. She spotted some stray grey hairs curling over her face, and knelt down to tuck them under her scarf. The loud-speaker buzzed and Maulana Haider's voice crackled through. They all sat down. Zahra was impressed with the maulana's improved English. He had to move with the times, she supposed. His subject was the Prophet's first wife, Lady Khadija. Zahra knew the story well. The Prophet, before he became the Prophet, was an orphan boy who worked as a merchant on the Makkan trading routes between Yemen and Syria. Khadija was his boss, a wealthy widow older by ten years – some reports even said fifteen. She admired her employee's honesty and noble features. She asked him to marry her, not the other way round, and he accepted her offer.

Zahra noted that their courtship was always reported from Khadija's perspective. It was rare for a woman's desires to be acknowledged in religious talks; but when the object of that desire was the Holy Prophet, it seemed acceptable, because the qualities Khadija saw in him were the very qualities all Muslims venerated. But what, she wondered, drew the Prophet to Khadija? Did she cover her face? Were shy looks exchanged over the ledgers? Had she been a gentle woman, or a commanding one?

Maulana Haider concluded his sermon with a familiar moral. Lady Khadija had placed absolute faith in her husband when he returned from the mountain cave with Allah's words ringing in his ears. She had supported him during his darkest times – even when he doubted himself and considered throwing himself off the mountain in despair. She was the model wife. A fugitive question crossed Zahra's mind about whether Khadija had truly been so trusting. Had she never once doubted when her husband told her visions from God were compelling him to start a new religion?

'We know from the Prophet's own words to Ayesha that he was feeling uncertain at this time . . .' said the maulana.

That was interesting. It had never occurred to Zahra to think about where these stories came from – about who had told them to whom. The story had been related to the chroniclers by Ayesha, one of the Prophet's later wives. She had heard it from the Prophet himself, during their pillow-talk, speaking of his first marriage to Khadija. Might this have affected how he told the story? Maybe the Prophet's devotion to Khadija's memory meant he remained silent over her doubts about him, and instead he had emphasised his own vulnerability? After all, she had saved him from the mountain top. Had he perhaps, out of love, protected her? Zahra liked her own interpretation; it made the story a lesson for husbands as well as wives.

The maulana began reciting the story of Khadija's death. Zahra glanced at the coffin. Mrs Dhalani had told her she rarely listened to the lectures, cheerfully confessing that they all went over her head, and that she had plenty of work in the kitchen. Zahra recalled her nervous energy at the wedding breakfast. At the time, Zahra had thought she was asserting control over her son – letting her know who was boss. But perhaps the truth was that she was a little intimidated by her son's new wife. Maybe she wasn't sure how to speak to a young woman with whom she shared a religion and a community, but not an education or outlook. Poor woman. She had probably only been trying to cover up her husband's bad jokes.

285

Zahra regretted her snobbish attitude towards the Dhalanis. She had seen them as the enemy in her project to drag Asghar away from his suburban religiosity – to raise him to what she thought was her level. People talked about mixed marriages as though they only existed between people of different religions or backgrounds: but every marriage was mixed, and every one needed the same painful compromises.

After the sermon, Maryam Auntie and the other women carried the coffin through the mosque. Zahra followed them. They walked past Fatima, who stayed in the back room to be comforted by her cousins. The girl's eyes were red-rimmed and her face pale. The coffin halted beside her. Fatima wiped her tears on the coffin's black covering, just as when she was a child Zahra would bury herself in her mother's oud-scented hijab in times of distress. Zahra wanted to say something to Fatima but didn't have the right words. She couldn't remember the proper Arabic condolences; and she didn't want to come out with some garbled version. Their English equivalents – 'I'm sorry for your loss,' or 'We're thinking of you' – might have been appropriate in the formal atmosphere of a church funeral held weeks after the death but at an emotionally charged mosque funeral they would seem emptily inadequate.

She slipped away from the coffin and walked to the window. Pulling aside the doily curtains, she watched Mrs Dhalani's body being hauled into the mosque's brown hearse. Mr Dhalani climbed into the front seat and stared straight ahead; behind him, Asghar was wedged in a small seat next to the coffin. The convoy processed through the iron gates and towards the graveyard.

For the women there was little to do except wait until the men returned. Relatives stayed to comfort the family, while others drank tea among their own friends or drifted home, their duty done. Zahra felt self-conscious in a place where she knew almost nobody but everybody knew her. She found a corner and pretended to read Quran.

She did not stay undisturbed for long. Maryam Auntie came over and asked for help in the kitchen. 'It looks better to be doing something,' she advised. Zahra followed her down the stairs and towards the bright kitchen, where the women were decanting the sweet chai into silver kettles.

'You remember these kettles from the old mosque?' asked Maryam Auntie, wiping steam from her thin-framed glasses. 'We still use the same ones.'

'We bought new ones for the old mosque,' she said.

'With sugar or without?'

'Oh, I never have sugar in my tea. Since uni.'

'No – I meant do you want to serve tea with sugar or without?'

'Without,' she replied bashfully.

'Good. Take this white handkerchief and tie it round the spout. Go to the diabetic ladies at the back first.'

Zahra picked up the heavy kettle and grabbed a tower of ridged, plastic white cups. Serving the old ladies, she remembered the satisfaction of pouring exactly the right amount of tea into a gratefully grasped cup. She waited patiently as one lady rummaged in her handbag for saccharine, before helping her dispense two tablets into her tea. She apologised to another lady who enquired after cakes or croissants: there would be food when the men returned from the graveyard. The woman thanked her.

When she finished her round, she returned to the kitchen and found Maryam Auntie resting on a stool.

'Now you can have a cup,' she said, pouring Zahra some chai. 'Is Mum here?'

'She's with her relatives in Exeter,' Zahra explained, pulling up another stool. 'She'll visit the family when she gets back.'

'I saw Dad here.'

'Yes – he wanted to come.' There was a pause.

'You remember I taught you Arabic at the old mosque.'

'Of course!' she said, though she wasn't sure if she did remember. Maryam Auntie sipped her tea and Zahra did the same. It was sweet and milky, flavoured with cardamom – a deliciously homely taste.

'It's a shame we didn't keep in touch,' she said. 'It was hard with the new mosque. I wanted to stay with your father at the old mosque but my husband insisted on moving. He said it saved us twenty minutes in the car.'

'Really?' said Zahra.

'It's coming up to his two-year anniversary,' said Maryam Auntie. 'You must have been at university then.'

'I'm so sorry I missed the funeral,' Zahra said, grasping for the right words just in time. She had forgotten that Maryam Auntie's husband had died.

'I understand you girls are very busy these days, especially with university. But please pray for him, next time you pray.'

Was there a sting in her words? Perhaps Zahra was imagining things.

'And your husband, Asghar, how is he?' she asked.

'We're separated,' said Zahra. She sensed Maryam Auntie wanted a hint that the separation might not last forever; that there was still hope. So she added, 'at the moment.'

'Such a shame,' she lamented. 'You looked so happy on your wedding day.' Had she been happy? Zahra could not recreate

288

her emotions of that day; it seemed as though it was someone else who had got married, not her.

'Asghar's grown up a lot,' Maryam Auntie continued. 'At the hospital, he was so calm and helpful. You know he spent the whole night reading Quran for her?'

'Sometimes things don't work out,' she said.

'It's happening more and more these days. You children have too many choices.'

'Not everyone could find a husband like yours,' said Zahra. 'You must have had a love match,' she teased.

'No, no!' Maryam Auntie put her palms on her cheeks in mock scandal. 'My father was too old-fashioned. One day he told me I was getting married to a boy from Kampala. I had to ask to find out his name. Other brides received letters from their fiancé or saw photographs. Not me! But,' she added proudly, 'my husband saw my photograph before he agreed.'

'And that was enough?'

'We loved each other because we had no choice.'

'Can that work?' she asked doubtfully, thinking of her own parents' troubled marriage.

'What choice did I have about my father or mother – or my brothers? I still loved them. But yes,' she conceded, 'with a stranger it's hard. Gradually they become like your family, and you love each other even if you argue. Yours was a love match, wasn't it – not chosen by your parents?'

'Yes, it was. In a way.'

'Well, people don't always know how to choose what's good for them.'

A volunteer interrupted, asking Maryam Auntie how much curry they should pour out and how much to freeze. 'We'll need enough for three helpings,' she said. 'The men are always hungry after a burial. Let me come and see.'

She bustled over to the other side of the kitchen.

Zahra watched the women working diligently around her. She felt lost and alone. Since she was a girl, she had fought to pursue a life away from the community: to study at Cambridge and work in the City; to ignore those religious precepts and cultural norms that made no sense to her. The cost had been a break with her past, her parents and her community. True, she still loved her family and was happy to be called a Muslim. She liked to tinge her Western sensibility with an Islamic hue. She brought Indian sweets to work the day after Eid, and at the office Christmas dinner emphasised to Sally the Quran's veneration of Jesus. She regarded herself as a role model who could straddle two cultures with ease. Yet she also felt like a fraud.

There were times when things were going well with Krish when she had secretly hoped her parents would retire to East Africa – just disappear from her life, even die. At least they would not live to see their daughter abandon their community. These selfish thoughts tormented her. How could she have been so cold-hearted? And now that her marriage to Asghar, the gamble that she had hoped would allow her to remain with a foot in the community even as she strode ahead to her destiny outside it, now that her marriage to Asghar had also failed, she had nowhere left to go. For sure, she would find it impossible to marry someone else from the community. The only men who married divorced women were divorced men – and she didn't much fancy her options there.

On the other hand, it also meant she had the freedom to slip quietly into the outside world. She knew of other women who had abandoned the community by engrossing themselves in careers or by moving abroad. Their personal lives were a mystery until one day you heard they had married a Sunni or converted an English guy. Such women's lives were not over, and once the scandal had cooled everyone moved on – in England few had the time or energy to enforce pariah status. Some even brought their mixed-race children to madressa on Sundays where the teachers cooed over their fair skin. Evidently they did not think they needed to be one thing or another. They did what they wanted and survived the messy consequences.

She agonised over whether she had taken the right path – but perhaps she needed to change her metaphor. Marrying Asghar might have been a mistake but was it a worse one than staying with Krish? Maybe the reason she pushed him away after that night in the college car park was not religious scruple or cultural taboo. Maybe, as Krish had said, she had simply not loved him. Did she love Asghar? His clumsy touch had not given her the same warm buzz she had felt with Krish. But at that Sunday with their families, she had seen something steelier in him. That afternoon she had admired his dignified solidity; he had, for once, not averted his eyes sheepishly. She had wanted to mould Asghar into the man she knew he could be: to fortify his good heart with a more impressive, assertive character. But she could not will such changes into existence – they had to develop organically. The bitter irony was that it had taken their separation to provoke the maturity she had needed to see in him from the start.

The women began to slosh curry into yellow buckets. One asked Zahra to fetch more ladles from the cupboard. The men were probably burying Mrs Dhalani right now, she thought. Poor

Asghar. Really, they should talk properly when all this was over. She checked her phone and found she had one bar of reception. Under the fluorescent light, she typed a quick message:

*I'm so sorry, today must have been really difficult. She was a really lovely woman, the kindest sort. Shall we possibly meet up sometime? Next week? We have to sort out a lot of things. Zx*

After pressing send she waved her phone in the air, hoping the message would get through.

Asghar gathered balls of earth in his hands – rolling the sand and mud between his fingers like morsels of rice and curry – and tossed them into the grave. At times, he felt as though he were playing a game with his mother, throwing her a ball like he did on those endless childhood afternoons. Except that she could not throw them back. She was being covered with English soil.

The other men helped by using their shovels with rough efficiency – all except Mr Dhalani, who remained in the hearse, frozen with grief. After twenty minutes the grave was half filled. Asghar was chanting the burial prayers when he heard a noisy mechanical digger approach. He watched as the driver – a rough-looking guy with a spider tattoo round his neck – used the controls to nuzzle the mound of earth with the digger's claw. Asghar stopped throwing and the men stopped digging. The driver pushed a large tranche of earth jerkily over the grave's edge; it landed on the coffin with a pebbly scatter. Asghar kept on chanting, but the mechanical roar drowned him out.

He slipped through the mourners and tugged Maulana Haider's cloak.

'What's happening?' he asked.

'Eh?' the maulana exclaimed, pulling on his earlobes to indicate he couldn't hear.

'Why is there a digger?' said Asghar loudly.

'People complain burials take too long,' he answered, with his mouth to Asghar's ear. 'They can't wait for one hour. More people come if it's quicker – so more benefit for the deceased. It was your father's idea originally.'

'But is it allowed – I mean, Islamically?'

He raised his hands in a gesture of impotence. 'This is the modern way.'

Asghar was not happy. Why should this sacred ritual be disturbed in the name of efficiency? The digger had nearly finished the job but there were still some chunks of earth left. Asghar grabbed a spade and waved it at the driver.

'Stop,' he cried out. 'Stop.' The tattooed driver looked at him for a few seconds; Asghar stared back defiantly. 'I'm telling you to stop.' He cut the engine. Asghar restarted the funeral prayers and turned round to encourage Maulana Haider and Dr Amir to join in. Soon they were all chanting vigorously. He scraped up the remaining mud with his spade and spread it evenly over the grave. The driver quietly disappeared. Asghar recalled the time they were on a beach holiday – in Tunisia perhaps, or maybe Syria – when his sister had buried him in the warm sand. His panicking mother had run from her shaded deckchair and dug him out with her bare hands. She had chastised Fatima for playing such a dangerous game. Such was the fierceness of her protective love. He poured water from the green watering can over the grave. Kneeling down, he spread the topsoil with his hands as smoothly as his mother would make his bed. The men around him approached in twos and threes to pay their final respects, as he continued to kneel and pray.

Asghar lifted his head. The men were wandering back between the graves, stopping at their own deceased relatives. He stretched his tired arms to the sky and watched the trees swaying coolly. He stood up and retreated to a nearby bench. In the distance he saw the neatly clipped hedges that marked the edge of a farm. Some horses grazed calmly while a foal dashed ahead of them. His mother would have liked this spot – so close to the English graves with their blossoming bouquets. Asghar recalled a family joke told by his father: could gravediggers pray for more business? Wasn't that praying for people to die? Fatima told him he was being silly; but his mother would take him seriously. People should pray for only a greater share of the deaths already decreed by the Almighty, she said, not a greater number.

Asghar found his mother's tissue packet and wiped his dirty hands. His phone vibrated in his pocket but he ignored it. Making his way to the entrance, he saw Maulana Haider imploring his father to leave the hearse and visit his wife's grave. He didn't appear to be having much success. Not to worry. If his dad wasn't ready now he could bring him tomorrow or the day after. He would pass his driving test and bring him every Sunday, and make sure there were flowers on the grave. As Asghar walked over, his phone resumed its buzz. This time he put his hand in his pocket. He looked at the message and smiled.